TRIP

THE SENSUAL PORTAL
BOOK 1

CHERIL N. CLARKE

METASOUL PUBLISHING

To the courageous women standing at the crossroads of obligation and desire: choose yourself. Be fearless. Seek pleasure. Create bliss. But...do it cautiously, tempered by wisdom. Sometimes, risking everything to satisfy an unquenchable thirst comes with unexpected consequences.

FLASH FORWARD

I didn't know if I was dead or alive when it kicked in.

My world went black, and my body went limp. Heavy. Detached. I'd plummeted out of myself into an ocean of darkness—free-falling into infinity. There were no sounds, sights, or smells. I was perplexed —not knowing where I was, where I'd end up, or how I'd acclimate when I arrived. Nothing I'd ever learned could prepare me for the shock of collapsing into such a void. It was deep and made me immediately lose sense of time. *Fuck!*

I didn't know if seconds, minutes, or hours were going by as I tumbled through the vast emptiness of life without senses. But eventually, objects came into view. Neon colors, geometric shapes, suspended letters, and an endless sea of unblinking eyes. They slowly, gently illuminated my surreal trip. But their arrival deepened my spatial disorientation. Everything was strange and entrancing, and I didn't know if I was sinking or flying, bound or free. *Maybe this is a mistake!* I panicked but could do nothing.

My metaphysical feet were off the ground. Hell, there was no ground, and I was on my journey. There was no turning back. *Let go. Don't fight it.* Somehow, the shaman's voice guiding my ceremony wafted into my mind, and I calmed down. *Release the urge to control, and know . . . just* ***know.*** I heard him faintly, and I scarcely sensed the tribal drumming that he'd started with. Suddenly, I willed myself to let go, and finally, my sense of falling transformed into one of floating. *Let go. Don't fight it...*

I was a fiery speck, a red ant, trying not to panic in a vast black ocean.

Soon after, I felt weightless, and my soul cracked open to a shaft of startling and seductive light. It pulled me in...pulled me in...pulled me in...like a sensual guide to an ethereal dimension—far away from the superficial, competitive and materialistic home I knew. Suddenly, the colors began intertwining like the tangled notes of a wind chime. Swaying. Mesmerizing. Captivating.

At that moment, I felt a connectedness to all things and a knowingness of everything big and small. I understood I was definitely *linked* to something grander than me. My sense of existence temporarily relaxed, and I entered a new gravity vortex. Then, I arrived at a pink, fiery, fluid portal. Scary. Orgasmic. Fascinating. Life-altering—it was my first Jump.

TIMELINE

9 Months Before...

1

CRYING IN PUBLIC

Longing.

The feeling took root in my heart, growing like a massive tangle of weeds taking over an abandoned playground. My spirit hurt. My heart hurt. My marriage. . . hurt. Wandering through the DeKalb Farmers Market, I felt like a ghost, my fingers tightly gripping the thin fabric of my gray jacket against the nippy air. It was January in Atlanta, Georgia. Not freezing, but not balmy either, and I searched for easy ingredients to stretch for a few meals. I didn't have the energy for elaborate dinners that week. I was tired.

My mind droned with a tumult of thoughts as I made my way through the market. *I should be happy, shouldn't I?* I wondered, noticing the sweet scent of freshly baked bread and roasted coffee beans filling the air. A beautiful home, a successful husband, and a gorgeous career and business that I built from the ground up. . .*But why did it feel like I was living a life tailored for someone else? Comfortable, but not quite mine.* I shuffled through the produce-packed aisles, picking things up and putting them down once I remembered the effort it would take to use them. I was disenchanted.

The market's aroma teased my senses, but I couldn't get as excited about it as I used to. Instead, I paused in front of a stand of vibrant flowers. Their colors popped, giving me a moment of aesthetic arrest. I was a sucker for beauty, no matter how dull my life had become. Running my fingers over a few of the velvety petals, I remembered when Jamie used to bring me flowers every Friday. Stargazer lilies were always my favorite blossom, their bold, pink-and-white blooms unfold like lovers' moans in the heat of a sultry night. Their fragrance was a distinct siren call to a passionate world I hated to have silenced. Even their dappled gorges hinted at a wildness that touched the primal parts of my soul. I missed them. Now, our flower vases sat under a dark kitchen sink—forgotten and gathering dust, sort of like our love life.

The chatter of happy couples around me was like a fly in my ear. They seemed so free and unburdened by the invisible chains I wore, and I couldn't stand the sound of their joy. Not in that moment. Because I felt trapped. I longed for intimate adventure and spontaneity. I missed my youthful, carefree days—before I'd fully conformed to a "picture of success." *What happened to me?* I used to always root for others regardless of how I felt, but I just couldn't, today. I felt envious yet hungry for what they appeared to have, and I didn't like it. I needed to break free. *This can't be life,* I thought, debating buying the flowers for myself. *It's too predictable. Too safe. Too. . .boring.* I sighed, walking away from the bouquets. I shouldn't complain, after all. People prayed for a life like mine, particularly my Jamaican parents. I shouldn't be ungrateful. It would disappoint them.

"Trish? Hey, baby girl, is that you?" a familiar voice called from behind as I grabbed bell peppers, onions, and avocados, staples to make Jamie's favorites.

I froze, the voice leaping into my ears like a jubilant echo from the distant past. My eyes widened, and my heart softened. *It couldn't be. . .* The voice was one I could pick out of a billion people. Slowly, I turned, simultaneously dropping the vegetables in my cart with shaky hands. I gulped, already feeling my mood shift, and there she was—Auntie Nia, with her beautifully contagious smile and wise eyes. Her presence was a patchwork of adventures, her silver curls framed her face like the rings of an old live oak tree, each telling the story of a year well-lived. She held herself with the ease of someone who has danced with life's ebbs and flows and moved to its unpredictable rhythm. The sight of her made the tears that had been threatening to fall well up even more, but I blinked them back. "Auntie Nia! Oh my god," I stammered, walking toward her with newfound energy. "Is that really you?" I was hopeful.

She laughed, her crown of curly gray hair enclosing her face like a silver halo. "Of course, it's me, child! My goodness, look at you! It's been too long since I've seen you, Trish." Her flowy turquoise dress and pink-and-yellow scarf made her the brightest, most vibrant woman in the market.

I rushed closer, momentarily abandoning my cart to hug her. "What brings you to Atlanta? I can hardly believe my eyes," I whispered, each word trembling with a mix of surprise and a deep-seated warmth.

She gave me a good, old-fashioned embrace that felt more like a lifeline than a hug. "I came here for some business. Didn't plan on cooking, but if I want a decent meal without going to a restaurant, it seems I've gotta make it myself. So, here I am."

My body shook, savoring the softness of her touch and the sweet smell of lavender in her hair. "It's so good to see you!"

A rush of memories flooded my mind. Auntie Nia wasn't a blood relative but a beloved family friend who had been a part of my life since I was a barefoot little girl running around my parents' South Florida backyard. I was always fascinated with the funny-looking ackee fruit that had fallen and was tickled that my parents called avocados "pears" simply because of their shape. My dad had planted the trees along with pineapples, coconuts, and sugar cane stalks to remind him of home and have easy access to produce that he loved. He and my mom had formed a rare friendship with Auntie Nia and one of her ex-husbands. It was unusual because they were immigrant islanders, and Auntie Nia was a "foreigner." They never usually clicked with African Americans, denigrating them as lazy and ungrateful people who couldn't see the economic opportunities they had in the US despite its horrific founding. I grew up believing I could outwork natives and overcome any obstacle because of my Caribbean parents and our little enclave in Carol City, FL. Regarding Nia, I'd always called her "Auntie" out of respect and affection.

"It's been too long since I've seen you!" she said, her eyes filled with genuine affection. "Look at you. How's Jamie? Your mom?" She quizzed.

"He's fine," I said, giving her the short of it. "And Mom is actually thriving—acting like a young woman again. Got herself a new beau and everything." It's funny; I felt safer telling Auntie Nia about my life than my mother.

"Get out of here!" she chuckled. "Good for her. I, for one, am done dealing with that gender for the foreseeable future. No shade; I just like my peace," she clarified. "Are you still doing interior decorating? I thought about you a while back when I walked into a house of horrors this man called home. Child, he was fifty-eight years old and still thought bean bags were appropriate furniture!" Auntie Nia's laugh was a melody that seemed to travel from across the globe, each giggle a story from faraway places, and her eyes held a depth that spoke of journeys and wisdom I had yet to discover.

I chuckled at her transparency. That was Auntie Nia for you! For as long as I could remember, she'd been a mentor, confidante, and source of wisdom to me. "I do. I love putting together beautiful spaces. Sensual spaces. Sanctuaries, you know?"

If everything else in my life had gone flat and dull, at least my job hadn't. My work in luxury homes and unique event spaces around Atlanta was the one thing left that gave me the aesthetics, seductiveness, and playfulness I craved.

"Well, are you in a hurry? I'd love to catch up with you more. Haven't seen you in ages." Auntie Nia placed her hand on mine.

I thought for a moment instead of defaulting to an instinctual urge to say I was busy. *Am I?* Not really. It was Sunday. I had long ago stopped working on the weekends unless it was an absolute crisis. Jamie was probably sprawled out on the couch, staring at football. He wouldn't miss me much. "Well, let's grab a bite to eat, then. I don't have to hurry home." I smiled.

We found an open corner with a rustic wooden table next to a charming little soul food restaurant. I bought us two bowls of pumpkin cream soup to enjoy while catching up. Just looking at Auntie Nia put me at ease. She was so colorful and breezy, so elegant with a hint of wildness. She was a mesmerizing picture of what aging well could be. I needed to know her secret!

"So, child, what's eating you up? Tell me the truth, now." Her eyes fixed on mine like a lantern illuminating a dark path.

I don't know why I didn't expect her to jump right into reading me. That's what she did. Auntie Nia could always see through my "I'm fine" white lies. I exhaled, my spoon hovering over the creamy soup. "It's just... Jamie and I," I began, my voice trailing off as I searched for the right words.

She leaned in, her expression a blend of curiosity and concern. "Go on. Whatever it is will come to an end. Everything does," she comforted.

I nodded and continued. "We've been wading in a rough patch for a while. No arguments or drama, just . . . nothing. It's flat. Our connection feels reduced to friendship rather than lovers. We're more like roommates, and it's tearing me up inside." My breathing quavered like a wavering flame as I gave voice to the quiet heartbreak I'd been nursing for nearly a year.

"From the looks and sounds of it, you've been in your own private hell, Trish. I'm sorry to hear that," she offered. "I know how you feel. It happens with long-term relationships, you know? It happens." Auntie Nia let out a gust of an exhale before intentionally taking a spoonful of soup. *Thoughtful.* She was always deliberate, not rushing to fill silence just because it was uncomfortable.

Tears spilled from my eyes. I couldn't stop them. My thumb twitched and tapped the table without conscious instruction from me. My body sank as I pressed my lids shut to slow the stream from my eyes. In the black of my closed gaze, I felt Auntie Nia's warm hand gently squeeze mine.

"It's alright. Let it out. It's okay." She ran her thumb over my hand before continuing. "You two have been through a lot. I know he had that terrible motorcycle accident a while back."

"He hasn't been the same since. His body is better, but emotionally—not so much. And he refuses to see a therapist," I told her, remembering the first time I brought it up and Jamie dismissed it with a wave of his hand. He insists he needs to figure things out on his own. It's exhausting."

She squeezed my hand to soothe me. "It threw his world off track, I know. One minute, he's this big-time orthopedic surgeon for Major League Baseball; the next minute, he's in an operating room with all kinds of fractures, broken bones, a foggy brain, and a devastated spirit." She exhaled. "And you, stopping everything to care for him and get him back on his feet. You did a good job. I wish I could have come back to help you juggle everything. I was going through my own issues at the time."

"I never expected you to."

"I know, but I would have if I could," she said. "Y'all have been married a long time. Since college, right?"

"Yeah."

"And you've just about seen it all except this. Health challenges like this strain couples when one of you can't quite bounce back. I've seen it."

"I knew he'd be down, but I didn't think he'd stay there. He's always been so tough. So strong. Such a fighter. I'm not used to this. He barely touches me beyond a morning hug and kiss. He's just not interested in anything he used to be. I think he watches the games out of habit. He doesn't actually care. His passion for life is gone."

Auntie Nia leaned back, her eyes fixed on mine, understanding and empathy shining through them. "Have y'all gone to counseling? What have you tried to help you get back on the right track?"

"We haven't, and I don't think he'd be interested. He'll just remind me that we don't argue or fight, so things are fine. That he'll come around—but he's not doing anything to show me he is. But something has to change soon. It's urgent. It needs to change now, or I don't know what I'll do," I confessed.

She nodded. "What about on your own?"

"Huh?" I quizzed. My vision was blurred by new tears.

"Have you taken any steps to care for yourself independent of him?"

"No . . . I . . ." The thought hadn't occurred. "I haven't, but maybe I should." A light bulb went off.

"You absolutely should," Auntie Nia confirmed. "These things happen, but it doesn't mean you're stuck in them, even if he isn't doing his part."

"But I don't want to give up on us."

"You don't have to. Love can evolve and transform to meet new versions of each of you. You'll have to work at it. Lots of talking, lots of patience, and lots of understanding."

I sniffled and wiped away my tears with the back of my hand.

"You don't need all the answers right now, just a willingness to take a step toward fixing your mental health. But Trish," she added, looking me squarely in the eyes, "your emotional health—your spirit—that's always going to be *your* job, child." She held my gaze. "No matter what. You got that?"

"Yes." I nodded, already feeling empowered by her words. "Well." I gulped down a few spoonfuls of soup before my meal got cold. "Enough about me. What about you? What have you been up to? It looks like life has been treating you fantastically!" Auntie Nia had a way of making even the heaviest burdens seem a little lighter, and I wanted to shift the mood.

As we continued talking and sharing stories of our lives, I realized reconnecting with Auntie Nia was a gift I didn't know I needed. She brought hope and wisdom back into my peripheral, reminding me of the power of love and resilience. She also brought immense intrigue, sharing some of her recent experiences with me including spiritual and psychedelic journeys.

"Wow!" I wasn't surprised, but I was curious. "What made you do it? Where did you do it? How was it? I have so many questions!"

Auntie Nia's eyes exploded with excitement as she recounted intense spiritual experiences that transformed her perspective on life, death, love, and purpose. "It was incredible!" she vocalized with glee. "Well, the first time was nerve-wracking and scary, but I did it with a group and a trained medicine man in Mexico," she gushed. Her excitement was infectious. "It ended up being the most beautiful and profound experience of my life." Auntie Nia's tales of travel and self-discovery gave her a stunningly youthful glow that defied her age.

"Amazing. I don't know anything about any of it, but I'm dying to know more." I was stunned. "It sounds like the jolt of energy I need in my life right now."

Auntie Nia spoke of moments of deep introspection, feeling powerful confirmations of knowing and accepting herself, a release of the need to control every aspect of her life and instead appreciate the flow of it. "Mostly," she said, "I felt love. Deep, all-knowing, chest-shaking, fearless LOVE. And it gave me strength. It gave me vitality. It gave me a shot of the feminine power that I felt when I was younger, but times ten. It gave me life."

I was speechless.

"I want to tell you more." She glanced at her dainty silver watch. "But time is getting away from me, baby, and I have to get going."

"But wait!" I didn't want her to leave. "Okay. I understand, but I don't want to lose touch with you again. I want to hear more. I *need* to hear more!"

Auntie Nia let out a hearty laugh. She gave me all of her new contact information and promised to share everything. She'd be in Atlanta only another two days and then was jetting off to Ecuador for a mystical retreat in the jungle. This woman was something else—such a firecracker at sixty-four years old. She lived in a coastal California town but seemed to be everywhere—free, floating, and fluid—the opposite of the rigid spirits my parents had become in their older years.

"I'm so glad we ran into each other," I confessed as she prepared to leave. "I'm serious about following up with you about your adventures. Your life sounds like a dream I'd like to jump into."

Her eyes instantly widened at my last statement. "What did you say?"

"I said your life sounds like a dream—"

"You'd like to *jump* into." She finished my sentence slowly, with a look of shock and fascination plastered on her face. Her lips parted, and she seemed to take an unconscious step backward before catching herself and moving closer toward me. She put her warm hand against my cheek.

"Yes, we will talk more. We must."

Her reaction to my words confused me. We'd covered so much, from Jamie and me to her quests to shed layers of societal expectations and unapologetically embrace her true self. What about my statement could have made her pause like that? I wouldn't find out immediately, because she floated away just as easily as she'd come up to me, only leaving me with, "Remind me to tell you about 'Jump' – it's something wild you might not believe!"

Huh? I had no idea what that meant, but I'd made a note to immediately bring it up the next time we spoke. Energized by my chance run-in with Auntie Nia, I returned to shopping, grabbing more items than I'd originally planned, so I could cook more thoughtful meals.

Auntie Nia had discovered a path to healing I hadn't explored. Her words resonated with me, kindling a spark of hope that things could turn around for me if I were willing to explore more ways to clear the weeds and emotional junk knotting my life. But it was her reaction to my casual comment that puzzled me. The way her eyes expanded in shock and awe left me wondering.

As I shopped, my thoughts circled back to that moment. I wondered what "Jump" meant to her and why my statement elicited such a response. *We will talk more. We must.* Her words echoed in my mind. What was it about "Jump?" I was determined to find out. Either way, I wanted some of what she'd had. I wanted passion. I wanted connection. I wanted more than love; I wanted ecstasy—the glow that seemed to engulf her. I desperately needed bliss back in my life, one way or another, or I might disintegrate emotionally.

2

BEAUTIFUL EMPTINESS

I smiled when I rounded the corner to my quiet home. Who knew my farmers market trip would deliver surprises? Muscle memory and daily habits had me clicking my garage door opener to smoothly pull my midnight-blue Porsche into my garage without much thought. *The grass needs to be cut*, I thought, after unconsciously glancing at it before easing in. I had a trunk half full of grocery bags and a heart packed with emotions.

The sun was setting, and I was glad to escape the evening chill into the warmth of my home. Jamie and I lived just on the edge of the Atlanta municipal line, which was still considered the city but felt more like the burbs. We had five bedrooms that I put my heart into designing, but they now often felt like empty canvases. The high-pitched chirp of our alarm system echoed as I entered the house.

"Hey, there!" Jamie called the moment my feet hit the house's interior. "I was just about to call you. What took so long?" he asked. "Let me get those." He came over and took the bags from my hands.

I smiled, grateful for the help and to see his handsome face. "I ran into Auntie Nia at the market." Slipping out of my shoes, I moved closer to give him a peck on the cheek. The stubbly new growth of his beard was rough but familiar and comforting.

"Auntie Nia," Jamie whispered, whisking the groceries from the nook between the garage and the main house to the kitchen. "Oh, whoa! Auntie Nia!" he repeated with sudden recognition. "I haven't seen her in ages! How's she doing?"

Before I could answer, Bentley, our senior Golden Retriever, ambled over to greet me. He was eleven and slowing down, but still full of love.

"Hey, big boy!" I gave him a loving head rub before returning my focus to Jamie. "Wonderful, it seems," I said, feeling remnants of her good energy flowing through me. "We ended up having lunch and catching up. That's why I was out longer than usual."

"Gotcha."

I knew better than to mention Auntie Nia's spiritual experiences to Jamie; he had always seen things like these as too abstract, too disconnected from the science he trusted. I remember him once remarking how people like her were chasing fantasies instead of facing reality—a judgment swiftly made with a shake of his head. So, I held back and let us fall into a pattern of moving efficiently around the kitchen, still having rhythm and sync despite our passionate disconnect. Though I decorated our home, Jamie made his mark in little ways, like lining up all the spice jars like soldiers. It was just like him to find solace in precision, his small act of control in a world that felt increasingly chaotic to him.

Bentley putt around us to complete the familiar family pulse. Jamie and I have been together for twenty-three years—married for eighteen. No children, although we did foster a boy over a decade before. It was a meaningful experience but reinforced that Jamie and I were content without creating our own children. For a long time, we traveled extensively, both for work and pleasure. We liked our freedom and knew adding kids would rip that away from us. Though we've both slowed down now, I had no regrets. Bentley was enough.

The soft glow of pendant lights bathed our marble island and cast a warm ambiance. Our kitchen had white cabinets with brushed nickel handles. A blue-green tile backsplash added a pop of color. The sound of a Falcons football game played in the background from our spacious family room as we put the food away. *Falcons overload the left side of the Patriots's offensive—line pass is picked! Intercepted!* the raucous TV announcers screamed. I tuned it out, straightening up our kitchen instead.

As the evening sun cast its stunning glow across the kitchen, I caught Jamie in a moment of stillness. Ignoring the TV, he held a distant gaze out the window. His body was a silent echo of the vitality he once had. *What is it, baby?* I thought but didn't ask. It wasn't the right time, but I was desperate to know. It used to be that an accident or setback couldn't keep him down. He's always found a way to bounce back, rise, or adapt to be the Jamie who tackled life head-on. But now, he seemed imprisoned not by hospital walls or physical scars, but by ones no medical team could heal.

Jamie used to light up any room with his deep, boisterous laughter. His touch was once a spark and flame, but that man seemed like a far-flung memory now. In his place was a shadow of the guy I'd fallen in love with. *When was the last time he looked at me deeply?* The question lingered in the air despite my not wanting it to. His hugs had become mechanical, and his kisses were more like brushes against my skin. *Why don't you try harder?* My inner voice pushed me, but I ignored it, leaving Jamie to his thoughts. The last time I snuck up on him his back stiffened in response. I didn't want to cause him any more stress, so I left him alone. Instead, I focused on the kitchen. *Does it have to be him who gives you pleasure?* The question shot through my mind like a violent thunderclap. Where the hell did that come from? My eyes widened in shock, and I quickly shooed the thought away.

Twilight seeped through the dense woods into the open windows of our home. They created shadows across a small potted succulent that adorned our breakfast table. Its vibrant green leaves added a touch of life to the room while a choir of crickets began their nightly serenade. The sound made its way through the leaves, doors, and windows—nature's song pulsed on Atlanta's outskirts. We had a small pile of junk mail that needed tossing. *Done*, I thought after chucking it into the trash. It was messing up the clutter-free space.

Our home was such a contrast from the bright and bustling market I'd just left. The memory seemed distant now that I was back in household territory. I wanted to wind down and enjoy a back massage. Auntie Nia had given me lots to think about.

"I think I'm going to relax in the spa room," I told Jamie after we'd put everything away.

"Alright." Jamie paused for a moment, a look of yearning in his eyes that quickly evaporated as he instead muttered, "I'll be here with Bent." Jamie smiled and strolled back over to our plush sofas, his attention split between his phone—likely a boring medical journal article, a glass of wine and the game.

I momentarily admired how his sweater fell snugly over his broad shoulders and back before I made my way upstairs. Running my fingers against the polished banister with intricate wrought-iron details, I juggled a mix of melancholy and yearning. Atop the stairway were built-in bookshelves filled with texts on architecture, small sculptures, and cherished family photographs. We even had a tiny collection of Cambodian pottery to remind Jamie of his mother. It was one of many micro galleries of our life together. To the left were double doors leading to the master suite, and immediately to my right was the spa room, its welcoming aura inviting me in with tranquil sounds coming from a wall-mounted waterfall.

I stepped into the spa room, immediately turning on the electric fireplace and surround sound system. The area was a small sanctuary filled with the elements of earth, fire, and water. The walls were painted in shades of sage green, and soft, dimmed sconces adorned the walls. The room's centerpiece was an extravagant, motorized massage table draped in crisp black linens. Surrounding the room were shelves filled with aromatic oils, scented candles, and cream-colored towels to create a full sensory experience.

Of all the special rooms I'd decorated with the intention to regularly use, this was the only one serving its purpose. I used the gym every now and then, but not nearly as much as I'd planned. Jamie rarely went in there anymore. Our pleasure room made me sad. It sat there, with plush shades of red and black, mirrors, different types of sex furniture, erotic artwork, bronze statues representing male and female figures . . . pillows, custom lighting . . . just so much! But all of it collected dust. We hadn't used it once. There was no passion. There was no adventure. There was no thrill.

I sighed and shook my head, returning my attention to the relaxation room and its mood. It was better. Quickly, I shed most of my clothes and opted for the massage chair instead of the bed—the chair was better at getting my legs, and I needed that. As soon as I sank into it, I felt relief. Mists of vanilla wafted into the room every so often from a programmed system. I picked up the remote control, activated the massage function, and immediately felt the respite of gentle, rhythmic movements kneading away the tension built up in my muscles. In that moment, I was lulled into a state of complete relaxation—from the warmth of the fireplace to the serene sounds of the waterfall and soothing aromas. I closed my eyes and smiled. It was heaven.

After a while, I heard the familiar chirping of my phone, signaling a message notification. *Damn it.* I'd broken my own rule of not bringing phones into the space. Reluctantly, I reached for it and checked the message. It was from Auntie Nia. Her message read, "Trish, hope you got in alright. Can't stop thinking about our chat. Let's catch up in a few days so you can get all your questions answered."

I set my phone aside and closed my eyes once more, letting Auntie Nia's words sink in. Psychedelics. Shamans. Spiritual journeys . . . and . . . "Jump?" She was a kaleidoscope of intrigue, and I wanted to explore every facet. "Absolutely," I finally typed back. "Let me know when you get settled back home."

As the massage chair continued working its magic, Bentley busted in. I chuckled, noting that I also forgot to close the door behind me. He was so slow and arthritic, but his tail still wagged, and his eyes were filled with affection. He licked my feet before lying down by my side.

"I love you, big boy," I cooed. He was an excellent companion.

"Trish!" Jamie called from downstairs. Clearly, my quiet time was coming to an end whether I wanted it to or not.

"Yeah, babe?" I responded.

"Do you know where the batteries are? The remote's dead."

I suppressed the urge to roll my eyes. He asks this every couple of months. "Bottom left cabinet, Jamie. You always forget."

"Oh yeah, that's right! Thanks!"

"Mm-hmm."

I brought my downtime to a close and headed to the master bedroom for a soothing, hot shower. That was my favorite part of every day. The stream of heated water pouring over my skin, the steam buildup, and the moments of solitude I could enjoy only in that private space; it was glorious.

~

JAMIE FINALLY CAME up while I moisturized my skin and prepped my hair for the night.

"Hey, sweetheart," he greeted me, his hazelnut eyes screaming he'd stayed up longer than he should've.

"Hey," I whispered, not holding his gaze.

He disappeared into the bathroom to do his routine while I reached for my e-reader to soak up a few pages before bed. This was our regular wash, rinse, and repeat, with Bentley slowly strolling back and forth between us before settling down once we were both in bed. But this night, I decided to break the cycle when Jamie came back into the room. "Jamie..."

"Yeah?"

"We need to talk..."

"Uh oh!"

"I'm serious."

He sighed, dropping his shoulders. "Okay. . ."

"I'm just...I'm lonely, Jamie."

"But I'm right here!"

"I know, but you're not. Not intimately."

"What do you mean? I kiss and hug you all the time. We are intimate!"

I exhaled. I didn't want to explicitly say what I wanted, but knew I had to. Auntie Nia always said I was responsible for my happiness and not to expect anyone to read my mind. "Passion, Jamie. I want passion. I want you to touch me beyond hugs and kisses. I want you to make love to me. Take me. Devour me...I'm...so lonely, baby. My body is starving for touch."

For a fleeting second, Jamie's facade cracked, and I saw the plea for understanding in his eyes before he masked it with a familiar nod. "Oh . . . that. Of course. Look, I'm sorry. I know, I haven't been giving you what you need. I'm aware, and I'm sorry. It's not that I don't want to, it's just . . . well, I don't know, honestly."

"I feel like we're roommates! What's wrong? What do I need to do?"

"It's not you. You don't need to do anything! It's me. I know it's me, and I'm embarrassed," Jamie admitted.

I sighed, resting my hand on his leg. "Babe, we're in this together. Whatever it is, we can work through it. You don't have to feel ashamed."

He glanced up to face me, and I could see vulnerability in his eyes. "Trish, I promise I'll figure it out. I just need some time to myself to sort through things."

"But you don't have to sort things out alone. Let me help," I pleaded.

He groaned and smiled weakly. "I know you want to, and I appreciate that, but this is something I need to get through by myself, at least for now."

I squeezed his leg gently. "Okay, I understand. Just promise me you'll try. And you'll tell me if you find it a struggle. I miss you. I need you."

He leaned over and kissed me softly on the lips. "I promise, Trish. I love you too."

I could sense his angst but didn't press him anymore. With a heavy heart, I turned on my side, facing away from him. I felt rejected. I know that's not what he intended, but it didn't matter. He wouldn't let me help. He rarely made advances anymore. He seemed to say only what he thought would make me happy, but it wasn't enough. This wasn't the first time we'd had this conversation. Every fiber in my being was famished for amatory affection, a yearning I hated getting used to. As soon as he fell asleep, I reached into my nightstand for the sex toy that had become my nightly companion instead of him. Quietly, I brought myself to a lifeless climax, but it would do. At least it was stimulation.

3

INTO THE UNKNOWN

The next few weeks passed with quiet persistence. Jamie retreated into his thoughts often, leaving a widening distance between us that felt insurmountable. As the days stretched into a monotonous routine, a sense of restlessness grew within me. I realized I'd gotten sucked back into the boring, day-to-day groove of things and hadn't called Auntie Nia. But it was time. One evening, when memories of our conversation cascaded over me, I gave her a call.

She answered after a few rings, her voice nurturing and welcoming. "Trish, hey, child! It's great to hear from you. How are things?"

"I'm hanging in there," I offered with a sigh, unwilling to convey the turbulent emotions I'd been grappling with—even though I knew she would see through me. "Auntie Nia, I've been thinking a lot about our last conversation," I said, wanting to get to the good stuff without dwelling on myself.

There was a knowing pause on the other end of the line. "I figured you would. I'm an open book; ask away."

"Well, what all have you done? How did you start? What is 'Jump?' And how do I even begin exploring the kinds of experiences you mentioned? I mean, you made it sound like you tasted God!"

She laughed without reservation. "Well, child, I felt like I did!" I knew she was speaking through a smile. It was contagious. "You're still a curious little bird, Trish. I love it," she told me. "It all started with something called a Changa ceremony."

"A what?"

"Chan-ga," she spoke more slowly. "It's a blend of herbs mixed with DMT—a hallucinogen from the vine of a plant called ayahuasca," she paused. "I know this probably sounds like a foreign language to you."

"It does," I giggled. "But I'm a fast learner, especially when I'm curious."

"Of course. Well, that was my first foray into it. It was a part of a ceremony with a group at a friend of a friend's house right there in Atlanta, believe it or not."

"Tell me more. I want details!"

She chuckled. "Okay. Well, it's sacred—not something to do recreationally on a whim—that's the first thing you learn," she explained. "So, the host started with a clearing of the space with sage and guided us into having positive intentions. There were about eight of us . . . maybe nine . . . and we gathered in a circle on the floor with pillows and blankets for comfort. The shaman was at the top midpoint of our round group—"

"Was he Native American?" I interrupted.

"No, Black, actually, but he'd trained in Ecuador and Peru for decades—he's well known in spiritual circles around there," she clarified. "Anyway, we talked and got the run down on what to expect, and eventually it started with drumming. Sweet, cultured drumming, which created a rhythm and consistent pulse in the room. It was almost hypnotic..." her voice trailed off as she recalled. "And then we inhaled this snuff stuff to further clear our minds and get our bodies ready. I don't remember the name of it...started with an R or something like that," she went on, her voice veering off again as though she were transporting herself back to a montage of this specific memory.

My ears perked up beyond belief as I hung on Auntie Nia's every word. "Okay..."

"You smoke the actual changa through a pipe," she continued.

"What!?" I was astounded. "Like a crack pipe?"

Auntie Nia got a good laugh. "I guess, but not really. You do smoke it. . . . It's tough to describe the experience, but I'll try. And you can look it up on YouTube," she added. "When the smoke gets into your system, it snatches you out of the here and now. Your body stays where it is—in fact, I felt like I'd gotten stuck sitting Indian style; I was like dead weight and couldn't move—there's a distinct separation in time and space in your mind and spirit. Almost like you drop into somewhere else filled with wildly intense colors, shapes and feelings. You laugh, you cry. You feel a myriad of emotions, and it's different from person to person. For me, it was mind-blowing and ecstatic." Her voice grew more expressive. "For others in the group, it was hard. They released a lot of grief they'd been holding in. It was cathartic."

"Wow." I didn't have the words.

"It lasts only about ten minutes, but it can feel like an hour. It depends."

"What made you try it?"

"I'd heard about it from some women in a tantra group I'd been going to."

"Excuse me?" I teased.

"We'll come back to that," she laughed.

I didn't know much about tantra, but I knew it had to do with sexuality somehow. Not that I wanted to think of Auntie Nia as a sexual being, but I was curious about the group—about it all! I wanted to drink from the cup of her wisdom.

"Anyhow," she continued, "that was the first psychedelic experience I had, and I was hooked after that."

"So, you've done it multiple times?"

"Yes. The first time opened my heart and mind so much that I never saw life the same way again. It was like a rebirth—a journey through my own consciousness, guided by the wisdom of ancient plants. It leads you to the point where you connect with God or whatever put us here."

"How so?"

"Well, not to sound dramatic, but it's almost like experiencing death. When you fall away from the present, you feel a sense of connectedness to the universe that words can't describe. And you realize there's nothing scary about death. It's like going home—wherever that is—and it's filled with pure love."

At first, I was speechless. And then, "Hmm" was all I could grunt. It sounded scary. "And what does that have to do with 'Jump?'"

"Nothing. I tried changa first and then went on to try ayahuasca sometime later. That's one of the more original plant medicines—going back thousands of years in indigenous populations. That experience lasted for eight hours. It was amazing, but not one I want repeatedly. It's not for everybody, seriously, just like I said changa isn't about recreation! Plus, I don't like the length of time that I feel like I'm out of the physical world with ayahuasca. And your body reacts during ayahuasca ceremonies."

"How?"

"You throw up. Go number two. Your body purges. It's not pretty."

"Oh. Ugh."

"Yeah. It can be taxing, even if euphoric and spiritually eye-opening in the end. I'm okay without it. And Jump..." she paused. "Is something new."

There was a heavy silence before she spoke again.

"It's experimental. A new discovery made by some folks who mixed properties from cactus, ancient vines, herbs, and some lab made, synthetic stuff." Auntie Nia continued, her voice taking on a cautious tone. "It's different, Trish. Unlike anything I've ever experienced before. It's a doorway to different dimensions, alternate realities, or who knows what else."

"Hold on, Auntie." I was entranced. "Can we switch to video?" I needed to see her for the rest of this conversation.

"Of course," she laughed.

With a quick screen tap, Auntie Nia and I went from a voice call to looking at each other. It felt better that way. "Is it legal? I whispered, unsure why because I was alone in my home office. Bentley lay at my feet, a comforting, nonjudgmental presence.

"No. The other stuff is protected under religious laws. Jump is so new and under the radar that there's no legal framework for it yet," Auntie Nia replied, her face serious as she gazed at me through the screen. "And it's not natural, like the plants alone."

"What happens when you Jump?"

Auntie Nia leaned in closer to the camera, her eyes intense. "It's like stepping into a portal that teleports you to another time, sometimes another dimension. It's as if you're physically there, experiencing everything happening in that reality."

"Like a dream state? How?"

"I guess you could say that. It's the power of the concoction, baby. I'm not completely sure. The herbs, plant alkaloids, and extracts, along with some carefully engineered compounds, have a unique synergy in Jump. They interact with your brain and consciousness in extraordinary ways, guiding your mind and spirit through the fabric of time and space. Suddenly, you find yourself living in another era as if the barriers of time have dissolved."

I sat back, my mind racing. "So, you're saying that with Jump, you can actually *live* in a different time period? Like, not just observe, but really be a part of it?"

Auntie Nia nodded. "Exactly. It's an inconceivable experience. You become part of history, and history becomes a part of you. You'll see, feel, and understand things in a way you never thought possible. It can be a shock to your system, though...depends on how you handle it when you arrive."

My mind was blown. "What about the butterfly effect? What about changing the course of history and its consequences? And what about the possibility of getting stuck in a different time?" I felt a mixture of fascination and fear. The idea of living in another time was both exhilarating and terrifying. "Is it safe?"

Auntie Nia's expression turned solemn. "Well, that's the thing,

Trish. It's still a big uncharted territory. The risks are unknown, and that's why it's not legal."

"Governments are still fighting over weed. This will never be legal," I laughed nervously.

Auntie Nia nodded in agreement. "And as far as I can tell, nothing in my present timeline has changed, but I'm aware of the possibility. Fully aware," she added. "And world leaders don't want people having these kinds of experiences—none of them, from time-tested plant medicine to Jump," Auntie Nia spoke passionately. "You're right that it'll never be legal. But the potential for self-discovery and spiritual growth is immense. Because you land with awareness and an eagerness to explore your deepest desires, temporarily embrace dynamic situations, and evolve."

As she continued explaining the intricacies of Jump, my curiosity ballooned, and a sense of adventure somersaulted within me. It was a journey into the unknown, and for the first time in a long while, I was excited about the prospect of something new.

"How would I start learning more? I've never done anything in this territory before."

"You would start by doing your research. Lots of it. Everything isn't for everybody, and I'd be remiss to lead you down a path without asking you to fully understand it. And before you start any plant medicine journey, you should spend time meditating and doing mindfulness practices."

"Hmm. This is a lot."

"It is. And you have to remember it's a deeply personal journey. Your mind and spirit need to be ready for anything. Because. . ." she paused, "when you drop into yourself, there's nowhere to hide. Who you are and what you want, to your core, leap out." She cleared her throat and continued. "Like it reminded me of the time I almost put down roots in Morocco on a whim. I'd fallen in love with a little casbah by the sea, but in the end, the wind called me back to the States. Sometimes, I wonder though," she rambled. "What if I'd stayed? Or the time I spent a month by a gorgeous lake in Guatemala.

If it weren't for me needing luxury in my life, I'd have stayed! It made me realize how much of a wanderer's heart I have."

"You sure do!"

She smiled. "That's what I mean by your essence flying out. Whatever parts of you that you may have ignored or forgotten about, resurface for you to face them. So, you must be ready for that," she finished speaking with a slump in her posture.

"Tired?" I quizzed.

"A little bit. I've been mentoring a few young ladies here and guiding another group online. It's rewarding, but I haven't had much time for my rituals lately. I need to slow down and breathe. To just *be* for a bit."

Her previous statements hung in the air, heavy with implication. And as I stood on the edge of a decision that could change the course of my life, I knew that the path ahead was filled with uncertainty. But I was ready to venture into the unknown. I was bored and disillusioned with what I knew—even though I didn't want to abandon it—and I hungered for adventure like a dormant volcano thirsting for eruption.

I HUNG up feeling ambivalent but courageous. I would do my research immediately. It was early evening, and Jamie would be home from the hospital soon. It had been almost seven months since his accident—Jamie meticulously tracked his progress and updated me with little milestones I might otherwise miss. And he was back to doing light rotations at the hospital. I was proud of him for being back on his feet doing what he loved, and I was grateful that he'd overcome the head injury and broken bones he'd sustained. He seemed to immerse himself in work as a distraction from everything, but at home, he was simply a shadow of his old self. He didn't hang out on the deck taking pictures of birds the way he used to. He barely played the vintage records he loved so much. And though I knew he loved me, he showed it in the most passive ways possible.

Guilt riddled me as I thought of everything I'd just learned and my eagerness to plow forward despite uncertainty. Was I a bad wife for being unable to wait for him to feel 100 percent himself again? What if he never did? What about me? What might my spiritual journey be like? And Jump—because I really wanted to try it—how would that be? Where would I land? Auntie Nia said who I was to my core would jump out. That's an impassioned and usually insatiable lover—what would I get into? How would I feel when I got back? So many questions gnawed at my soul. I was ready to learn more.

4

A JOURNEY BEGINS

After Jamie and I did our usual evening routine, I crept out of bed when he fell asleep. I couldn't rest. Thoughts of mystical journeys and curiosity whipsawed in my mind like a rainstorm. I had to take a step forward, and I needed to know more or else I might do something impulsive to quench my burning desire for sensual touch and adventure. So, I tiptoed in the dark to my office and went down the rabbit hole of video and text search for hours.

I read about everything from magic mushrooms and psilocybin to Changa, Ayahuasca, Peyote, DMT, and Ibogaine. They were all medicines used in historic spiritual practices. I persisted until exhaustion weighed heavily on my eyelids. As Auntie Nia mentioned, Jump was a new drug, and I could find chatter about it only on obscure forums and other dark corners of the web. It wasn't revered along with the sacred plants. In fact, some folks detested it as a capitalistic exploit on ancient traditions. If it weren't for Auntie Nia telling me about Jump, I would've run away as fast as possible. There was one discussion about Jump feasibly causing quantum entanglement—an unusual connection where things far away are mysteriously linked, like when two friends always seem to know what the other is thinking, no matter how far apart they are. I still had much more to research, but so far, it seemed mushrooms might be the best thing for me to try first. Jump was too advanced.

It was still dark when I eased back into bed. Jamie slept soundly, unaware that I'd even gotten up. Despite fatigue, my mind spun in the flickering blackness, bathed in the soft glow of moonlight seeping through the curtains. In the quiet, I watched Bentley's chest rise and fall with each breath. He loved sleeping by the windows on my side of the bed. Gazing at him, I noted how much his peaceful slumber starkly contrasted everything going on in my mind. *At least those two are sleeping well,* I thought.

At some point, I finally dozed off, and too soon after, signs of the morning—birds, garbage trucks, and daylight spilled into the room, waking me up again whether I wanted to rise or not. *Fucking hell*, I lamented. Jamie was buzzing about in the bathroom. I could hear him shaving and listening to a sports medicine podcast—he was always studying his field. I sighed, and an unprompted smile spread across my face. I loved him so much and wished we could return to how we were. It just felt so out of reach and slipped farther each day.

Jamie was a handsome silver fox with chai latte skin, a chiseled jawline, and curly hair from his mixed-race heritage. Part Black and part Cambodian, Jamie was alluringly attractive. The tattoo sleeves on his arms always caught people off guard, especially since he was a surgeon, but they were as old as our relationship. He'd started getting them when we were younger and he played baseball. And even though Jamie didn't work out how he used to, remnants of his solid physique remained. I would ravish him in bed if he'd let me. But he always gave me a few pecks before delicately pushing me away. I wanted to scream sometimes because I was so bored and needy, but I didn't want to keep pressuring him. I'd just have to find pleasure another way.

~

What if I ended up in slavery? I jotted down in my journal over the next few days. I had to think of everything that could happen, right?

But what if I ended up in a world of unimaginable passion and ecstasy? a contrasting thought rapidly followed. Jump was about joy and getting what you deeply needed and wanted, and I was sure that didn't mean dragging me to a Southern cotton field under colonizing White rule. And I'd tear up a plantation if I knew I wouldn't be there for long! Fuck that! Master my ass! *Or would I?* I liked to think of myself as being tougher than I am now, but that was unlikely. Plus, I wondered how my behavior in dream states would impact others after I returned to my real-time home. That's where that quantum entanglement and possibly the butterfly effect might come into play. It was a lot to think about, and I needed to talk to Auntie Nia again. I figured she would be able to answer some of these questions, or at least know someone else who might.

My mind soon drifted back to more pleasant thoughts. *What if my soul's journey through time helped me find the passion I'd yearned for, but it meant cheating on Jamie, even if only in my dreams?* Could that even be considered cheating? It would be in another realm! The possibility ate away at me, a double-edged sword of desire and guilt.

A rumble of Bentley's barking pulled me out of my thoughts. He didn't get too worked up these days, so I was surprised to hear him make such a stir. Someone was at the door, and I could see from the doorbell camera linked to my phone that it was a young man in his early twenties. His demeanor was confident and purposeful, and he had a stack of papers in his hand. I jogged downstairs and opened the door cautiously. Bentley's growls faded to suspicious grunts behind me.

"Can I help you?" I spoke immediately. It was chilly and overcast out.

"Yes, ma'am. Thanks for opening the door and not talking to me from behind it. My name is Derrick Covington, and I'm part of an organization called ATL Solidarity. We're out trying to get support for a big food drive for local shelters. I'm not asking for any money, but if you have any canned goods or nonperishable items that you don't mind donating, it would really help a lot." He handed me a pamphlet with a hopeful smile.

I was impressed with how concise and informative his pitch was. "That's a commendable initiative," I replied, noticing the Morehouse College emblem on the top-right corner of his shirt.

"Thank you. Just doing my part to plant seeds of change."

"Planting hope for a brighter tomorrow." I smiled. The words flowed from my lips with ease.

"Yes, ma'am." A unique, vintage-looking microphone pendant hung from a leather cord around his neck. It had a mysterious charm to it, and I couldn't help asking him about it.

"Interesting necklace you have there."

"Thank you. Heirloom, I guess you could say. They say it came from my great-grandma," Derrick shrugged.

"It's nice," I complimented. "Alright, let me see what I have. Would you mind waiting out here for a bit while I grab a few items?"

"Of course not. Thank you so much!"

I ended up filling an entire reusable bag full of canned goods and nonperishables. It warmed my heart so much to make the donation that I also promised to go online and contribute more to the cause. I didn't think college kids like Derrick still cared much for door-to-door activities like this, so it was a pleasant surprise.

"We appreciate your support," he said before lugging the bag to his car by the curb.

"Anytime!" I smiled before closing my front door. The interaction did me good!

After making my way back upstairs to my office, I gazed past all the interior design books on the shelves to the outside window. Derrick had long gone, and a thick blanket of low-hanging clouds shrouded the sky, filtering the weak winter sunlight into a dull, grayish hue. The street was damp and glistening from intermittent showers. My fingers nervously tapped the desk as I went back to my psychedelic search. *Where can I safely get mushrooms?* I wondered. Unlike weed gummies, I couldn't think of anyone I knew locally who might be into shrooms. I didn't have a big circle of friends and definitely wasn't close enough to any of my neighbors to ask. I'd have to get creative without Auntie Nia around to provide them. *Or, you could visit her.* The thought popped into my head, but I quickly ushered it out. Something didn't feel right about doing a California drug run to my play auntie who was twenty-five years my senior.

Determined to find answers, I began searching for any local events or gatherings related to psychedelics. I lived in Atlanta, and it might not be as liberal as most of California, but it wouldn't be too far-fetched to find something! My search led me to a symposium happening at Georgia Tech later that week. *Perfect.* The event featured Dr. Randolph Reynolds, a renowned neuroscientist, as one of the keynote speakers. *Come on, universe!* I cheered internally, grateful for the timing of it all. His talk was on the potential therapeutic benefits of plant medicine. Without hesitation, I bought a ticket. I was eager to learn more from an academic perspective. After all, it might be life-altering. I needed to know as much as possible about the world I wanted to enter.

As I sat there, scouring the internet for answers, a soft chime from my phone signaled a new message. I glanced at the screen and saw it was from Auntie Nia. My heart skipped a beat; her timing couldn't have been better. I opened the message, eager to see what she'd said.

"Trish, darling, I had a vision last night. Something important to tell you. Let's connect tomorrow via video call, say around noon your time."

My eyes expanded as I read her text, and I felt a mix of excitement and apprehension. What kind of vision could Auntie Nia have had?

5

THE SYMPOSIUM

I had a big job with wealthy clients up in Roswell, Georgia, the next day, but I made sure to slip out to my car to call Auntie Nia at noon. I was desperate to hear about the vision she'd alluded to. In fact, it was 11:58 a.m., and my heart raced as I settled into my vehicle for our video chat. The midday sun cast welcome rays to warm up the winter afternoon. As the clock struck noon, I called her, whirring in anticipation. The line rang several times, each second feeling like an eternity. Then, finally, Auntie Nia's smiling face appeared.

"Hey, child!" She greeted, a mix of cultural artifacts in the background of her frame.

"Hey, Auntie!" I returned the grin, relieved to see her. "You've had me on the edge of my seat with your vision talk. What did you see?"

Auntie Nia spoke as if preoccupied with something else. "Trish, close your eyes and imagine this: It's early morning. Warm. A full moon is still showing despite the sun. It may be spring. You're by the ocean at daybreak, mesmerized by its allure. Carefully, you explore the shoreline, looking for tranquility and peace. And as the waves' sounds wrap you in an embryonic embrace, you stop now and then to swaddle yourself—smiling, relaxing. Then you come across a pocket watch with a shattered glass cover." She paused.

I opened my eyes. By now, she'd given me her full attention.

"That's what I saw." She finished. Even across the screen, Auntie Nia's presence felt commanding. It was obvious how she'd become a mentor to many.

"What do you make of it?" I quizzed, glancing at the time to make sure I wasn't away from my client's house for too long.

"Not sure; beyond time, baby. But I wanted you to know so you could think about it. It could mean you have a lot of time or a little—or that time is an enigma. In any case, you've gotta decipher it. Trust your intuition."

"Auntie, I don't know what to say. I've done so much reading and watched so many videos, and I'm sure I want to step into this world. I'm just trying to figure out the safest way. Thought I'd try mushrooms first since they're the least intense, but I don't know where to get them.

"You're a brave soul, Trish," she spoke calmly. "And if you're sure, I might be able to help you with that."

"Seriously?"

"Yes. I can make an introduction to some folks I know and trust there. That way, I know you're in good hands. Otherwise, I'd invite you out my way. It's important you're surrounded by good people with great energy. Have you been journaling and working on mindfulness?"

"Yes, ma'am, I have. It's been helpful. Thank you for encouraging it. Not sure why I hadn't done it all these years."

"It's a good practice, especially if you're going to journey down this path. You'll want to log your experiences so you can analyze them later," she paused. "I've been writing about my life for decades. Every wrinkle and silver strand I have has a story behind it, I'm sure. They're marks of a life fully embraced. I think you might want to do the same," she emphasized.

"Hey, Trish!" One of my assistants called from the home we were designing.

"One second, Auntie." I held up a finger to let my helper know I needed a second.

"Actually, I have to run, darling. I know it's the middle of the day for you, and you're probably working.

"I am!" I grinned. "But thank you for this. And I'll take that introduction to your contacts, if you don't mind. I'll text you later to catch up on a few other things."

"Sounds good. Take care."

"You too. Bye." I hung up. Our call left me feeling curious yet a bit more at ease. Auntie Nia's words were comforting but still a little mysterious.

I still had a full day ahead of me, so I couldn't dwell on her insights for too long now. But on my hour-drive home, I'd surely ponder them.

Days later, I found myself in line to enter the symposium to hear Dr. Reynolds speak. His being an accomplished scientist who studied the effects of psychedelics and consciousness was something that made me eager to listen. I'd read through his long list of accomplishments more since I bought my ticket and knew that many called him too skeptical and quick to overlook metaphysical and spiritual interpretations in his studies, but I was interested regardless.

Meticulously groomed with a crisp haircut and clean-shaven face, Dr. Reynolds was likely in his early 50s. His rimless glasses and tailored navy suit were accentuated by a burgundy tie. I listened intently to his presentation, making notes when he discussed brain chemistry and altered states of consciousness. I was curious about the potential for adventure and deeper connections with oneself and others from different psychedelics. There was no mention of Jump during his talk, which wasn't surprising since it was so off the radar for most people.

"I don't believe psychedelics are a magic cure," he answered doubtfully when someone in the audience asked about their potential to treat depression and addiction.

But isn't life's magic found in the wild corners of the soul, not in a sterile lab? I wondered. From everything I'd read, I could totally see psychedelics being a healing tool.

Dr. Reynolds continued, "There's been some studies that allude to them helping, but not enough research to make me feel confident enough to give an enthusiastic yes," he added.

Tuh, that's something Jamie might say, I thought. Although Jamie might be even more critical. He'd likely hate the fact that I attended this event to research the bewitching side of psychedelics.

"What about compounds in new elite drugs like Jump?" another person asked.

Dr. Reynolds seemed caught off guard. "Well, first of all, I would stay very far away from any illegal drugs," he spoke firmly. "Regarding the compounds, I only know that the ones in Jump supposedly interact with the brain's quantum properties, particularly the sensation of quantum entanglement—the compounds act as a conduit. It supposedly leverages that feeling to allow users to connect to the past. That's all I know about it. Nothing concrete. And I strongly advise against it," he belabored, pushing his glasses up the bridge of his nose. Dr. Reynolds stood with an air of conviction and assuredness.

I groaned. While I appreciated his educated approach, I was wary of medical professionals who seemed overconfident in clinical research to validate everything. I didn't think life could be boiled down to what can be picked up on tests or measured scientifically. There had been times when all of my medical scans and bloodwork showed me to be perfectly healthy, but I knew I wasn't. Stress, anxiety, emotional unrest, and spiritual turmoil can't be understood by most scientists, so I took what I needed from his lecture and left what I didn't. His stance was not shocking, unfortunately. A gatekeeper like Dr. Reynolds would likely never want to discuss non-clinical treatments. He probably listened to classical music and collected vintage medical instruments for fun.

When I got home, I saw Jamie had cooked dinner.

"Surprise!" He smiled proudly. "I know you had a long day today, so I took some initiative." He panned his hand toward a set table as if he were on a game show announcing grand prizes.

"Thank you! That was so thoughtful," I beamed.

"Mm-hmm! So, put your things down and come enjoy. I made honey-glazed salmon with mashed potatoes and asparagus. Healthy yet tasty!"

I nodded with approval. The gesture warmed my heart.

As we sat down to eat, Jamie's affection and care for me were evident. He'd even fed Bentley ahead of us so he wouldn't sniff around us while we ate—I loved the dog but hated that even in his old age he still did that.

"You won't believe what happened today," Jamie chuckled, taking a bite of salmon. "I had one of the Hawks's basketball players come in for a consultation. Six and a half feet tall, muscles everywhere, a freaking giant! Guess what he came in for."

I raised an eyebrow, intrigued. "What?"

Jamie grinned incredulously. "He had a sprained pinky toe, Trish. The whole team was worried he couldn't shoot hoops properly with that li'l ugly pinky toe bothering him. He actually thought it was broken."

I burst out laughing. "A pinky toe? Seriously?"

Jamie nodded, still chuckling. "Yep, he was convinced that his entire career depended on that tiny digit because they're heading into the playoffs, and he couldn't be off his game."

We both erupted into laughter, imagining the towering basketball player fretting over his pinky toe.

"To be fair," Jamie added. "A broken toe would be a huge problem for him and the team. It was just the contrast of this 6'7" muscle-bound dude reduced to a sobbing man-child over a tiny toe," he chuckled.

We continued chatting and making plans for the weekend, discussing a possible trip to the North Georgia mountains. I'm more of a beach girl, but Jamie adores the mountains.

"There are some nice trails we could trek. I checked them out already," he said, his voice taking on the precise tone it did when he discussed surgeries and treatment plans for his patients.

He didn't sound excited or passionate, but he was taking the initiative to do something outside the house, which I appreciated. I also loved the thought of him being in nature. Jamie had partially grown up just east of Winston-Salem, North Carolina, a stunning and mountainous region. He attended Appalachian State University for his undergraduate studies, where his athletic prowess shone through as a star baseball player.

Balancing his academic ambitions with his love for sports, Jamie excelled in both arenas. After earning his biology degree as an undergrad, he joined the Army, following in his father's footsteps. Jamie's transition from civilian life to military service marked the end of his competitive baseball days. Still, he continued enjoying and playing softball whenever he had downtime in the military. He knew athleticism from both sides, and his challenges while serving our country added to his unique combination of skill, discipline, training, and rigor. It laid the foundation for his eventual career as an orthopedic surgeon specializing in treating elite athletes.

Before his motorcycle injury, Jamie always found ways to be athletic when off work. Somewhere along the way, he'd fallen in love with bikes and cycling—traditional and motorbikes. He was the kind of guy who kept a bicycle in the trunk of his car in case he finished up early at the hospital and it was a nice enough day to hit a trail. It was hard to watch him shrink into this new version of himself. Still caring, but inactive and a shadow of who he once was.

He cleared the table after dinner and pulled two personal slices of coconut cake for dessert. My favorite!

"I know you like your sweets to put the final touch on a meal," he said proudly and gave me a new fork. Jamie lingered for a moment as if he had more to say, but instead, he just handed me the cake with that characteristic restraint in his eyes.

"Thank you. Yes, I do!" I dug in.

"You're welcome, babe...you know, this feels nice, me doing something normal," he said softly. But he didn't expand. A tiny smile of satisfaction tried to spread across his face but it didn't get far.

Dessert was delicious. We even went for a family walk around our neighborhood with Bentley afterward. The weather was clear, with a gentle breeze rustling its way through the few leaves that remained on trees. Our development was relatively quiet, with most residents in their fifties or up. Jamie and I had met only a few other families where the couples were in their early forties. Each home, including ours, stood as a testament to personal achievement, with luxury cars parked in garages and driveways, showcasing the neighborhood's material success. We lived in one of the few communities where most people didn't leave after moving in. It had history—on the south side of Atlanta where Black professionals once chose to live after being shunned on the more affluent, White side of the city.

One thing most outsiders of Atlanta didn't realize was that the city was still segregated. Despite all the jokes about it being a Black mecca and a cultural melting pot, it's not. Not when you dig in and realize the races rarely mingle. Racism is quietly rampant. There's confusion around the difference between tolerance and acceptance, and equitable integration. Atlanta is a great Southern city for various reasons, but it does not live up to the ideals outsiders have projected.

As Jamie, Bentley, and I strolled around our all-Black, upwardly mobile community, it wasn't lost on us that if we lived in Roswell, Buckhead, or Alpharetta, houses like ours would be worth nearly double. But it was fine. We liked our location. It was close to the airport, not far from downtown, and we were surrounded by caring neighbors who ensured our area was clean, safe, and respectable.

"Hey there," a neighbor called as we walked by.

Both Jamie and I smiled and nodded in acknowledgement. We often saw others while walking Bentley. Heck, even the two former mayors of Atlanta lived in our development. It was a great place to call home, publicly devoid of the pretentiousness that seemed so loud in Midtown and Buckhead.

After getting two miles in, we began heading back home. Bentley kept stopping to look at the path we'd walked, which was also our signal from him that he was ready to call it a night.

"So...how...have you been feeling lately? You know, overall," I asked Jamie. "Tonight seemed like it was a good night for you. I appreciate the dinner."

"Okay, you know. I'm okay."

I took his hand in mind, caressing his fingers. "And about us?" We stopped to let Bentley relieve himself.

"About us...I'm working on it. It's really about *me*," Jamie said. "You're great. I know that. But I'm working on myself so I can be the man you want me to be."

"I just want you to be the man you used to be."

"Well, see, that's the thing. I don't believe I can do that. He's gone," Jamie spoke somberly as we picked our pace back up. "But that doesn't mean I can't improve who I am now. It doesn't mean that I can't work with what I've become."

"What did you become?" His wording threw me off, and I felt a slight shiver from the cloud cover that had started rolling in.

"Depressed," Jamie spoke without hesitation. It sounded as if he'd been eager to spit out the word.

I stopped again. Shocked. I knew he was sad; yes, of course. But the way he said it had weight. It sounded resolute.

"You know what I really want?" he continued. "What I think I need?" He squeezed my hand nervously. With a big exhale, he said, "I just want to lie in your lap some nights in silence. I—I—" he stammered. "I want to take a depression nap in your arms without judgment. I want to cry because I . . ." His voice rattled as he pulled his hand from mine to wipe his tears. "Not yet. Not here. Let's get inside," he explained, and we hastened the pace for the final stretch home.

Bentley glanced at both of us as if he knew something was stirring.

Once in the house, Jamie cracked open. "My feelings align with the symptoms of clinical depression—persistent anhedonia, intrusive negative thoughts, apathy...I've analyzed it every which way..." he admitted and sank to the floor.

"Anahe what?" I had no idea what he was referring to.

"I feel like I can't experience pleasure, sorry. And I'm not sure. I probably shouldn't diagnose myself, but it's all I can think of. I keep trying to pull myself out of this quicksand of negative emotions, and I can't, Trish. I put on a happy face as much as I can, but the truth is there are a lot of days I wake up disappointed that I did."

My eyes enlarged in shock. Though I knew his spirit took a bigger hit than his body after his accident, he'd never seemed so defeated. I suddenly felt guilty for wanting to find pleasure outside of him. I felt anxious and wanted to console him. For decades, Jamie had been my protector and the picture of strength. He'd been a paragon of virility who would take on anything no matter the odds. But now, I didn't recognize the man on my kitchen floor. My heart rocked in my chest. I wanted to nurture him.

"I've always had a plan, a protocol to follow for when I feel out of control, but this—there's no manual for navigating the chaos in my head right now."

"Come here." I pulled him between my legs, guiding his head to rest on my chest.

"I just...I've always relied on things being certain and, in their place, but now, everything's just falling apart—I feel like I don't even know who I am anymore, Trish!"

In that moment, he bawled. He shook his head negatively as a rush of tears fell from his eyes. "What happened to me?" He asked repeatedly, not waiting for me or giving me time to answer. "I just want to feel peace, baby. But I can't find it. My thoughts are loud, and they won't listen to me. I can't control them! What happened to me?"

Bentley moseyed over, knowing something wasn't right. He sniffed around us and licked Jamie's salty, tear-stained hands before resting his head in Jamie's lap—his own offering of comfort. For all our years together, this was the first time I'd seen Jamie break down. He'd survived military deployments as a medic, rigorous medical school, working in trauma hospitals where every day was a tornado of chaos and death. He rarely showed signs of helplessness, but now he was openly struggling. Moments like this reminded me everyone has a breaking point. No one is invincible. I shouldn't even need reminding. Every night, I felt like I was dying inside from lack of touch. But I didn't actually *want* to die. Jamie's admission scared me, and I had to take the lead now. He needed me to.

I didn't see weakness in the tears falling from Jamie's eyes, although I knew he probably felt I did. I saw courage to finally look his shadow in the face, even if he was afraid of it. He met its gaze. And as I held Jamie, my inner conflict deepened.

Guilt eroded me, and I began to question the inevitability of my journey into Jump. Jamie had given me everything I'd ever wanted for years: love, stability, and a partner who truly cared about my well-being. I had no reservations about doing the necessary to get him back on safe mental ground, but how long would that take? And what about me? Was I an awful wife for still wondering? I had no idea how long his mental health journey would be, and truthfully, I wasn't as stable as I'd wished either. Most days, I was distress draped in designer clothes and stilettos—Chanel bag and all. It wasn't just the lack of intimate touch that buried me in sorrow. It was the *connection* that lack had to my mood, creativity, well-being, and self-worth that dragged me further into hell. But for now, I had to focus on helping Jamie find his way back to himself. And maybe, just maybe, I could find a way to heal myself too.

"Would you consider giving therapy a try now?" I asked cautiously.

He sighed and kept his gaze on the floor. "Sure."

THE NEXT MORNING, I made a series of calls to find a psychiatrist for Jamie. He was right; he shouldn't self-diagnose, so I got the ball rolling to find the help we'd need to get through this. He was the love of my life, and I refused to let him sink further into depression without trying everything at my disposal to help him. I decided to keep researching Jump and other psychedelics but delayed trying Jump, specifically, until Jamie was on a stable therapy plan. The last thing he needed was me taking a black market woo-woo drug and having an adverse reaction. I trusted what I'd learned so far, especially with Auntie Nia vouching for it, but I had to think of all possible outcomes.

From what I'd uncovered about magic mushrooms, however, I thought I needed them now more than ever. I needed to feel the profound emotional connection that so many others claimed they'd experienced. I needed something to help me be strong enough to help my husband, and hoped shrooms might be it. That night, I decided to take Auntie Nia's offer to connect me with someone she trusted.

6

UNKNOWN GROUNDS

My night was restless. I had hot flashes and cold sweats, tossed and turned, and barely slept for more than five hours. I was worried about Jamie. I was antsy about what a psychiatrist might say or prescribe, and I was conflicted about the path I'd chosen to navigate, both for myself and for our relationship. When my alarm clock went off, my eyes had already been open for two hours.

Jamie had left early to prep for a seven AM surgery he'd been scheduled to perform. By the time I peeled myself out of bed, he'd likely already be scrubbed and with his team, working hard to put his broken patient back together.

"Come on, get up, get out of bed!" I amped myself up. It was a new day and another chance to tackle my uncertainties. Even if I was only wearing one sock—because that was the best way to regulate my body temperature throughout the night—I had to give everything my best shot.

A part of me felt the return of the weight of being a partner and caregiver, but I would have it no other way. I was determined to help Jamie find his way back to himself despite questions hammering at me like persistent doubts in the back of my mind. After grooming and dressing to look, smell, and represent a million bucks, I pushed myself to go out and give my best to new and existing clients. In between work calls, I managed to nail down a mental health professional who I thought would be a good fit. He'd worked with many athletes and high-performing individuals with demanding careers, and I hoped Jamie would be receptive. Just in case he wasn't, I reached out to two other specialists to have backups.

Days later, we'd found ourselves in the office of a middle-aged, three-piece-suit- and purple-bowtie-wearing psychiatrist who greeted us with an enthusiastic, "Good morning, folks!"

He ushered us to a comfortable seating area, where Jamie and I, holding hands, settled into plush armchairs. We both had a sense of anticipation but also an underlying unease. I hoped Jamie was wrong with his self-diagnosis and that he wouldn't need medication or a long-term care plan. The therapist, Dr. Rowe, was a man of experience, and his office bore the marks of a seasoned pro. The midtown workspace was adorned with books, calming artwork, and soft lighting to create a serene atmosphere. A polished, glass-topped coffee table in the center of the room gleamed from the sunlight pouring through the tenth-floor window.

"Care for some water?" he quizzed.

"Sure," Jamie and I answered in unison.

Dr. Rowe smiled, handed us each a chilled bottle, and took a seat in a chair across from us. He adjusted his glasses and looked at us with kind eyes before continuing. "So, tell me how you're both feeling today," he spoke calmly and reassuringly.

Jamie and I exchanged glances, and then he spoke up, his voice wavering slightly, "Doc, I've been feeling . . . *different* lately. Like I'm in this deep depression." He paused, but no one filled in the silence, so he continued. This time, words hurried out of him like a river rushing downstream. "I can push myself to get through most days after a lot of heavy mental lifting and pep talks about all the people who depend on me, but it gets harder every second. I get exhausted with living. Annoyed with it, actually, but I know I shouldn't. Because I have a great wife and a good job. I could have died already, but I didn't. I should be grateful, not miserable, but I can't shake the low feeling."

Dr. Rowe nodded empathetically. "Thank you for sharing that, Jamie. I'm sure it isn't easy."

Jamie's leg shook nervously, but he seemed more eager to talk than I thought he would be.

"Trish, how about you? How have you been coping with Jamie's feelings?"

"Oh, me?" I wasn't expecting to contribute. This wasn't a couple's counseling session. "Um..." I took a deep breath. "Well, I didn't know the severity of his feelings until last week. That's why we're here. Once I knew, I realized I may not be enough to help. I want him to get his spark back." I placed my hand on Jamie's knee. "I'm nervous but hopeful that this is a rough patch and unexpected stretch of recovery from his motorcycle accident last year."

Dr. Rowe leaned back in his chair, scribbling notes on a pad. "Tell me more about that," he requested.

After a brief pause, Jamie recounted the Wednesday he'd left the hospital early after a successful surgery. It was just before the July 4th weekend. Hot and humid, but not too bad when you're going fast on a lime-green Ducati. He'd said he just wanted to enjoy a ride before the holiday weekend. Jamie felt a little lightheaded, he admitted, but thought he might be dehydrated.

"I was literally slowing down so I could go to a gas station and grab some Gatorade when it happened," he recalled. "But after that, I don't remember much. My world went dark. I woke up in the trauma unit of Grady Hospital with broken ribs, a fractured shoulder, a cracked leg, and a head injury because my helmet flew off." He stopped, unable or unwilling to discuss what he remembered after waking up in a hospital bed.

"They think he passed out," I added. "And unfortunately, first responders believed his helmet wasn't securely fastened, which is why it didn't stay on and absorb most of the impact. They found him face down, bleeding and unconscious in a thick patch of grass, with his mangled motorcycle behind him, smoking."

"Treatment was rough. I was in and out of consciousness from the ambulance ride to the hospital. I remember only slices of that day. They rushed me to surgery, where the medical team worked hard to stabilize me. I'd lost a ton of blood and was a sack of shattered bones."

"A bunch of scans, tests, and emergency procedures," I added. "It was really scary. They initially told me the surgery would be three to four hours, then it went to six, and then it went to nine. I was a nervous wreck."

"A trauma hospital means constantly hearing "code red," or "code blue" over the loud system while stretcher after stretcher of wounded patients streamed in. Nothing about it alleviates stress, and I hate to think about the panic she felt while I was under," he grazed his fingers over my arm. "But I pulled through, obviously. I had a great team working on me."

We continued talking about that day and the aftermath. All the physical therapy Jamie had been through up to his return to work. He'd come a long way physically, but not so much mentally. Dr. Rowe listened and made notes. As the session continued, he guided us through a series of questions, helping us articulate all our emotions and concerns.

"How do I know if this is clinical depression or just a rough patch?" Jamie was eager for answers.

Dr. Rowe leaned forward, his expression empathetic. "Valid question, Jamie," he began. "Depression can often overlap with rough patches in life, but there are key differences. With a clinical diagnosis, you experience persistent symptoms such as a deep and prolonged sense of hopelessness and changes in appetite or weight. You'd experience sleep disturbances, fatigue, difficulty concentrating, and a loss of interest or pleasure in things you once enjoyed. It can be overwhelming and impact your daily life."

"He still eats like his old self, that's for sure!" I chimed in.

Jamie chuckled. "Correct. No changes in my weight either. I sleep okay most nights," he admitted. "It's when I wake up that's the problem."

"And why is that?" Dr. Rowe asked.

"I feel disappointed that I did."

"Oh?" His gray eyebrows rose.

The moment Jamie confessed his feelings, I felt a tinge of regret. It didn't dawn on me until that moment that his admission may impact his ability to work—his career. Who wants a depressed surgeon operating on them? Did Dr. Rowe have an obligation to tell on Jamie? I got anxious. *Maybe we should have thought about this more before coming in*, I thought. Jamie didn't seem to think about it. He seemed more relieved to get his thoughts out and eager to find a solution. *Maybe this is a good idea? He clearly didn't want to die. He just thought he did . . . right? Is there even a difference?* I was unsure.

Dr. Rowe glanced at his watch before speaking again. "You went through a traumatic event. And after years of being the savior for others, suddenly *you* needed to be saved. I gather this was a new experience for you. The vulnerability. Relying on others. Not being able to move for months."

"The isolation during recovery," Jamie injected. "I had Trish and a home health aide sometimes, but I still felt alone. That did something to me . . . knowing how easy my life could splinter to pieces," Jamie finished.

"Of course. Few people know what that feels like, Jamie. So, give yourself some grace. I would say since you're back to operating . . . even if at half capacity, and you're not experiencing the other changes I mentioned, you're not clinically depressed."

"Is there a test I should take to be sure?"

I chimed in, sharing my concerns. "He's not the same as he was before the accident, Dr. Rowe. He used to be so confident and upbeat, but now..."

"I understand, but if you aren't feeling the things we mentioned every day for weeks on end, I think we can work through this in traditional therapy—without medication—because I don't believe you're clinically depressed, Jamie."

A broad smile spread across Jamie's face.

"The most important thing right now is providing you with the support and tools you need to navigate your emotions," Dr. Rowe said to Jamie.

Jamie glanced at me, and I could see hope in his eyes. The path ahead felt more manageable, and we were taking the first steps toward understanding and healing. In the weeks that followed, Jamie's therapy sessions would become a crucial part of our lives. I didn't attend anymore, but he told me what he felt comfortable sharing, and I felt good about his direction.

WHILE JAMIE WORKED on his mental health, I couldn't shake the need to take the fork in my road. I contacted the folks Auntie Nia had referred for mushrooms. They were a couple named Yasmin and Amara. They quietly grew their own plants. Auntie Nia swore by them and had also vouched for me. I was nervous to meet them but felt I had to. I needed to know what was so magical about the experience and wanted to take the first step in my journey.

One afternoon, we'd agreed to meet at an event held by a local tantrika named Lena. Yasmin and Amara wanted to get to know me before any kind of transaction and thought the workshop might be a great start, especially once I explained why I wanted to try the shrooms. The event was on breath control and how it could help create spiritual experiences connected to erotic pleasure. I was excited to attend and grateful that they told me about it.

"We want to introduce you to a community," Yasmin had said the first time we spoke on the phone. "It's not just about getting high or going on a trip," she explained, regarding the shrooms. "We take it more seriously than that. It's sacred to us, especially if you want to work your way up the psychedelic chain," she continued.

Hmm. Community. It was a word I rarely heard anymore, save for the young man who had rang my doorbell soliciting donations. I liked the sound of it, though. I often felt like I was on my own running my business, tending to Jamie, taking care of Bentley, and just generally in life. I didn't have a sisterhood or many friends. The thought of meeting other women who were interested in things similar to mine exhilarated me. I liked Yasmin and Amara before I'd even met them!

Walking into the event made me nervous at first, but I quickly started to relax when Lena, the facilitator, warmed everyone up through guided small talk and house rules for phone usage and privacy. Soulful, dreamy, and contemplative music played softly under her voice. The vibe was peaceful, welcoming, and affirming.

Dressed in an earthy-green-and-brown-print kimono, Lena exuded confidence and control. Her hair was braided and fell to the middle of her back, with a few locs being red while the rest were dark brown. She sauntered around the room with no shoes and an infectious smile before starting with relaxation exercises.

"Alright, everybody, I'd like you to get seated, get comfortable . . . whatever feels best for you. Please just settle into that," Lena began. "I want us to begin with a few clearing breaths. And by that, I mean inhale through the nose and exhale through your mouth. But we're going to do it with intention . . ." she continued. Her voice was deep and smooth, like a glass of bourbon.

Yasmin and Amara, both of whom I recognized from a photo Auntie Nia had sent me, arrived late. They sat on the other side of the room, so I didn't get to speak to them until everything was over. Before then, however, I was introduced to conscious breathwork and how it connects to both spirituality and sexual awakening. I learned how crucial breathing was to being present in the bedroom, expanding orgasmic experiences, and tasting the intersection of desire and transcendence; an axis point that until then, I'd never considered. Lena talked about ancestral healing tools our bodies already knew that could empower us to enjoy erogenous experiences beyond the norm. She talked about breath control's ability to release tension and make you feel safe, its relation to the vagus nerve, and so much more. I was entranced by her lesson and wondered why it took me so long to stumble into this kind of environment. I guess I didn't know what I needed.

"You must be Trish." Yasmin looked up from her phone and at me with a happy greeting. She and Amara came over after the workshop was over and folks had started mingling.

"I am," I grinned. "Nice to meet you." I outstretched my hand to shake theirs. Suddenly, it felt like an awkward gesture in a room full of women hugging to greet and say goodbye to one another. The handshake felt sterile and impersonal, but it was too late to retract my hand.

"Likewise," Amara chimed in. "How did you like the class?" She inquired.

"It was amazing. I don't think I've ever thought about all the ways conscious breathing could help me connect with my body's sensations and desires. I don't think I really thought about it at all, you know? I just breathed without thought...until now," I laughed.

"Love it," Yasmin giggled, happy to see me happy.

"I'm definitely going to attend more of her sessions," I added.

Before we could chit-chat longer, we got audible cues that we didn't have to go home, but we had to get out of the space. Outside, Yasmin and Amara introduced me to a few other ladies who were in attendance that night. They seemed to know most of the students and Lena's staff. "Community" was right. There were a handful of men there, but overall, the energy was of sisterhood. It was of togetherness for the betterment of all present.

"Thank you so much for inviting me to this," I gushed. I meant it. That was one of those evenings in life where I knew my life would change because of the experience I had and the people I met. I would absolutely journal about what I felt and what I'd learned.

"It's our pleasure," Amara said. "Your aunt said a lot of great things about you."

I was grateful for the segue. "She's the best. Like a second mom. I'm closer to her than to my actual mother. I love her to pieces," I confessed. "How did you all even meet?"

"At one of Lena's events in Mexico," Yasmin recalled.

"She travels," Amara injected. "Does retreats in and outside the country."

"That sounds amazing!"

"It is. Definitely get on her mailing list," Yasmin suggested. "I think she has one coming up in Cuba. Anyway, we met Nia at an event a while back and hit it off. She sort of became everybody's auntie, having more experience than many of us. Told us all about her journey to fulfillment and how she landed on the shores of California by way of Florida to backwoods parts of Georgia."

"Heck, I might need a refresher on those stories!" I was surprised. Auntie Nia and I still had a lot to catch up on.

Yasmin, Amara, and I chatted for a while. We left Lena's event venue and met up at a popular café not far away. We talked more about plant medicine and what I could expect. They shared with me their journeys into the space and why they'd become so passionate about being a resource for trusted others who wanted to try it. I didn't know what I was expecting from someone I was supposed to buy drugs from, but it definitely wasn't this. It wasn't seedy, secretive, or suspicious. Yasmin and Amara were informative and attentive. Cautious, yes, but more so protective of the experience and their plants. Apparently, they grew mushrooms and peyote.

By the time I left them, I had three grams of shrooms and instructions to remember it's all about mindset.

"Try not to go into it with any specific expectations. You usually don't get what you want, but what you need," Amara said. "It may make immediate sense when you come out of it, or it may take some time to click."

"And have water. Lots of it. Like a gallon, and some chocolate to diffuse the taste," Yasmin added.

"Yeah, shrooms kind of taste like ass," Amara piped.

We all laughed before they continued to run down a list of dos and don'ts, from what to wear and the type of space—clutter-free and open, outside if possible but with someone to watch over me—to what kinds of emotions to expect. It was a lot, and admittedly, I was afraid of trying it alone for the first time.

"What's wrong?" They could read my face.

"I want to do it responsibly, but my husband doesn't know." The moment I spoke the words, I regretted them. I didn't want to alter their perception of me, but it might have been too late. I hoped they weren't judgmental.

Neither woman pried. "Well," Amara began, "if you're positive you want to do it, we can maybe . . ." she paused. Thinking. Glancing at Yasmin.

"We can hold space and facilitate for you," Yasmin added. "But we do think he should know. Don't get me wrong," she quickly added. "You are your own person and obviously can make decisions independent of him, but . . . if you guys don't have any problems and you think he'd understand, why not—"

"I don't think he'll be receptive. Plus, he's got his own issues he's working through."

"If it's emotional or mental, you could try it together," Amara suggested.

"Not yet. Not now. Maybe later. I don't know."

They acknowledged my hesitance in silence and went back to offering to help me with my first experience.

"I'd really appreciate that!"

With a double-checking look at each other and a sigh, they agreed. I'd made up my mind and now had guides. I knew Jamie might not take it well if he knew I was experimenting with this. He tended to look at healing more clinically. Although lately, that was shifting due to his own need for help. Still, I didn't believe he'd be open to my trying something "illegal," but I didn't want to suppress my desires to appease him. Not for this. I needed this, especially to clear the path toward trying Jump, and I would deal with any consequences later, I decided.

7

A SLOW DANCE WITH NATURE

Surrender is required. That was on-site reminder number one. A few weeks had gone by since I initially met with Yasmin and Amara. I had to find the right time to link back up with them that wouldn't arouse suspicion from Jamie. It took me a while to figure out my story since he and I spent so much time together, but eventually, I told him I was inspired by Auntie Nia to go on a spiritual retreat. But it was local and for only a day. As expected, he had no interest in going, but he did ask lots of questions about where I'd be and what it was all about.

I'd told him about the breathing workshop I attended before, so this wasn't completely out of the blue. By now, Jamie understood that Auntie Nia had lit a fuse in me to experience something new. He was okay with it, even if not personally interested. Plus, his weekly therapy sessions were going extremely well, and I could see changes in him. Sometimes he see-sawed with emotions, but overall, I thought he was heading in the right emotional direction. I, on the other hand, was a playground swing of feelings. I was excited, curious, and mildly apprehensive.

To Yasmin and Amara, this wasn't a big deal. But to me, it was monumental. I met them at their place, an adorable ranch-style house on the west side of Atlanta—just fifteen minutes or so from where Jamie and I lived. Their street had a completely different look and feel than my neighborhood. It was more vocal, with their home proudly displaying giant Black Lives Matter and LGBTQ pride flags above its entry steps. Not every lawn on the block was well-manicured, but theirs was. And a lone preteen aimlessly rode his bike up and down the otherwise empty street.

It was a Sunday, sunny but frosty outside for early Spring, and I followed their instructions to pull into the driveway instead of parking on the street.

"Send a text instead of ringing the bell, please," Yasmin had requested. "No need to get our dog riled up. He goes ballistic from the chime every time like he's never heard it before."

"No problem," I'd texted back. And soon, I was pulling into their home. *Deep breath*, I coaxed myself. I wanted to be relaxed.

"Find the place okay?" Amara greeted me with a smile.

Returning the good vibes, I said, "I sure did."

"Normally, we'd prefer doing it later in the evening, but since you've got to get home, we'll start around noon," Yasmin told me after welcoming me inside.

Their place seemed curated for relaxation. Pillows everywhere, a vintage record player softly crooning neo-soul melodies in the background, and the distinct scent of incense wafting through the room. Art of beautiful Black women adorned the walls, making me feel right at home. Shortly after I arrived, I watched Yasmin and Amara use a pestle and mortar to crush the pieces of mushroom into a fine powder. We chatted while I watched. They also showed me a tray of six button-sized cactus with furry white tufts.

"Those," Amara pointed out, "are peyote plants."

They were spineless cacti revered for their healing ability, but admittedly, I couldn't remember everything I'd researched—only that it was too advanced for my comfort level just yet. They were cute though.

"But advanced," Yasmin added, confirming my initial thoughts.

"We're going to have some as a tea with lemon and ginger, but we think you should just eat it with chocolate. It'll get you past the taste faster," Amara told me. She let their tea steep for half an hour while telling me stories about their trips—both physical and metaphysical.

"Oh, man, I remember the first time I did shrooms. It was back in college, actually," Yasmin volunteered, a Yin-Yang pendant dangling from her necklace. "No one warned me about the taste, and I had no idea what I was doing dosage-wise. My trip was more comical than anything. I couldn't stop giggling. I laughed until I couldn't breathe, and I was dangerously dehydrated. It was fun, but I was so ignorant of what the plant could really do. It would be more than fifteen years later when I tried it again with maturity. I've been hooked ever since."

"It's fascinating how much there is to learn about these plants—as natural remedies, I mean."

"Absolutely," Yasmin hinted with an air of mystique. "The world of plant medicine is vast and not always what it seems. There's a lot under the surface, kind of like most people, you know?"

"Girl, Yasmin loves her mysteries and abstract interpretations, but at the end of the day, it's all about a healing journey, Trish. That's what we're helping you start today, hopefully."

"Thank you. I appreciate the hand-holding," I admitted.

"No problem. That's why we grow. Safety is paramount for me," Amara added. "Sometimes we go on full trips, but most days we just microdose."

My eyebrows furrowed. "Microdose?" I'd gotten used to their calling the feeling of being high on shrooms a trip, but this term was new.

They explained how taking tiny doses every day improved their mood and heightened their creativity. "You don't need a lot to feel a difference in your system," Yasmin explained. "Why take anti-depressants, anti-anxiety meds and all of the lab-created, synthetic pills pushed by pharmaceutical companies when you can literally eat something that naturally comes from the earth?"

"No asking your doctor for permission or prescriptions," Amara added. "Just taking care of yourself with what is innately available to you. That's a whole other political discussion though," she course-corrected, deciding she didn't want to go there now, I guess.

I'd read and studied so much that I was aware of the splitting opinions on psychedelics and drugs in general. From the academic perspective to the religious to the libertarian, I'd observed a mosaic of viewpoints. To me, indulgence should be up to an individual—after they learn the potential risks and rewards—to determine if they want to try anything or not. Everyone wasn't smart. Some people would jump in without a clue because they wanted a good time. Everyone wouldn't be thoughtful, and everyone may not know their pre-existing conditions and do the thorough and necessary homework to be cautious before partaking in something new, which could easily make them a burden to society. Perhaps not with psychedelics, but drugs universally.

Every substance, whether legal or illegal, has pros and cons, but addiction is a real problem that shouldn't be ignored. Life was hard, and drug use wasn't new. It goes back thousands of years, with people using it to numb pain or reach enlightenment. Finding balance and avoiding paternal interference should be the goal, but of course, it wasn't. Social control was. At least, that was my opinion.

"You know," Yasmin opened up, "Amara always says to take things slow, to let the journey unfold naturally. But sometimes, I wonder if we're too cautious—if we're restraining ourselves from deeper experiences."

Amara sighed. "Yas, there's wisdom in patience. Beauty too," she added, tossing locs of her hair back. "We know that every journey isn't a good trip. So, it's important to respect the process and a person's readiness."

Their back-and-forth made me a little nervous. "Is there a right pace for this kind of experience?"

Yasmin gave me a comforting smile. "It's different for everyone, Trish. What's important is listening to your inner voice, even if it leads you somewhere unexpected. Sometimes, what we think is caution might be fear in disguise."

"You're here. Something in your soul already told you that you're ready. It's a person-by-person pace, of course, but you're safe with us. We're here to guide, not push you," Amara took over, making me feel better.

As the clock ticked farther into the afternoon, the three of us sat on pillows on their living room floor. Amara played ambient music that she said had the precise beats per minute to induce deep relaxation. It was a mix of Native American, and Indian strings, pure drumming and nature sounds like thunder, rain and flowing rivers. My nervousness began to taper off, but every now and then returned when I remembered I lied to Jamie about where I was. I felt guilty. Why couldn't I have told him the truth and given him the chance to respond for himself instead of assuming? *He would have a fit, that's why.* My inner voice responded like a violently selfish shadow wanting to snuff out thoughts of Jamie.

"Here's your chocolate-covered shrooms," Yasmin kidded as she handed them to me. "And some water."

"Thanks," I smiled, hesitantly taking a bite.

Amara and Yasmin sipped their tea while I ate the pieces they gave me. The texture was harder and grittier than I expected.

"Hmm. Okay," I chewed and swallowed hard. "These damn sure aren't portabellas!"

Both women cackled out loud. "Not even close!" Amara wheezed.

"Nah, sis, I guess we forgot to tell you about the consistency," Yasmin spoke through a smile. "You get used to it."

"All good," I said and hurried to swallow the rest.

I followed them through a meditation to clear my head and relax as much as possible. Overall, I felt like I was in a good headspace. For a time, everything felt uneventful. It wasn't for another half an hour or so that I started to feel anxious again. I worried about having a bad trip or that I'd taken too much too fast for my first time, but it was too late. I wasn't going to throw it up. I calmed myself, remembering I was in good hands, and before I knew it, I started feeling something. Amara and Yasmin had closed the blinds in their house to make it feel more like evening and I began feeling like my vision got sharper.

"I think something's happening," I vocalized. "I feel nauseous." *Oh fuck.* That was exactly what I *didn't* want to happen.

"Breathe..." Yasmin placed her hand on my shoulder. "Just breathe...slowly. It'll pass."

The feeling was horrid and lasted longer than I wanted. *Don't vomit. Don't vomit. Don't vomit!* I rocked the words like a mantra in my head, in synch with the background music. Soon enough, the feeling did pass. Shortly after, however, is when things got bizarre. The room became more dynamic. It felt alive, and the dull white walls of Amara and Yasmin's house developed moving streaks of color. They appeared like veins under skin. Green. Pink. Blue. They grew into a repeating pattern of symmetrical shapes with five sides. They looked like spinning stop signs, only they weren't red, and they didn't evoke a feeling of danger or any need to stop.

I sank into the music, which felt like it was vibrating in the molecules of my blood. I didn't just hear it, I felt it. I was it. And soon after, I became intensely aware of the remnants of chocolate on the plate before me. I could smell them as if they were fifty times their minuscule size. My mind was blown. I couldn't tell the last time I'd been so in tune with my senses. It was overwhelming, and I felt the urge to lie down. I had to. Sitting wasn't steady enough for me. I needed to close my eyes. My mind was a scattered mess trying to process everything, so something had to give.

"Can I lie down?" I heard myself mumble. I was aware of my surroundings and not gone mentally, but I couldn't control my brain's urge to take in everything. It was a confusing moment.

Yasmin and Amara guided me back on pillows resting against the couch. I felt them watching over me, protective, while still enjoying their journey. With my eyes closed, I continued seeing lines, shapes, and various colors, especially green. It was GREENING, and together, they glowed and mesmerized me. The background music felt like a nurturing embrace.

"How do you feel?" Amara quizzed me softly.

"Okay," I whispered. "I'm good. I see a lot. Sense a lot. It's hard to describe though…" my voice trailed off because I found it hard to converse.

Once again, I closed my eyes. I could still see the outlines of both ladies behind my lids. They dissolved into floating shapes like sugar crystals in warm water. Soon, I was in the aquatic dance too. I'm not sure how long I was submerged in this feeling, but eventually, all the shapes and colors went away, and I felt calm. I wanted to remain completely still. I didn't want to drink or talk. I felt introspective, only wanting to untangle all the sensations I'd experienced. I was hyper-aware of everything—the texture of the pillows against my skin, the very air I breathed, and every individual instrument in the music. With my eyes opening and adjusting to light, I noticed tear smudges against Amara's cheeks. She was there with us, but clearly not completely present. Without words, I sensed happiness from her. Yasmin was attentive to me, very much present and aware of everything.

"I think it's fading away," I told her.

"That's fine. Let it go just as easily as it came," Yasmin advised.

As the day turned into early evening, I found myself extremely at peace in my mind and body. I came down gradually without any major breakthroughs or feeling like my life had dramatically changed. There was no dissolution of my ego or anything transcendent, but I did feel peace. I felt like everything—all things…would always be okay. My mind was clear like a haze had dissipated. I felt like whatever might happen with Jamie, we'd be alright—even if he found out about me doing this. We'd always be fine. I hoped that were true.

In the moment, I couldn't feel anything negative so nervousness couldn't present itself. And I didn't notice it until I was in my car heading home a few hours later, but I was mildly aroused. Between all the sounds, shapes, colors, smells and other sensations, I missed my body's subtle and physical response. Actually, I didn't know if it was a response to the drug or to my state of relaxation. Either way, I appreciated the stimulation.

Yasmin and Amara told me they gave me a low dose to start. My psychological safety was the most important thing. I thanked them from the marrow of my bones for exposing me to the experience. Even though I didn't have any massive changes happen, I was certain I wanted to try it again. The inner peace and clarity of mind were enough to make me want to take another trip. I was excited to see where I could go.

8

INNER CROSSROADS

My drive home wasn't long enough. I maneuvered the highway without thinking about traffic because my mind overflowed from my trip with Yasmin and Amara. There was a lot to process, and I was starving. It's funny, they told me that I'd lose my appetite, but I felt the exact opposite. I could eat a three-course meal! The moment I got home I fixed myself a sandwich and grabbed a bag of chips from the pantry. The soft glow of twilight filtered through the kitchen window when I stepped inside. Thankfully, I arrived at an empty house. Jamie was attending a work event, leaving Bentley and me alone in our cozy haven.

I glanced down at Bentley while scarfing down my makeshift dinner. My faithful four-legged companion took his time greeting me this evening, and shortly after, he plopped down at my feet. He'd been slower than usual the past few weeks, and a slight limp in one of his front legs had surfaced. Jamie was scheduled to take him to the vet in a few days. I hoped it was nothing serious.

"Hang in there, boy," I spoke to him softly while running my feet over his fur. His deep brown eyes met mine, filled with love and loyalty.

We'd had Bentley since he was eight weeks old, and he was truly like a son to me—a child who never got annoyed or complained; rarely got an attitude, and only wanted companionship, love, and fun. I hated seeing him in pain and tried comforting him while finishing my meal. Meanwhile, my mind drifted back to my inner journey.

My first mushroom trip with Yasmin and Amara had struck an ember within me, and confirmed I wanted to go farther. I could still see the glowing shapes and letters swinging freely, held in place by incredible cosmic threads. I wished I could tell Jamie about it, but I wouldn't dare. I didn't have the courage. Nor would he have the appreciation I do. I should have done it before doing what I did, but it was too late now, and this secret was just for me. It had to be.

I knew that I stood at a crossroads where my next set of choices would shape my path likely more than anything else. But I wanted to taste glory, and it wasn't at home anymore. I wanted to drink heaven, but my chalice was filled with mundane, tasteless water. I had peace, but no passion. I had stability but no spunk. I had loyalty but no luster. With a sigh, I rose to my feet and crossed to the window, peering out to the backyard we rarely used because palmetto bugs—roaches as I always knew them—resided in the trees. I hated that about Atlanta and should have listened to my cousin who told me not to buy a house backed by woods. "They live in the trees!" she'd cautioned, "I'm telling you! Those nasty motherfuckers live in the trees!" But I loved this house and bought it anyway. Now, above the arbor line, the evening sky was painted in gorgeous shades of pink and lavender.

As I swam in and out of psychedelic reveries, the soft chime of my phone cut through the silence. It was Jamie, checking to see how my evening progressed. I hesitated for a moment, swallowing the knowingness that I hadn't been completely honest with him. The truth was sour—bitter and disgusting, but I answered with a honey-sweet tone, "It went well! 😊" I typed and paused, letting out a giant breath. "Eye-opening and reflective," I continued, my heart pounding with the weight of my dishonest words. "I'll tell you all about it when you get home." *Great.* I thought. Now, I needed to figure out what I was going to tell him!

BENTLEY SIDE-EYED me when Jamie came home later, almost as if his furry little mind knew I wasn't shit for my choices. I made up a tale about a meditation session where we visualized our inner fears as colors and shapes.

"It was pretty abstract, but strangely soothing," I told him.

My story was simple and enough to not provoke deep questions. Jamie took my word and shared details of his evening. He'd met other surgeons from across the state and connected with a pioneer in orthopedic research, "someone whose work could revolutionize joint replacements," he told me. All in all, we'd both had a great day.

Guilt ate away at me that evening and several others that followed, but I could not bring myself to tell the truth or stop myself from going forward. Even calls with Auntie Nia couldn't help. I'd told her about my decisions, and she explicitly thought I was going about it the wrong way, but also believed my right to choose my path.

"What will be, will be, child. Things always have a way of working themselves out however they're meant to," she'd said. "Just know you control the direction of your life. You can always change course if you feel like it's the right thing to do."

"I know, Auntie," I gave in. "I know..."

Her words reverberated in my mind, reminding me of personal choices and consequences. But my desire was too strong to "do the right thing." For Jamie, that is, because this was the right thing for me, I thought. I couldn't just observe and learn about others enjoying something so intoxicating and not immerse myself in it too. I wasn't strong enough.

Weeks later, I found myself in a group of twenty people for another trip, or more like a gathering for different kinds of trips. I didn't want to over-rely on Yasmin and Amara, so I sought a community to join, and supposedly there would be different guides for distinctive ceremonies present. I remember Yasmin once saying, "Expand your horizons, be open to meeting all new faces in the journey," and I took it to heart. A hushed part of me wondered if her horizons were as broad as she claimed. Was she guiding me or nudging me towards a specific path? Despite the doubts, the allure was too tempting to resist. I went for it.

The gathering was in an old church, of all places. The pews were gone, and the belly of the building was hollow, but we were surrounded by stained glass windows, old arches, and folding tables. Several dynamic souls filled in, each draped in their unique essence. From colorful and flowy moo-moos to ripped jeans and too-big sweatshirts. Short-haired, rebellious women converged with perfectly dread-styled ladies. It was ninety percent women and ten percent a mix of everything else folks identified by these days—I'm getting old, and struggle to keep up with the labels. Honestly, I don't care. That's the truth. I just want people to be what they feel they are without the intense need to make me put "she/her" on my nametag. I didn't say that out loud, but the compulsion annoyed me even though I considered myself gender fluid. I digress.

Early in the event, I overheard a fellow attendee gossip to another to "Be careful with Yasmin. I've heard things...she's not always what she seems." Because I was being nosey, I couldn't be sure they were talking about the Yasmin I knew or someone else. The words sent chills down my spine, and I hoped it was someone else. Yasmin and Amara weren't even there that night.

There was a raw, unpolished beauty about the attendees, a stark, contrast to the glossy veneer of my usual crowd. One goddess-looking being floated in wearing all white, an updo, and dainty earrings. The rest were a medley of liberating energy that I found surprisingly infectious. Lena the tantrika was there—the one who did the initial breathwork class I'd taken to meet Yasmin and Amara. Her smile was bold, and her attire was a questionable red half-shirt that read "Respect Heaux" and black sweatpants. She looked comfortable, already out of her shoes and walking around with black ankle socks that had the balls in the back. *Whew! It's a lot going on right there*, I thought of her outfit, noticing sleeve tattoos on both of her arms and another on the small of her back. But Lena was free, moving through the crowd with grace and a not-giving-a fuck attitude. She was interesting and magnetic, with a super cute and curly frohawk hairdo. I was used to people constantly taking selfies and asking how they looked. Lena's edge was hard to ignore. I watched her interact, her demeanor shifting subtly when she spoke to certain individuals.

I found myself drifting towards the heart of the gathering, where a lively discussion about changa and toad medicine caught my attention. "Changa, huh?" I didn't know what the hell toad medicine was, but the former rang a bell. The word rolled off my tongue like a secret incantation.

"It's a different journey." A woman with eyes like ancient forests turned to me. Her gaze deep and rooted, as if they held timeless wisdom. "It's more intense, more immediate," she explained. The idea of accelerating my journey sent an electrifying thrill down my spine.

"And that's available today?" I quizzed, eager to try.

"I believe it is," she said with a warm smile and nod toward a small group near a window.

"Thank you!" I returned the grin and casually made my way to the direction she signaled. *Why not?* I thought. I know I probably should have gone with a higher shroom dose first, but I wanted to speed up the voyage to ascension. My heart pumped with a mix of excitement and trepidation as I introduced myself to the others, actually recognizing a woman I'd previously met at Lena's event. Lena was in this tiny faction too. That made me feel better. She had a motherly presence that comforted me.

"Have you done this before?" She asked, the depth of her voice reminding me of Maya Angelou's—not necessarily the cadence, however. But the resonant texture was relaxing.

"I have not," I grimaced bashfully. Me trying to hide my eagerness and angst was like trying to put a Band-Aid on a waterfall.

"You're in for a treat," Lena winked and cheerfully walked off.

As I watched the participants, Lena caught my attention again. She was conversing with a man who seemed out of place, his attire more formal, his demeanor reserved. I couldn't help but eavesdrop. He sounded like he'd read every book in the Harvard Law Library.

"Sorry, this isn't your scene," Lena said abruptly, her tone dismissive. "Maybe find a group that's more... suited for you."

Taken aback, the blonde-haired man, merely nodded and walked away. *Well, that was rude,* I thought. I watched Lena roll her eyes as he left. Her behavior struck me – was this the free-spirited Lena I admired, or was there a side to her I hadn't seen? *What was up with that?* I wondered, but their interaction was over just as soon as it had started. It probably took a lot for him to come into a room where no one else looked and sounded like him, and that was the welcome he got? Sad, and typical of Atlanta. But it wasn't my business, and I only saw part of their interaction, so I stopped myself from judging further. Besides, he'd ambled off to find friendlier folks, I guess.

From there, a corkscrew-curly afro-sporting medicine woman prepping the herbs and guiding the ceremony acted just as Auntie Nia had described her first time, with a cleansing of the space and an explanation of the experience. This went on for at least twenty minutes before our corner of the church quieted and the sounds of light drums and tribal flutes overpowered all else. The mushroom folks had disappeared to another part of the sanctuary, so it was just us, seated on pillows below rays of colorful lights coming from the stained-glass windows. I took deep breaths, remembering Lena's teachings on control and embodiment. I could feel my body shaking but managed to quiet it as it became closer to my turn to smoke the changa.

The first thing I wasn't prepared for was the snuff, rapé. Pronounced "rapay," it was the powder Auntie Nia couldn't recall, and I found it harsh. The medicine woman blew it up each of my nostrils using a long, skinny blue pipe, and I hated it. My eyes immediately watered.

"Breathe from your mouth," Soledad coached—she was the medicine woman in charge. "Breathe from your mouth," she repeated.

I'd never snorted anything a day in my life, and having the ground-up tobacco and other herbs forcefully blown up my nose made my nasal passage burn. *How the fuck do people do cocaine?* I questioned. Completely different drug, of course, but it was my first thought after taking the dust up my nose. Jamie would have a conniption that I let a stranger blow something up my nose post-COVID. I hadn't thought that part through but hoped for the best. It was too late. The train was creeping out of the station. *Whew!* I did not like the process, but I did like the feeling it quickly produced. It cleared my mind. I couldn't even think about him for a second longer, and instead sat comfortably on the floor with my knees pulled to my chest.

I closed my eyes, sinking into the relaxed feeling. As it became my turn to do the actual changa, it felt like stepping into a river, not knowing the depth or current, but eager to be swept away.

"Kuh-uh, kuh-uh." I coughed horribly on my first attempt to smoke from the small glass pipe.

"Let's do it over," Soledad spoke patiently.

Once again, I tried but could only take in the smoke half-way. My attempt was dismal, but I still felt something. Others in the group who hadn't gotten their turn yet looked on. Those who had already experienced their trip sat contemplatively. It was exciting to watch other attendee's responses, from ecstatic laughter to seemingly well-needed cries. I had to get my third try right, because after the second attempt, I hazily felt between worlds, but mostly in the present. I wanted to leave. I was ready to escape! The music continued and I felt myself getting heavy.

"One more time." Soledad leaned forward, bringing the pipe to my lips. This time, she held my nostrils shut to prevent me from accidentally breathing out the changa smoke. It worked. "Close your eyes..." was the last thing I remember her saying.

I couldn't move and was unable to tap any of my senses for input, but my spirit and soul felt animatedly alive. The experience was nothing short of transcendent, with childhood memories appearing and disappearing. I heard my seven-year-old-self laugh giddily when my mom twirled me wildly in our garden, skirts flying, under a shower of mango blossoms. I felt the Miami heat radiating out from the core of my being. Colors and shapes danced before my eyes, and time seemed to fold in on itself. Though I couldn't sense my body, I had the feeling of trembling. And then I was floating in soft water, a sea of emotions, each wave crashing under me with the strength of newfound understanding. I was on the shores of heaven.

In those moments, I touched something divine, something ineffable. It made me feel a deep sense of longing to be wild and free, because that's what I truly wanted to be. I didn't want to be civilized. I wanted to return to Eden, to freely walk naked and express myself. I wanted to do this and not feel burdened by the gaze of others so repressed; they couldn't fathom my freedom. I wanted to dance, which was odd, because I never danced. I desired to sing. And I hungered to play. I wanted to feel the liberation of a child filled with wonder for the world. Under the changa, I saw a vision of how life could be, were it not for the cycles of social conformity and the capitalistic slavery I'd unconsciously entangled myself in. I tasted bliss.

My eyelids fluttered as the effects waned, and slowly began to sense my legs again. One at a time, with the left taking longer to feel normal than the right. Darkness gave way to light and sound became more audible. I was in a loopy in-between state for what felt like a minute before reality seeped back in. But it was altered, however, like a street painting that had been touched up by a masterful, unseen hand. I exhaled heavily, reacclimating to the present. *The walls aren't moving*, I thought. *Good.* I was back. Since I was the second to last, most eyes were on me. And I no longer felt like I was among strangers except for Lena, I was with fellow travelers on a bizarre and beautiful journey.

Lena's silky voice pulled me to the moment, "You've now seen a glimpse of what's possible, Trish. Take your time processing it."

"Mm hm," I mumbled quietly. I hadn't found my voice yet. It was so much to take in that I felt like I needed to lie down.

Her words lingered in the air as I gathered myself. She was the last person to go, so I politely moved out of the center so she could take up the space. I knew my journey was just beginning, that there were canyon-deep truths and revelations waiting for discovery. I checked my phone and there was a message from Jamie, simple but laced with concern. "Hope your day was enlightening. I haven't heard from you, but can't wait to hear about it. Love ya!" he said. I stared at the screen, still not ready to process day-to-day conversations. The words blurred with how much I had swirling in me. I'd have to share something with him, but clearly not the truth.

"Love you too," I typed back, a gong-bang of guilt knotting in my stomach, pulling me back to reality even faster. I wished I hadn't checked my phone. His message was a buzzkill. "We'll talk soon," I finished. I would remain at the church for at least another hour before heading home. By then, I was completely back to normal and felt no trace of the magically altered state. As I wandered to my car, the evening felt different, charged with the electricity of my experience.

THE NIGHT AIR, once unnoticeable, now felt like whispers caressing my skin. I was different, kissed by the moonlight and adored by the Gods. I felt reborn and knew my life couldn't remain the same. When I got to my car, however, I noticed a small note on the windshield. My stomach plummeted as I unfolded it. "Saw your car. We need to talk. – Jamie." My breath caught in my throat. What did he know? What was he thinking? How did he even know where to find me?

I'd initially wanted to call Auntie Nia to tell her about my experience, but Jamie's note sent me into a panic. I was afraid to go home but knew I must.

"Fuck, fuck, fuck!" I muttered and pounded the steering wheel. How could I have fallen from heaven so fast? I wanted to enjoy myself and revel in the experience I just had but reality whipped against my face like a sandstorm. I couldn't see straight from the shock of it all. Tears instinctively built in my eyes at the thought of confessing to him. I couldn't do it. There's no way.

Not only did I not want to face the truth with him, I didn't want to halt my journey. I liked where I was going and didn't want him blocking the way. "Fuck, fuck, fuck!" I started my car, angry at the intrusion of reality into my newfound realm of freedom. *Don't tell him.* The thought penetrated my mind like a needle through silk. I was in too deep now, and Jamie...he wouldn't understand. He couldn't. His world was so opposite mine, so structured and unyielding.

Driving home felt like crossing into another realm, one where my newfound liberty clashed with the familiar confines of my old life. Each traffic light seemed to interrogate me, throwing flood lights on my dark secret. I'd have to bury it more. As I pulled into our driveway, the house loomed worryingly. I had to pull it together and stay committed to my lie. Jamie's Range Rover was there in the garage, waiting, just like his note. I sat in my Porsche for what felt like an eternity, trying to anchor myself. The words I'd need to tell him pranced in my head, each more false than the last.

Finally, I stepped out, my legs shaking. I knew I had to hurry up or risk him coming to the garage door to greet me. I wasn't ready for that, but the moment the door started going down behind me, I felt his presence. Sure enough, he was leaning against the wall immediately after the entry when I stepped inside. His expression was a complex motif of concern and suspicion.

"Trish, where have you been? I saw your car at that old church off MLK. What's going on?" he questioned.

I took a deep breath, steadying my voice. "Jamie, I..." I paused, the truth clawing at my throat, begging to be set free. But I smashed it down, stomping beneath a mound of half-truths. "I was at a meditation session, a different kind. It was... intense. A group thing, very spiritual. I just needed some space, some time to think."

He stared at me, his eyes prying for more. "All night? At a church? None of that makes sense, Trish. You're not telling me something. What is it?"

I forced a smile, a brittle mask. "I know it sounds crazy, but it was just a group of people looking for some peace, that's all. We lost track of time."

Jamie's gaze softened slightly, but the seed of doubt was planted. "Okay, I just worry about you, that's all. You've been so distant lately."

I nodded, hugging him with one arm while my mind did backflips. "I know, and I'm sorry. I'm just trying to find some balance, you know? Explore some new things. I'm on a spiritual journey."

He scoffed. It was slight, but I noticed it. As Jamie hugged me back, I felt the weight of my secret pressing between us, an invisible barrier that kept me from fully returning his embrace.

The rest of the night passed in a tense silence, each of us lost in our thoughts. Jamie's suspicion had awakened a new fear in me, a realization that my double life was fraying at the edges, and I'd need to create a stronger seam. I lay in bed that night, staring at the ceiling, wondering the best ways to do that and if I could keep it going long enough to find bliss before the fabric of my lies tore apart completely. I had to. I wanted to Jump.

In the middle of the night, I found myself creeping into my office to journal. I recounted my changa trip, the sensations, and memories it awakened. I wrote down the questions in provoked. *What happened between adolescence and now—I'd gotten everything I wanted but it turned out those things weren't enough. So, now what? What did I* need? I scribbled down the childhood experiences the ceremony unearthed. My mother and I were never super close, but the particular visuals I got reminded me of one of my happiest times with her. Smiling. Carefree. Why didn't I try harder to be closer to her? My first response was that "we're just too different," but was that a cop-out? I explored all my feelings on paper.

I even flipped through a somatic healing prompt book that I'd purchased to help me better understand my body's connection to my emotions, and answered questions like "Think of a recently emotive experience that jarred your body—list specific areas where memories of it make you feel tense, tight or relaxed at the thought of it (your jaw, your shoulders, your back, etc.). Describe them." All this work in exploring the connections to my emotions and my being was new to me, but I liked it. It pushed me to be more aware of my interconnectedness in ways I'd never imagined. I could thank Lena and her workshops for that. I'd never even heard the word "somatic" until I meandered into her world via Yasmin and Amara.

The next morning, I called Auntie Nia as soon as it was a reasonable hour for her. I still needed to share my journey with someone who would understand. Not wanting her to take on a more parental tone, I opted out of telling her about Jamie's suspicion. Instead, I focused on my experience.

"Auntie, it was like touching the sky…feeling every emotion I've ever had, all at once, and then some."

"I'm so glad you got to experience that. Just remember, every high has its descent, and you never know what it might be. Be prepared for whatever comes next. I'm sure you'll do a lot of reflection."

"Yes. I already started journaling about it."

"Good. Well, look, baby girl! I've got to run. Got a plane to catch, actually."

"Where are you heading?"

"I'm going to India for a few weeks."

"What?" This woman was always jetting off someplace.

"Yes, it's been on my list for a while, and I'm not getting any younger."

"Are you going alone or with a group."

"With a group."

"Good." I felt better knowing she wasn't doing this as a solo trip.

"But I do have to go, Trish. My car is waiting to take me to the airport."

"Alright, Auntie. I'll talk to you soon."

We said our goodbyes, and I knew she'd come back with a dozen and a half stories about this adventure. As things cooled down to a manageable temperature with Jamie, and I got back into my weekly groove with work, I decided I wanted to dive deeper. It was the most unfamiliar urge—to go it alone—but I wanted to learn more about the toad medicine I'd heard about, though I didn't feel pressed to try it. I only wanted to educate myself. However, I did want to Jump. I just needed to figure out how, especially with Auntie Nia out of the picture for a few weeks. It's a shame I didn't ask her for a Jump contact before I let her go.

The more I thought about everything, the more I realized I'd always been too timid to define and go after what I needed to be happy. For too long, my joy had been deeply enmeshed in pleasing others, especially Jamie. It wasn't his fault. He never forced me to do anything, but I defaulted to it because I thought devoting myself to him would make me the perfect wife. I'd been living my life for him, my clients, and professional circles for decades and it was time for a change. I wanted to know more of who I was, feel more of what I craved, and be more of who I could be if I stopped caring so much about the feelings of others. What would that look like?

What would it feel like to break free from fear of judgement—and stop judging myself for times when I steal little moments of pleasure? How much sweeter could life be if I stopped suppressing my deep-seated desires for adventure, sensuality, and freedom and just go claim them as my birthright? I wasn't ready to be open about these thoughts at home, but in my newfound circle, I decided to baby-step into living unapologetically. Maybe Yasmin and Amara might call this microdosing on liberation.

The revelations from the changa had me ready to take a solid step forward—finding a contact for Jump. I hated to bother Auntie Nia on her trip, but I texted her to let her know I was ready to try it. Hopefully, she was paying attention to her messages during transit.

9

BEYOND BOUNDARIES

There was a cacophony of noise in the background of Auntie Nia's voice mail message to me. Traffic, people, and probably animals—the sounds of India confirmed her arrival to the exotic country. I couldn't make out a word she said and let her know via text. I hated being a bugaboo on her trip, and figured her talking into her phone was easier than typing, so I ended my note with "No rush," despite desperately wanting the information now.

To alleviate my anxiety, I took Bentley for a stroll outside of our community. It was good for both of us to switch things up sometimes. And as the morning sun spilled golden light across his amber fur, it also cast long shadows across me. I stood there, as he sniffed random weeds and wildflowers, lost in thought. Today, I was not just Trish Gregory, the interior decorator with a predictable routine. I wasn't just a woman trapped in a passion-less marriage. Today, I was a committed explorer at the cusp of expanding my life with magical experiences. The realization cascaded over me like a spectacular waterfall of shimmering stardust.

My phone rested in my pocket, a silent timekeeper, counting the moments until a message from Auntie Nia came through. As Bentley sauntered ahead, moving despite the clear discomfort in his joints, a sense of adventure bubbled within me. I thought about Auntie Nia's voice, lost in the vastness of India. How she, too, must have once been tethered to the ordinary, only to break free and embrace the extraordinary. I smiled, deciding to head home to give Bentley medication Jamie had gotten from the vet to ease his pain.

I looked at my phone again, eager to see a text from Auntie Nia, but there wasn't one. Surprisingly, however, there was one from my mom. It was a shock because she almost never reached out to me first, which got annoying but there wasn't much I ever did about it. I didn't like confrontation, and she'd just get defensive if I mentioned it. So, I accepted her behavior. But I felt different today and didn't hurry to return her call. With every step I took, I shed a little layer of the old Trish, the one confined by expectations, routines, and maybe even some fear. I was eager to step into a new role. One where I wrote my own story, and confidently declared what I wanted.

"Hey, Trish!" A neighbor driving by yelled out of her car. She had a broad smile, and it was a welcomed greeting.

I waved and grinned, knowing she wouldn't hear my voice now being farther ahead of me. The air felt fresher, my steps lighter, and my heart bolder. Jamie was out of town for a conference, so I didn't have to worry about tip-toeing around his suspicions. Hopefully, he'd be so distracted he'd forget about my quest. His kiss goodbye didn't even linger on my cheek the way it normally would have. I was happy to be alone. Happy to have space to expand and explore. I was happy to chase the possibilities of vibrancy and passion I craved. I loved him, of course, but the part of me who had been waiting for more had an existential foot out the door already.

The moment I stepped back into my house, my phone buzzed with a message from Auntie Nia. "His name is Dr. Kaelan Murdock. He's the best person to guide you through Jump." *A doctor?* I was perplexed. I don't know what kind of street person I expected, but it surely wasn't someone with a PhD. "He's a biochemist and pharmacologist who went rogue," a second message tumbled in. "People call him 'Doc K' for short, and he usually works side by side with his wife Zephyra and a shaman named Jelani," she added, and then left me another voice message from a quieter place and told me the best ways to contact him. He lived in California. *Obstacle number one*, I thought. How the hell was I going to get ahold of Jump if I had to go across the country to get it? Shipping it wasn't an option that felt comfortable.

As the clock ticked on, each second felt like a heartbeat, pounding with the promise of what would come. But how? *Relax*, I reminded myself. You don't have to figure out everything right this second! I paced the length of my living room, my thoughts as constant as my steps. Bentley, sensing my restlessness, followed me with his eyes, his head tilting slightly every time I turned. Deep down, I knew that if I wanted to experience Jump—or even just learn more from a trusted source, I'd have to make a trip to the west coast. It was a daunting thought but exhilarating too. Jamie wouldn't be back for another week, and the idea of a secret journey both thrilled and scared me.

My decision didn't come lightly. After learning about Doc K that night—I spent hours and found pockets of information about him buried on decentralized video platforms and outdated-looking forums. There were no current photos, email addresses, or public contact details. It's as if his username and digital footprint vanished from the internet eight years ago, but quiet chatter about him took place in ambiguous, niche online communities. As the evening went on, I found myself repeatedly drafting and deleting texts to him. It wasn't just about getting the substance; it was about understanding it and experiencing it safely. I was about to leap into uncharted waters, and the magnitude of that decision pressed heavily on me.

Finally, I hit send on a text: "Dr. Murdock, this is Trish G. My auntie, Nia, spoke highly of you. I'm interested in learning more about a unique subject of interest. Could we possibly discuss this further?"

His response came the next morning. "Good morning, Trish. Nia is a great friend of mine, and she gave me a heads up you'd reach out. I'd be happy to talk to you. It's important to understand what you want to step into. Let's arrange a video call?"

My heart hurdled. I gulped. *Do it*, my inner voice goaded impatiently. And with that gut push, I scheduled the call for later that evening. Jamie would only be gone for a week, so I had limited privacy. Hours later, I clicked the 'join' button, my breathing slow, measured and jagged. Doc K looked the same age as Auntie Nia—early 60s, but that's where the similarities stopped. His hair was a tornado of gray, as was his beard and handle-bar mustache. He wore a sage-green button-down shirt under a worn white lab coat. Behind him was a wall of beakers, intricate lab equipment and a wall of herbs, and obscure compounds. His demeanor was calm and his gaze was piercing, yet kind.

After exchanging pleasantries, we talked at length; he explained the science behind Jump, its effects, and the importance of being in a controlled environment, especially for a first-timer.

"You need to be somewhere safe, with a trip-sitter, as I like to call it—someone to watch your physical reaction and guide you through the experience," he advised. "Your body temperature and heart rate may elevate, although I'd do my best to give you instructions and a dose to suit your body type."

I nodded, taking in every word. Like the mushrooms, but even more crucial, it was clear that I couldn't just acquire Jump and try it on my own. The risks were too great.

The call ended with an invitation from Doc K. "If you decide to try Jump, I can facilitate your experience here with my team in California. I normally wouldn't extend that offer, but because you're family to Nia, I feel obligated to. She's important to me," he said, his eyes almost drifting off to a distant memory.

"I would love that," I gushed. "Thank you so much!"

On second thought, my brows began to furrow in suspicion, but I suppressed them. I knew a special connection between two people when I saw one, and there was something about his last statement that made me wonder if he and Auntie Nia were more than casual acquaintances. *Mind your business and focus on your own love life.* My shadow self was so rude and intrusive.

"Do you know when you'd like to come?"

"Soon," I spoke faster than I wanted to. "It's just I have a window over the next week where I'm not working and can take time off," I tried covering.

"Oh, you mean right away," he slowly nodded his head in understanding. "Well, I'm available. Just let me know when you'd like to arrive, and I'll take care of you."

We didn't discuss the cost, but I didn't care. Money wasn't an issue for me. I spent half the night in a daze, contemplating my next move. With Jamie being away, it really was the best time to explore Jump. Yet, the idea of taking a deeper dive behind his back paralyzed me with guilt. Bentley wandered over to me as I deliberated. I felt like he was judging me but wasn't sure if I was reading too much into his watery-eyed stare. I needed a drink!

After much thought and several cocktails, I decided to book Bentley a short stay in doggy daycare so I could go to California, but with a clear intention. I would meet Doc K, learn about Jump firsthand, and if it felt right, experience it under his supervision. This wasn't just about seeking pleasure or an escape; it was a quest for deeper understanding, a journey into the buried parts of myself. I texted Doc K with my decision, and he responded with a meeting address and a request for a quick chat about the fee. I obliged, bracing myself.

"Regarding the cost," Doc K. said, "normally, I charge $3,000 for a session. But for Nia's family, I can offer a discounted rate of $2,000. This includes all preparations and guidance throughout the process."

Whew! The price tag almost made me jump out of my skin for free! I don't know what I was expecting but it wasn't that. Yet the experience could be priceless. I anxiously bit at my lip, contemplating the investment before I finally responded. "Okay, I can work with that. Thank you so much for the discount. I do appreciate it." Jump definitely wasn't your run-of-the-mill street drug. It was exclusive. It was for those with means...or at least the right connections.

"You're quite welcome. I wanted to be upfront with you," he finished.

Shortly after, I caught Auntie Nia up on everything. Though shocked at my speed, she assured me I was in excellent hands. "Be open, be safe, be you. Enjoy the ride," she said, and sent me a few pictures of her riding a camel in a desert. "You only live once! Sort of!" was her last message.

"Oh my God!" I squealed, startling Bentley. A surge of excitement snaked through me, mixed with a tinge of apprehension. This was it. The moment of truth. I took Bentley out for a late-night walk with a newfound resolve. I couldn't believe my trail of decisions. It was like I was a new person with new guts, new confidence, and new determination to go on a journey. I felt like I couldn't stop myself despite all the risks to my carefully built life. I needed this. There were parts of me suppressed for so long that the promise of light fortified them, pushing me to explore the terrains of my being. A crescent moon hung in the sky like a silver hammock, cradling the stars. This week was the one I'd cross into new realms. My heart was calling, and I was ready to answer.

I booked my flight, convincing myself this was a necessary step in my journey to passion, adventure, and self-discovery. As I packed my bags two days later, a hurricane of excitement and fear barreled through me. I dropped Bentley off and made my way to Atlanta Hartsfield Airport. I was about to wade into a world I never knew existed just a few months ago. If all went well, I was about to jump back in time—or maybe forward. I didn't know! There was no telling where I would be lead, but I was ready to Jump.

10

FEET OFF THE GROUND

The hum of the airport was a medley of movement and angst, mirroring the cyclone of emotions inside me. As I hustled through Clear, TSA Precheck and the seemingly never-ending walk to my gate, the heaviness of my decision fell on me like a blanket of lead. I was about to do something most people couldn't even fathom.

I found myself scanning strangers' faces, wondering if any of them had even known possibilities like this existed. The thought brought a slight smirk to my face. Here I was, an ordinary woman on the brink of something extraordinary. Was I courageous or crazy? Visionary or misguided? The line seemed thinner than ever.

My phone vibrated with a message from Auntie Nia, a simple heart emoji followed by a lotus flower, reminding me of the promise of renewal and growth on this journey. I replied with a picture of my boarding pass, adding, "Here goes nothing. . .or everything!"

Soon, I eased into my first-class window seat and downed two bottles of water. I'd drank too much the night before and wanted to flush as much alcohol out of my system as possible. From my view, I watched baggage handlers fluttering around like a colony of bees. As for me, I was eager to takeoff and watch the world disappear beneath me. When the plane ascended, my heart raced in sync with the rising altitude. It was early morning, and the flight wasn't just a physical journey from Georgia to California to me; it was a bridge to a different world of experiences.

While my seatmate fiddled with the on-board entertainment, my mind ping-ponged from thoughts of Jamie to my run-in with Auntie Nia that started this whole expedition. I was never more grateful than now that Jamie balked at the idea of us having GPS locator apps on our phones. I'd have to explain being unavailable for six hours if he happened to call while I was in the air, but otherwise, he'd never know I wasn't in Atlanta. The guilt was getting easier to swallow. Replaying the last few weeks and the unraveling—or expansion—of a life I thought I knew through and through to something I never saw coming. It's funny how a chance encounter can thrust you on a completely different path if it happens at the precise moment you're silently crying for help.

But deep down, beneath the layers of apprehension and excitement, a kernel of truth resonated within me. This was more than a search for lost passion or an escape from the mundane. It was a pilgrimage to the unknown, and that thrilled me.

"Ms. Gregory?" The flight attendant brought me back to reality. He leaned down with a tiny notepad in hand to confirm my drink and meal request for the flight. "Beef short rib with creamy herb mashed potatoes, is that still your choice?"

"Yes, it is. Thank you." I smiled at him.

"And to drink?"

"Just water, thanks."

"Alrighty!" He nodded and moved on to the woman next to me.

Left to my thoughts again, I wondered about the world I might jump into—one where the rules of time and space didn't apply and where history and future could intertwine in a dance of wild possibilities. The contemplation was mind-blowing. Eventually, I fell asleep and woke to the pilot's announcement that the plane was beginning its descent into San Francisco. I took a deep breath, bracing myself for what was to come once I got to Bolinas, the small hippie town where Doc K apparently lived. He wasn't too far from where Auntie Nia rested on Stinson beach, she'd told me. We had exchanged a few more texts since yesterday.

The hour ride from the airport to Hotel Frisco, a boutique lodge where I was staying and the first place I'd meet Doc K, was agonizing. Traffic was horrible, and with each second that passed, I began questioning my decision to come. It had been a long day including the flight and final leg of drive time—long enough for the bitter taste of guilt to rise like bile and disgustingly flow onto my tongue. Jamie called while I was in the back of my reserved car service.

"How's the conference?" I worked hard to keep the conversation on him.

"Busy. Lots of running back and forth between sessions and to impromptu meetings."

He sounded tired, which was a good thing. I hoped he didn't want to chat before bed. Jamie told me about a few of the folks he'd met and one of the sessions that resonated with him, and I was excited to hear him sound so upbeat about everything. Therapy was working for him. Before we could chat for too long, however, he said he had to go participate on a panel. Thank God. By the time we hung up, I wanted a glass of wine but ignored the desire. Doc K was on his way over to meet me, and I wanted to be clear-headed.

Finally, we pulled up to an elegant and welcoming façade and my driver unloaded my small carry-on bag with a polite nod. I'd only be there for one night, so there was no need to travel heavily. Stepping out into the crisp San Francisco air was refreshing, and the lobby greeted me with the warm scent of vanilla and a hint of citrus. It was heaven to my senses, instantly compelling me to relax my jaw and take a slow, intentional deep breath. The staff was fast, welcoming and attentive, quickly checking me in and sending me to my room. The hotel looked even better than the photos, a blend of modern chic and timeless grace, but I didn't spend long taking in the details. My mind was on the upcoming meeting with Doc K.

In my room, I paced, used the bathroom and paced more. I was so far away from everything familiar and on the brink of something that was either a fantastic idea or one that could collapse my entire world if it's not worth it and Jamie finds out. Either way, I'm fucked if Jamie learns about my actions, but I'll deal with that when it happens. And until then, I planned to fight like hell to keep it from him. Already, I felt like I was slipping into being a bad wife, but I just wanted to be good to *me*. Was that so wrong?

A few hours later, I found myself heading down to the property hotel to meet Doc K. It was time. Clad in a loose-fitting, plaid, button-down shirt and khaki pants, Doc K's presence was light and reassuring. He was shorter than I expected and full of energy. *What's in the water over here?* I thought, noting how youthful he and Auntie Nia appeared.

"Trish?" His voice was deep and steady.

"In the flesh," I grinned.

Doc K smiled warmly, extending his hand for a firm shake. "It's a pleasure to meet you in person, Trish. Nia speaks very highly of you."

We found a quiet corner in the hotel bar, a spot that felt private yet open. A low drone of conversations around us provided a discreet backdrop to our own. Doc K ordered an herbal tea, and I opted for a bottle of sparkling water.

"So, Trish, Nia tells me you're ready for a special journey," he began, his eyes twinkling with a mix of curiosity and caution.

I nodded, feeling adrenaline pulse through me at the mention of the trip. "Yes, I am. But I must admit, I'm equally nervous and fascinated."

"You must be! That's a natural reaction, Trish," he replied. A smile revealed itself from under his bushy gray mustache. "What you're considering isn't a typical experience. It's not even well known. It is transformative, however, and with transformation comes uncertainty."

We talked for hours, delving into my reasons for seeking out this experience, my fears, and my hopes. Doc K listened intently, occasionally interjecting with insightful questions or sharing anecdotes that helped ease my apprehensions. The more we spoke, the more I understood him as a man who straddled the worlds of science and spirituality with ease. His wisdom bridged the gap between the tangible and the mystical, making the unbelievable seem within reach. From mentions of quantum mechanics to astral planes, chakras and ley lines, each word he spoke was like a skeleton key unlocking parts of a world that until recently, I didn't know existed.

The conversation shifted to the Jump tincture and the experience it enabled. "It's important to understand," Doc K said earnestly, "that this is not an escape from reality. It's an exploration of it, a way to perceive and interact with the world in the most unique way ever known to man."

As the evening wore on, my anxiety was replaced by a sense of anticipation. Doc K was more than just the keeper of the tincture; he was a guide. Eventually, it was time to part ways.

"Tomorrow," he said as we stood up, "we'll meet at my lab. My wife will be around to help keep an eye on everything, and that's where your journey will truly begin if you want it to."

Back in my room, I lay in bed, the city lights casting shadows across the ceiling. My mind was a tsunami of thoughts, but beneath it all lay a seed of exhilarating anticipation. Tomorrow, I would step into a new world, and there was no turning back now.

FINDING DOC K's place the next day was an adventure in itself. He warned me that locals took the street signs down to keep tourists from discovering it, but it still came as a surprise that Google Maps led me there without even a physical post to tell me to turn right or left. It was as if it was a ghost town, but it wasn't. It was a sacred treasure to residents who didn't want their quaint beach town overrun by outsiders who would ruin the experience. *This isn't a trip or an escape; it's a journey through the very fabric of time.* I recalled one of Doc's statements from the night before and felt like the voyage began before I drank anything—getting to him was surreal.

Nestled in the heart of Bolinas, his house was as light and airy as him. Tucked away at the end of a winding, narrow road, the home was a charming, somewhat eclectic mix of Bohemian and rustic styles. Its exterior was a weathered, driftwood gray, and the yard was accented by a collection of native art and whimsical wind chimes that danced in the coastal breeze.

Doc K's wife, Zephyra, greeted me with a mischievous grin, her eyes sparkling with a kind of lively wit that instantly put me at ease. "Welcome to our little circus of curiosities!" she quipped, gesturing around their home with a flourish.

The house was a quirky labyrinth of rooms, each corner filled with a varied mix of artifacts and books that seemed to have their own tales to tell. As we navigated through the maze, her lively banter was peppered with humorous anecdotes about their adventures and the unusual trinkets they'd collected, making the whole experience unexpectedly entertaining. I was still deathly nervous in the back of my mind, however. I was in a stranger's house across the country about to take an illegal psychedelic that would thrust me to an unknown time and place in history unbeknownst to my doctor husband. But I couldn't stop myself! I had to keep going!

Doc K's lab was in a small yurt-shaped building behind the main house, was a stark contrast to the rest of their whimsical abode. The space was an alchemist's dream, a fusion of ancient wisdom and modern science. Circular walls lined with shelves were filled with meticulously labeled jars of herbs and obscure compounds, just like I saw in our video call. *Hawaiian Baby Woodrose. Ayahuasca Vine. Damiana. Mugwort. Salvia Divinorum.* I skimmed the label names as I followed Zephyra and Doc K. Some of them I'd heard of, others were as foreign to me as the world I might jump into.

"And this...is Jelani," she introduced me to a short, bald, fair-skinned man who was already in the lab, sitting in a chair next to two small tribal drums. He stood up to greet me.

"Hi," I smiled.

"Hello, Trish. I'm here to assist with your journey today." He spoke slowly and didn't blink, but he did return a warm grin. Jelani looked part black and part something else. I couldn't tell. He was dressed in black yoga pants and an oversized green shirt and a well-worn fedora. His forearms were covered in ethnic tattoos.

"We all work together," Doc K said. "Jelani has a way with drums that'll help you relax before you take off.

"Got it," I whispered, and went back to surveying the space.

The room was suffused with the subtle aroma of exotic plants and the sterile tang of chemicals. Patterned light poured in from a massive skylight and trees towering over it from above. Doc K's lab was a sanctuary of knowledge, a place where time and tradition met the cutting edge of science. It was here, amidst this blend of the arcane and the modern, that I might leap into the unknown. Standing there, a maelstrom of apprehension engulfed me. *Breathe.* I reminded myself. *Slowly. Inhale. Exhale.*

The lab, a well-lit confluence of ancient wisdom and modern technology, vibrated quietly around us. I noticed an Anna's Hummingbird, its iridescent feathers glinting, flitting outside a nearby window. Doc K motioned me towards a gigantic maroon rug and set of comfy chairs in the center of the room.

"Please, have a seat, Trish," he said, his voice steady and reassuring. Zephyra, his wife, lingered nearby, a kind presence with a motherly smile. Her long gray hair was somewhat straight-somewhat dreadlocks. I wasn't sure of her nationality, but she looked about the same age as Doc K, with laugh lines and a sun-kissed glow that told me she might have been a longtime lover of the outdoors and active. She was short, but fit, draped in an eclectic mix of clothing and layers of handcrafted jewelry.

"Thank you," I said, settling into a chair. I noticed a trio of metal singing bowls resting on a sleek, metallic table. Months ago, I had no idea what a singing bowl was but since I've gone head-first into this new world of spiritual exploration, I instantly recognized them from one of Lena's online workshops. I'd enjoyed her breathwork class so much, that I joined her community and experienced her sound healing sessions too. The harmonious tones were soothing and took me into states of deep relaxation. I wondered how Doc K used them in his lab and if it might accompany Jelani's drumming.

"Do you use those as a part of the process," I pointed at them.

"Oh no. Doc fancies himself a musician when he isn't creating scientific concoctions," Zephyra joked with a playful twinkle in her eyes. "We play together for fun sometimes, but we don't usually use them when he's working," she added.

"Gotta have hobbies!" He chimed in. "Don't get me wrong, I LOVE science, plant medicine and metaphysics, but I do need creative outlets for when I'm resting my mind."

"Don't we all." I understood exactly what he meant. For me, downtime was in romance novels and cheesy rom-com movies.

"This is where your journey will begin if you're positive you want to move forward with this today." He explained, his hands gesturing towards a comfy-looking sofa with half a dozen pillows. It was flanked by plants and side tables with books and clay figurines. "The Jump experience, while brief in our time, can feel expansive for the Jumper. It's an odyssey of the mind, really. And you'd only be 'gone,'" he said using air quotes, "for about twenty minutes."

"So, a few minutes feel like days?" I asked, trying to mask the tremor in my voice. "How?"

"It's the nature of the compounds to alter your perception of time," he replied, his dark brown eyes reflecting decades of knowledge. "Your consciousness will cross different planes; unbound by the constraints we're used to here."

Zephyra added, "It's like dreaming, but 10,000 times more vivid. You'll be safe, but the experience will be intense. Every person's body responds differently, which is why I'm around to help watch over you." Her posture was relaxed, yet confident. "Jelani has studied in Ecuador and Mexico."

"You're safe," Jelani spoke again. He was a man of few words, but his presence spoke volumes.

Doc K nodded, "Exactly. And remember, I'll also be here, monitoring your physical state. We'll ensure your safety."

My heart jack hammered. What was I doing? This was insane. What if it killed me? What if it didn't but Jamie finds out and kills me himself? Why was I here? Was it really that serious? I felt pummeled by fear and second thoughts, but I wanted to know more. I felt powerless due to my fascination and hunger for excitement. "What should I expect to see or feel?"

"It varies," Doc K said, picking up a small, intricately carved box. "Some experience profound emotional revelations, others journey through historical or fantastical landscapes. It's unique to each individual and their current mental state. The more relaxed you are—and I know that might be hard given all the new information you've absorbed in a short time—the better."

Zephyra leaned in, genuinely wanting me to voice all my concerns. "Ask as many questions as you'd like. And remember, you don't have to do anything today if you need more time to let everything sink in."

But I don't have more time, I thought. Not when Jamie's distracted. This had to happen now or possibly never. I might lose my nerve if I didn't do it today.

Zephyra cut through my thoughts, her voice soft, "Jumping is a dive into the depths of your psyche, an exploration of your innermost desires and fears." Her words mirrored those of Auntie Nia's. "And you'll blend in wherever you land."

We talked a while longer and I learned that they'd known Auntie Nia for nearly five years and had initially met at a spiritual retreat in Big Sur, where they connected over a shared interest in shamanic drumming and plant medicine ceremonies. They became close very fast because of their similar transient backgrounds—Zephyra and Auntie Nia—and their age. They spoke of her with deep fondness, an intimate knowing that I couldn't put my finger on, but it was clearly a special friendship.

"Let me show you the tincture," Doc K said, pulling out a small vial containing a shimmering gold liquid with innate inner light.

Immediately, I was transfixed by the fluid. It pulled me in like an irresistible force. I looked at the vial, then back at Doc K. Back at the vial and then at Zephyra. "Can I. . . touch it?"

"Sure," he answered without hesitation and gently handed me the tiny vial.

The bottle was warm. It felt alive, as if the liquid could sense being in my hands and greeted me like an old friend. I turned it gently between my fingers, watching the light play off its surface, casting tiny rainbows around the room. It was mesmerizing.

"This," Doc K began, his voice a blend of reverence and scientific curiosity, "is the essence of Jump. It's not just a psychedelic—it's a master key to opening doors within your own consciousness. Doors to other times, places, feelings that might reintroduce you to parts of yourself you've forgotten about."

Right then and there, I knew I was going to do it. I didn't care what it cost. I wanted it. "It's beautiful," I murmured. The thought of ingesting something so enigmatic was both thrilling and outlandish. I couldn't believe I was sitting in this room, holding this bottle, about to jump out of my timeline. I handed the vial back to Doc K, feeling a surge of adrenaline. "I want to do this. I'm ready to Jump."

"Are you sure?" He quizzed.

"Yes."

"Positive?" Zephyra double-checked.

"Absolutely," I confirmed.

Doc K nodded, taking the potion, and placing it back in the box. "Then let's begin the preparation. It's important to approach this with the right mindset and environment."

I took another deep breath, steadying myself. This was it—the moment of truth. I sent him half the payment electronically in good faith and would send him the balance when I completed the experience.

"Let's move to this recliner over here. It will offer you the best support and comfort because the effects come on fast." He explained.

As I shifted to the lounge chair, its soft embrace welcomed me. Zephyra adjusted it gently and handed me a soft blanket, ensuring I was at ease. "Sometimes people say they feel cold after it kicks in."

Doc K then fitted a small, discreet heart monitor onto my wrist. "This won't interfere with your experience but will allow us to keep an eye on your vitals. Just a safety measure. I've never had a problem with anyone," he reassured me, his voice calm and steady.

"Okay," I whispered.

"Now, I want you to relax and focus on your breathing," he instructed gently. "Close your eyes and let go of any thoughts or distractions. You're in a safe place, and we're here with you."

Jelani cleared his throat and reached for his drum. Slowly, he began to beat a simple four-count rhythm. Boom. Boom. Boom. Boom. "Don't fight anything," he told me while playing. Boom. Boom. Boom. Boom. "Release the urge to control anything, and know...just **know**. You are safe. Boom. Boom. Boom. Boom. He sped up slightly, and began chanting words I didn't recognize.

The subtle whirr of the lab faded into the background and faint, ambient sounds of flutes and waterfalls took its place, along with Jelani's drums. It was all in a good flow, and I took deep, measured breaths, feeling my body relax more with each exhale. Jelani banged the drum faster until the rhythm felt like it was in my blood, pushing energy through my body. The recliner cradled me comfortably, and the light blanket added a sense of security. My hands trembled. Still nervous.

"Deep breath," Doc K coached again.

I felt ready in my spirit, but my mind was sounding alarm bells and sirens. A flutter of anticipation raced within me.

"Remember, let go of all expectations. Let the experience guide you," were the final words I could recall from Jelani before hearing a whisper from Zephyra that it was time to drink. Faster. His drums carried me to an open and receptive state.

"Okay..." Instinctually, I opened my eyes to unscrew the vial, raise it to my lips and take a sip. The moment the liquid slid down my throat the room blurred, the carpet started breathing, and everything soon went completely black. I didn't have time to panic, I was spinning in a tornado of dizzying colors, motions, shapes, and forms. It felt like I'd gotten shot out of a cannon and got caught in a funnel of energetic stardust. There were haunting, atmospheric sounds. And then everything brightened from a shaft of pure white light. It pulled me in...pulled me in...pulled me in. *Oh shit!* If riding a rollercoaster while the earth gave way was a feeling, this was it.

I felt myself grip the arm rest of the recliner to try and steady myself. Everything was blurred and distorted. I didn't even know if my eyes were open or closed anymore. My cheeks were wet. Was I crying or laughing? I couldn't tell what emotions I was expressing. Nothing, absolutely nothing I did to research that moment could have properly prepared me for the time the tincture fully took hold. It felt like every damn cell and emotion in my body exploded like the Big Bang. BANG!

Fear. Love. Hope. Excitement. Terror. Bliss. Confusion. *Is that fire?* I gasped at the sight of humongous spinning flame balls. *Is this hell? Am I dead? Where the fuck am I?* I tried not to panic. I tried not to fight it. "Let the experience guide you..." I heard Doc K very faintly again and tried relaxing.

I felt the urge to run, but I couldn't sense my legs. Not long after, it felt like I had wings for shoulders and began flying for a day straight. The sun rose and it set, and I was still soaring in and out of some sort of nebula. I went from feeling like a supreme goddess to a petrified child under a bed. The trip made me dizzy and exhausted. It made me feel faint, and just as I thought I would pass out, everything stopped spinning. I no longer felt the yo-yo sensations of falling and flying. I think . . . I arrived at a pink, fiery, fluid portal that sucked me right into a new world. I. Had. Jumped!

My sphere was fuzzy. I could hear sounds, but they were faint. It was like when you're coming off general anesthesia and you're there, but not quite there yet. Slowly, I began making out movements around me. People. *Okay, I'm alive. There are people here!* I took a step, feeling as sure of myself as a toddler their first time trying to walk. The sidewalk and signs started to come into view. *Okay, okay, okay! I'm somewhere on earth* and *I'm alive!*

As objects became clearer, I hesitantly reached out to touch a nearby lamppost. Nervous, I half-expected my hand to pass through it like a ghost but to my shock, my fingers met the cool metal. *Oh my God.* My heart somersaulted. I was there, tangible and real in the era! Did I look as ragged as I felt? I needed a mirror and a place to gather myself. *Holy shit!* I'm in the past! *Was I visible to others yet?* I wondered.

Glancing down, I noticed my attire had morphed into something befitting the period—a modest but stylish taupe day dress, typical of the 1920s. It fell below my knees and was accented by a chestnut belt. The fabric was soft, and the color was safe enough to not draw attention. I walked over to a storefront to look at myself in a window, and I couldn't believe my eyes. The woman staring back at me was unmistakably me, but with a vintage twist—like a photograph someone may have taken of my great-grandmother in her prime. A dainty brown bow accentuated my hair and my make-up was flawless. I wore a light jacket to shield me from the cool spring air. *Not bad.* I admired and smiled. *Not bad.*

I found myself nodding positively in response to my attire. Gorgeous copper fabric earrings adorned my ears, and I wore sensible, low-heeled shoes. The only thing that didn't change was my wedding ring. It was still there, a reminder of my real life and relationship with Jamie. Shit.

It already felt like I'd been gone a few days just to get here, but I remembered Doc K saying time perception would be different, so it may have been just a few minutes back home. I sure hoped so! Fully immersed now, and with everything clearly in view, I noticed the street was alive with the sound of jazz drifting from open windows of brownstones, and the chatter and laughter of people. I smelled cornbread and other teases of soul food wafting through the air. This was Harlem. The alto sax player soulfully delivering the blues confirmed it for me. It was booming with energy and everything together told me I was smack dab in the Harlem Renaissance. Despite my initial shock, I felt an exhilarating thrill from blending into a vibrant part of history I'd only studied in school.

"Beautiful day, isn't it?" A woman in a similarly styled dress offered a friendly greeting as we crossed paths.

I managed to smile and nod but couldn't find my words. The simple interaction solidified my presence at the time, making me just as anxious as I was enthralled. I wanted to explore but didn't know where to start. Quickly, I thought of what could be "must dos" if you had a chance to visit during this time. A jazz and blues club, that was for sure, a speakeasy and possibly a poetry reading. I didn't know how long I'd be there and what my journey back home might be, so I wanted to make the best of it.

As I walked, absorbing the sights and sounds, a quaint café caught my eye. The aroma of fresh coffee was inviting. The trip here wore me out, and I was surprised I hadn't thought of something as basic as having a drink or bite to eat yet. I was overwhelmed but needed sustenance. Stepping inside, I approached the counter and ordered a coffee, only to freeze when the cashier asked for payment.

"Well, pretty lady, that'll be thirty cents," a cheerful waiter stated.

A sinking feeling hit me as I patted my dress, finding no purse, no wallet—nothing. Embarrassed, I mumbled, "I'm so sorry. I must have forgotten my wallet," and quickly looked down, my cheeks burning.

"No worries, darling." He paused and gawked at me. "My word, I don't think I've seen you around here before, but I'll tell you what... I'll be here all afternoon. Come on back and I'll have a new order ready for you! The name's Percy," he added. "Please ask for me if you don't see me," he joked.

"Thank you so much," I said quickly and slinked out of the café. I was so mortified I couldn't even blush.

The realization that I was without money flustered me to no end. It made me feel isolated, lonely and confused. What was I going to do with no money? How would I get around? Where would I sleep? How would I eat? Panic enveloped me but before I could get too down, my attention was drawn to a vibrant mural across the street. It depicted a hummingbird, its wings a blur, hovering over blossoming flowers. The sight of it reminded me of the bird I'd seen at Doc K's lab, an echo of familiarity in this foreign timeline. It also ushered a sense of calm and entrancement.

Compelled by a strange instinct, I followed the path the mural's hummingbird seemed to be guiding me towards. *Forward and to the right.* I felt a gut feeling and followed it and the streets soon grew quieter, the lively energy of Harlem softening into a peaceful hush. I didn't know where I was going or why, but it felt right, so I continued until I saw another hummingbird, this one sculpted in metal, marking a gate that led to a tree-lined but dead-end street. Despite my cautious nature, an intense energy pulled me forward. It was daytime and didn't feel like a shady neighborhood, so I chanced it.

At the block's end stood a small house, its door adorned with a brass hummingbird. The symbolism was too strong to ignore. I approached and gently knocked. "Hello? Anyone home?" Part of me was screaming that I was insane for this entire trip. The other part sank deeper into the world. There was no answer to my call. Slowly, the door creaked open on its own, as if inviting me inside. I stepped over the threshold, my heart hopscotching with a mix of curiosity and caution. Something pulled me here!

"Is anyone home?" I called out again, my voice echoing slightly in the quiet space. The interior was cozy, decorated with items from various eras. My attention was drawn to a small table by a vintage lamp, adorned with a drawer featuring a carving of a hummingbird, mirroring the one on the door, the street's and Doc K's.

Hesitantly, I opened the drawer and found a stash of money, seemingly from the 1920s. My eyes widened in shock. *Get out of here!* Twenty-first century me told me to get the hell out of there before the owner came home. *It's yours, Trish.* The 1920s me felt a flood of bewilderment and relief. This money immediately fixed my penniless problem. But should I take it? My hand hovered over the green bills, uncertain, until I noticed a small, elegantly handwritten note tucked between the bills. "Jump money," it read.

"Whoa." My reaction was vocal. I was thrown by the little memo and looked around to see if anyone might be watching. *Take it and go.* I heard my inner voice again and listened. Doc K never mentioned this. I'd have to ask him about it when I got back. The note quelled my guilt and ignited a sense of destiny. "Just enough for today," I muttered to myself, as I carefully picked a few bills, leaving the rest undisturbed and the note in the drawer. Slipping the currency into my dress pocket, I carefully left the home and stepped back into the vibrant Harlem streets. I would keep an eye out for hummingbirds from here on out. Clearly, it was some kind of spirit guide for me.

My confidence was popping now. I looked amazing, had money in my pocket and was floating through the Harlem Renaissance! Seeing people whom I'd only known through books and movies in real life gave me a special kind of high. I couldn't get enough! I was heading back toward the café to grab a bite to eat and that's when I saw her. Drop. Dead. Gorgeous. I couldn't stop my head from craning in her direction if I tried. She walked with an air of confidence and grace, commanding attention without seeking it. Her dress, a flowy, bright yellow covering danced around her as she moved. Her eyes met mine, and there was an instant spark, an unspoken magnetism. She slowed down; she held my gaze, compelling me to stop.

"Are you new here?" she asked, her voice smooth like honey and warm as the sun.

"Yes, I guess you could say that," I replied, captivated.

"Welcome to the neighborhood. I'm Imani," she introduced herself, extending a hand that I hesitated only a moment to take.

"Trish Gregory," I said, feeling a jolt as our hands touched. She wore a beautiful charm bracelet with music symbols and a microphone pendant. It looked shiny and new, bouncing light off from the sun.

"Trish Gregory," she repeated. "Got it."

Imani was more than beautiful; she was radiant, with hair cascading past her shoulders like water. Her smile was infectious, and I found myself inexplicably drawn to her, captivated by an allure that was mysterious and enchanting.

"You look like someone who appreciates good music. I'm singing at a club tonight, The Velvet Crescent. Right up the street from here. It's a fundraiser for a local community center," Imani explained, her eyes reflecting a deep sense of purpose. "We're trying to create more spaces for art and education in Harlem. It's part of a larger movement for change."

Intrigued, I responded, "That's a commendable initiative. Art and education are vital, especially in communities like this."

"Thank you. Just doing my part to plant seeds of change." Imani's smile broadened, a glint of gratitude in her eyes.

The moment the words left her lips I had a sense of déjà vu.

We've had this exchange before. Not here, but not like this, but it felt deeply familiar. My train of thought was broken by a vision of her intoxicating smile and eyes. She was a goddess. The sincerity in her words and the cause she supported resonated with me, making the invitation even more compelling. "I'll definitely be there," I assured her, feeling an irresistible pull.

"I appreciate that," she said and glided off just as elegantly as she'd appeared.

My heart pounded in my chest and butterflies ran relay races in my stomach. I hadn't been so enchanted by a woman since I was in college. Imani took my breath away on sight. She made me forget I needed to eat. As the early morning transitioned to afternoon, I began feeling exhausted and hungry. I needed a place to rest. A place to collect myself and regroup. I didn't know how long I had in this Jump but I knew I couldn't run off adrenaline alone, so I finally got myself to a restaurant.

As luck would have it, I found myself at an open and airy establishment adorned with photographs of Langston Hughes, Zora Neal Hurston and so many other prominent writers of the time. They'd all dined there, I supposed, and hoped any of them would pop in while I was there! After being seated in a corner booth, my eyes and attention were called to a young woman passionately reciting poetry on a small stage. She snatched my attention with her first two lines...

Carry me on a chariot
Through lands of passion
And valleys of vulnerability
Across roads of trust...
Bring me over mountains of bliss
Into peaks of writhing screams
Down into cascading streams
Into the swirling waters of love.
You must
Join me on a pilgrimage to pleasure
Where ecstasy creeps out of fingertips

And dances against skin
Where the journey is the destination
And the exchange of love never ends
Where veneration and homage to natural states of being "just is"
Bring me home and stay with me for a while
Let our reverence for one another
Make us the epitome of restorative lovers
Living in the now.

"Thank you," she said, her voice rippling with an undertone of vulnerability and strength before stepping off the small stage.

"Quite something, isn't she?" a gentleman at the next table remarked just before the room broke out into applause. Before I could respond, he was joined by two other young men and a woman.

I sat oddly alone but savored the poet's words. They were a vivid blend of longing and advocacy, painting a landscape of deep passion intertwined with a desire for equality. The poem was much bolder than I would have expected from a woman at the time, and it was beautifully shocking to hear. The lady captivated the room, resonating with many listener's hearts, including mine. *This is incredible!* I thought, overjoyed at the experience! Being in a space where the pulse of creativity and resistance beat strongly was mesmerizing.

"Here's a menu for you, gorgeous." A handsome waiter appeared at my table. He placed a glass of ice water down. "Wow," he stared into my eyes. "I don't reckon I have *ever* seen you around here before!" As I took in his crisp, white shirt tucked neatly into high-waisted black trousers, he studied me just as curiously. I looked the part but didn't know if anything else about me gave me away.

"I guess you could say I'm new in town," I said, getting the courage to engage. I could feel my heartbeat in my throat.

"Well, welcome! We gon' treat you right around here. My name is Ronald," he added before glancing to my left and nearly doubling backwards at the sight of my wedding ring. "He sure is a lucky man. And judging by the size of that rock, you're a lucky woman. I'm just gon' do my job and leave you be this evening," he said playfully.

Instinctively, I wanted to flip my ring around, so it wasn't so noticeable. It must look colossal for the time—either fake or that I belonged to some kind of business tycoon or goon.

"Today's special is smothered chicken with homemade gravy, slow-cooked collard greens seasoned with a hint of smoked turkey, and sweet, buttery cornbread. But there's more on the menu if you don't fancy that."

"Thank you."

"I'll just need a few minutes to decide."

"You got it. I'll come on back around in a little while, sound good?"

"Yes. Thank you," I said, and watched him dash off in shoes polished to a shine on the wooden floor.

I glanced at the menu on my table, which was draped in a rich, deep red tablecloth. My mouth watered at all the options: Fried catfish, collard greens with andouille sausage, sweet potato pie, and okra stew. Red velvet cake with cream cheese frosting. . .I wanted to eat everything! Finally, I settled on the catfish and collards with smoked turkey. I'd have to wait and see if I even had room for dessert after all of that.

While I waited to place my order, I smiled in gratitude. I had stepped right into a living, breathing moment of history. The restaurant ambiance was a fusion of a cozy at-home vibe and raw energy. Dim lighting cast a warm glow over patrons engaged in animated conversations. And outside the window nearest me, little girls in bright cotton dresses and leather Mary Jane shoes played with boys in knickerbocker pants and suspenders. It was incredible to witness, as were the jazz posters inside the restaurant. They were brand new here but looked vintage to me.

While waiting, my mind drifted back to Imani. She clutched my attention without effort. I could still see her smile, her eyes and hear her dulcet voice. She was an allure wrapped in a riddle of warm elegance. The way she floated over to me made her presence seem like the sun's caress on a river's surface—just sparkling, vitalizing, and captivating. I loved the way she repeated my name to ensure she remembered it. Intention and attentiveness were always appreciated in my world.

"Hello there, ma'am. I'm back!" My waiter, Ronald enthusiastically announced his return. "Ready order something"

"Yes, I am," I told him and gave him my choices.

"Alright! I'll get it to you as soon as possible." He smiled politely before walking off again.

Immediately, my mind went back to Imani's fluid movement. Everything from the slow blink of her eyes to the graceful way she handed me the flyer reminded me of slow-flowing water. Her eyes radiated light, I couldn't wait to look into them again. The clink of glasses, the murmur of voices, and the rustle of the next poet going on stage brought my mind back to the room I was in. When my food arrived, the first bite tasted like the Promise Land. I mean, Atlanta had good soul food, but God Almighty, this meal was like a jazz riff for the taste buds – unexpected, soulful, and leaving me wanting an encore! *So, this is what our grandparent's food tasted like*, I mused, *before all the hormones, additives, boxed substitutes to speed up production and modern twists on old recipes*. It was nirvana.

As the afternoon wore on, I finished my meal, settled my check, and headed out to explore. I wanted to soak in as much as possible, knowing my time was limited and not wanting to squander it sleeping. Hell, I paid thousands of dollars for this trip and didn't want to miss a second! I visited Mount Morris Park and was amazed by so many people's semi-formal attire. Everyone looked so well put together and in the moment. There weren't any cell phones. There weren't any digital cameras and there weren't any noisy cars blaring music. I watched painters methodically create vibrant artwork that captured the essence of the Harlem spirit. I saw street performers playing jazz and blues, their music filling the air with life and energy. In between it all, I thought of Imani. Thankfully, her set was early, and I wouldn't have to wait too much longer to see her.

The sun began dipping, casting long shadows on the bustling streets of Harlem. The anticipation for the evening's event at The Velvet Crescent was building within me. It wasn't just about the music anymore; it was about her—Imani. Her image was etched in my mind, and the hours until I could see her again felt like an eternity.

I freshened up at a public restroom, trying to look presentable for the night. The streets were alive with anticipation as people in their evening best headed towards various destinations, their laughter and chatter adding to the vibrancy of Harlem at dusk.

As I approached The Velvet Crescent, the pulse of music and the crowd's buzz reached me, sending a thrill through my veins. The line outside was long, and the glowing neon sign beckoned. Just as I was about to step forward, a hand on my shoulder stopped me. Turning around, I found myself face to face with...

11

HARLEM'S HIDDEN HEARTBEAT

"Pardon me, ma'am. I'm so sorry, I thought you were someone else," a dapper young gentleman apologized.

The buzz of people around The Velvet Crescent transfixed me. Everyone looked so stylish, and elegant and spoke with such a sweet cadence. Suits and bowties. Flapper dresses and feathers. Top hats and shiny shoes. The air was fragrant with a blend of cologne and the faint smell of tobacco, creating a heady mixture of intoxication and nostalgia. I was in the middle of Harlem's upper class, and each jazz note weaved through the air with undulated energy. I didn't just hear the music; I absorbed it in my soul.

The club was alive with laughter, clinking glasses, and an atmosphere thick with anticipation. I felt more emboldened with each step and set of eyes I met. It was exhilarating, like walking into a different life where I could be anyone I wanted. As I moved through the crowd, I caught glimpses of animated discussions and lively debates—it was a hub of intellectual and artistic enthusiasm.

Soon enough, I found a spot close to the stage, my thoughts still lingering on Imani. My mind was a merry-go-round of eagerness, and a warm flush crept up my cheeks at the thought of her entering the room. She must have been backstage, preparing to captivate the audience with her performance. The idea of her voice filling the room sent a slither of excitement down my spine. From my solitary spot, I could feel the electricity in the air intensify as the moment for Imani's performance drew nearer. The anticipation was tangible, and each time the curtains to the wing area of backstage opened, I found myself unconsciously leaning forward, hoping to catch a glimpse of her.

I noticed a striking painting of a stargazer lily on a wall adjacent to the bar. *My favorite flower*, I thought with a smile. It had been so long since Jamie bought them for me, and the sight of the art made a flashback of Auntie Nia in the farmer's market appear in my mind. I'd seen similar flowers there, too, and noticing them here was a strange confirmation that I was doing what was best for me. The lily was more than just a painting; it felt like a silent nod to my unmet desires and a secret acknowledgment of my journey. That random run-in with Auntie Nia started this excursion, and I had no regrets. In fact, I felt revitalized. My soul was happy with my decisions.

As I waited, a figure caught my eye—a debonair older man sitting alone at a table in the shadows, his gaze fixed intently on the stage. He occasionally broke his intense focus on the performance area to habitually stroke the patch of hair on his chin. He nodded approvingly at people moving near him, making him seem more embedded in the world than a spectator or participant. He looked at me and blinked slowly with a half-smile as if trying to process my presence. Something about him struck me as oddly familiar, yet I couldn't place where I might have seen him before. *Hmm. Was he from the present, or did I see him earlier in my Jump?* I wondered, trying to place him, but I couldn't.

Just as the lights dimmed to signal the performance's start, he turned, and our eyes locked. There was a flash of recognition in his gaze, a knowing look that suggested he understood more about my presence here than I did myself. His dark brown eyes seemed to pierce through the low lighting, reaching out to me with an unspoken message. Before I could ponder any further, the spotlight hit the stage, and the room erupted in applause as Imani stepped into view, radiant and commanding.

"Good evening, Velvet Crescent!" she greeted the excited crowd with a voice that dripped with sweet nectar.

My breath caught in my throat when she began singing, her melodies weaving jazz notes like a river of marmalade and a sea of silk. She was spellbinding. Her entrance and opening lines were like shafts of golden light in the club. She exuded an ethereal grace, dressed in a stunning emerald green dress that shimmered under the illumination. Her vocals were a siren's call that hushed the crowd, and each song took me on a new journey of auditory pleasure. Imani's voice blended raw power and delicate vulnerability, leaving the audience rapt. As the set continued, the man, now reseated, watched discerningly, nodding along to the rhythm and occasionally exchanging whispers with others around him. I felt a connection to him but didn't know why.

I lost myself in the music as Imani's set continued. Her movement, her smile, her eye contact with me—all of it made me feel more alive than ever. Every time she looked at me, I felt a heat between my legs. *Holy shit.* I wasn't expecting that, but she kept looking at me with those beckoning eyes. Between songs, Imani shared stories and insights. Her passion for change and love for Harlem was intense in every word. She wasn't just a performer but a force, a voice for her community.

"Thank you, everyone, for coming out tonight," Imani began, her voice flowing like a gentle stream. "This evening, our melodies embrace more than just the ears; they touch the soul of our community. Each note I sing is a tribute to Harlem, a lullaby for the dreams we nurture here." She paused, her gaze lingering on the audience with a tender intensity.

Patrons listened intently. Even the breaks and pauses she took had a powerful effect.

"Our cause tonight is to fund a new arts program for our kids, to give them the canvas to paint their futures, a stage to dance their dreams. We must build a place of our own that nurtures their creativity and lets them be the architects of their destinies. So, whatever you can spare tonight will be appreciated. I'm essentially up here for them, giving most of the proceeds to this project." Her words flowed like warm water from a spring.

The applause after Imani's final song was thunderous. We gave her a standing ovation. As the room buzzed with energy, Imani's eyes scanned the audience, landing on me. Our stares locked, and my mouth slightly became ajar. I think she winked at me, but I wasn't sure. I was probably hallucinating. It was the 1920s, and that was highly unlikely. . . or so I thought. At that moment, the world around us faded for me, leaving only the two of us in a bubble of mutual recognition.

Suddenly, the man in the shadows rose and approached the stage. There was an air of confidence about him, a poise that spoke of a bold life. As he reached Imani, there was a brief exchange—a smile, a nod, a shared moment that seemed to hold history. The interaction was fleeting, yet it spoke volumes. Who was he? What was his connection to Imani? My curiosity piqued.

Imani descended the stage, her eyes still locked with mine as she moved gracefully through the adoring crowd. She smiled and hugged a few people while walking in my direction. The energy in the room shifted. I suddenly felt nervous. As she approached, my heart rattled in my chest, each step she took closed the distance between us. The noise of the club completely muted into the background now.

"Trish Gregory," she said, her voice a soft melody, as she stood before me. "I'm glad you made it!" She clasped my hand in a soft clamshell shake between hers.

She remembered my whole name. Immediately, Imani stole my breath.

Her proximity was overwhelming, her scent a mixture of citric zest and something uniquely her own. I leaned in to reply closer to her ear. "I wouldn't have missed it." The connection between us was electric.

She turned, so our faces nearly touched, and responded, "I was hoping you'd make it—"

Our moment was interrupted as that familiar stranger reappeared, a charming smile on his face. "Imani, that was a phenomenal performance. Your voice isn't just a melody. It's a movement," he complimented, his eyes briefly flickering to mine with a hint of curiosity and a subtle, protective assessment.

"Thank you, Charles," Imani responded, her stare glimmering with appreciation. She touched his arm in a gesture of familiarity and turned to me. "Charles, this is Trish. Trish, Charles is an old friend and a great supporter of the arts here in Harlem."

"Hey, hey, young lady, who you callin' old!?" Charles joked.

I extended my hand, and he took it in a firm grip. "Pleasure to meet you, Trish. Any friend of Imani's is a friend of mine," he quipped, and I noticed a small brass hummingbird pin on his lapel.

I couldn't stop my brows from furrowing in recognition if I tried. Who was this man, really? His demeanor was intriguing, and a mysterious blend of confidence and paternal. I was eager to know the nature of their relationship and the easy rapport they shared. And I needed to understand more about the broach he wore.

"That's a nice uh..." I hesitated. "This a nice pin you've got there." Words found the courage to leave my mouth.

"I appreciate that. You know, the hummingbird is such a funny little creature. Always flitting through time and space, seeing more worlds than we ever can. I've had a fascination with them for a few years now," he finished.

I was taken aback. Imani seemed lost and Charles pivoted quickly. "Anyway, Imani, I think you'll raise quite a bit of funds tonight. Great job."

As the conversation flowed, I found my attention increasingly torn between Charles and Imani, but mostly drawn to her. Her laughter. The glint in her eyes. The peak of her collar bones from her dress. The rouge in her lipstick. Her insights and her scent. While chatting, two other patrons called her to gush over her voice and ask questions about her project. This momentarily left Charles and I alone.

"So," he began. "I've learned you're new in town. Hopefully, your trip wasn't too stressful." He spoke in a way that made me stand up straighter and listen harder.

"It was...uh...a journey."

"I imagine so. Look, I saw when you came in. I know you're still adjusting and likely have lots of questions."

My body stiffened.

"You're a Jumper. It's okay. Most folks around here have no idea what that is or that it's possible, but I do. You're about the fourth one I've run into. Damn near had a heart attack the first time I saw one. We were both just as confused and frightened. I didn't believe his story but when it happened again with somebody else, I started believing. Seems like you all land on the same corner, in front of the same shops. I've been fascinated ever since—actually wondering if somehow that serum could make its way back here. I'd sure like to go back and relive time with my wife."

My mind spun as he spoke. *Jumpers...we have a nickname?*

"That house where you found the money is safe. And the funds there are communal. You did the right thing by only taking what you needed and leaving what you didn't. That'll serve whoever lands here next."

"Wait, so—" before I finished my statement, I noticed Imani returning. "Does she know?" I asked hurriedly. Nervously.

"No! But I know when she's smitten with someone. She's ahead of her time in so many ways and can't hide her desires. She's like a daughter to me. Different and misunderstood by most folks, but I've taken a protective role over her so...knowing you won't be around long please find a way to be up front about that. She won't listen to me if I tell her to leave you be."

"How long will I be here?"

Imani came within footsteps of us.

"Can't say. It's different for everyone. The hummingbird will guide you." Charles slipped in an answer before we were a trio again.

Fuck. I wanted to talk to him more. How much did he know? Were other Jumpers there while I was or did we drop in one at a time? I had so many questions.

"Charles! Hey, hey, Charles, man!" A boisterous young man yelled for him drawing him away from us. The room was abuzz with greetings and chatter.

"He's a great guy," Imani motioned towards Charles a few feet away. "I don't know what's up with him and birds. Ever since his wife passed, he's been into bird watching and symbolism." Her gaze reflecting a deeper, unspoken thought. "Anyway," Imani's hand brushed against mine again, a simple touch that made the hair on my arms stand up. "Would you like to go somewhere quieter?" she asked, her eyes inviting me into her world. "I'd love to chat with you more."

I hesitated, unable to find the words. So much was happening at once. For a fleeting moment, the invitation thrilled me, but then a wave of apprehension washed over me. The idea of leaving with Imani was enticing but also unearthed a deep-seated fear. I was in an alien era, navigating through the Harlem Renaissance with its own set of rules and unknowns. As captivating as she was, the thought sent a shiver down my spine. What if I was pulled back to my time unexpectedly? The unpredictability of the Jump was a wild card I hadn't fully considered until now.

Suddenly, my life back home flooded my mind. Jamie. Bentley. My home. The familiarity of my routines. The contrast between that world and this vibrant, unknown Harlem night struck me sharply. Jamie's face flashed in my mind, his voice, our last lukewarm goodbye – all a stark reminder of the life I had momentarily abandoned. The weight of my wedding ring felt heavier, a tangible link to a family that seemed so distant now. I wondered if she even noticed it. I'd spun the diamond around so only the two bands showed. Less flashy. Less conspicuous. Though her question caught me off guard, it did highlight a dilemma I had for the night. I had nowhere to stay. And then I heard Auntie Nia's voice echo in my mind, *Whatever parts of you that you may have ignored or forgotten about will resurface for you to face them.* I hadn't been with a woman in so long, the thought aroused my mind and body beyond belief!

"My place isn't far," Imani broke through my thoughts, perhaps sensing my hesitation. "It's safe, I promise. We can enjoy another drink and chat a bit and you can go on back to your place. Where are you staying anyway?"

Shit. I couldn't even lie because I had no idea the names of any places.

"You do have a place, right? I know you said you're new in town. Are you not situated yet?"

"I—I was going to rent a room. At one of the boarding houses on Lenox Avenue."

Before she could respond, Charles reappeared next to me.

"Say, before it gets too dark. Why don't I walk you home, Imani?" He asked. "Trish, if you're in the area, I can get you to your place safely too."

"I was just about to invite Trish to my place. There's no need to stay in a boarding house, especially since you don't know if they have any space tonight. I have a little extra room. You shouldn't be wandering the streets at night looking for a place at the last minute." Imani's voice was a warm mix of concern and courtship.

Her offer was surprising and welcome. In these times, a free-spirited woman like Imani felt like it should have been a rarity, yet she seemed unburdened by the conventions of the era. "What do you say?" she asked me.

Fuck it. *This is why you jumped right?* I asked myself. "I'd like that," I found myself saying to Imani, pushing aside thoughts of Jamie, my fears and the complexities waiting for me back home.

"So, that's the plan?" Charles quizzed.

"Yes," I confirmed.

"Alright," Imani grinned. "Come on. Let's get out of here. Thank you, Charles!"

She led us through the dapper crowd to the cool early evening air. I felt the urge to take her hand but didn't dare. As we walked, I noticed the shift in Imani's demeanor. The confident, radiant songstress on stage was now showing a more tender, vulnerable side. Charles hovered more like a shielding but ultimately powerless father.

"So, Trish, you said you may not be around long, right?" he startled me with his question, but I rolled with it. He knew more about my visit than I did, apparently.

"I don't think so."

"Then we should make the most of it," Imani added. "I don't know where you're heading next, but I'm glad you touched Harlem for a spell. Would love to hear all about your journeys," she finished. "Maybe you'll decide to stay a while after experiencing it more."

The city lights sparkled around us, creating a magical backdrop.

"You know," Imani spoke softly, "nights like these make me dream of a better world. One where our voices are heard, our art is celebrated, and all love is free from judgment."

Her words resonated with me, echoing my own yearnings for freedom and expression. In that moment, I felt a deep connection to Imani, a bond that transcended time and place. I was eager to be alone with her.

"So, where are you from? What brings you around these parts? And thank you again for coming out tonight."

"You're welcome. I'm from uh...Georgia—Atlanta, Georgia. And I guess you could say I was looking for a new experience. Something fresh. New opportunities...like most others, I guess. Something... free." My words were flowing now.

We continued walking, our conversation flowing effortlessly. Imani shared her dreams and aspirations for art and change, her voice imbued with infectious passion. She spoke of her activism, her music, and her hopes for Harlem. I listened, captivated by her spirit and the raw honesty in her words.

As we walked, I couldn't help but wonder about the ticking clock of my return, adding an edge of urgency and intensity to every step I took with Imani.

IMANI'S APARTMENT was less than a ten-minute walk from the club. As promised, Charles tipped his hat and bid us goodnight once we safely reached the entryway. Imani and I were alone now, and our shared energy was palpable. Her unit was on the 17th floor and had a view of the Hudson River, albeit through tiny windows. Her place reflected her spirit: vibrant, welcoming, carefree, and filled with symbols of African heritage and artistic expression. The sound of a radiator hissing streamed from a corner where her tile floor had a crack in it. The noise took me back decades from my current life. It reminded me of my grandmother's old house in Connecticut.

"Want some lemonade or a real drink?"

"Lemonade will do." I didn't know if alcohol would have any interactions with the Jump serum and didn't want to find out the hard way.

Imani and I talked for hours, and I found myself opening up to her in a way I hadn't with anyone in a long time. I told her about my love of architecture and design. Textures. Patterns. Colors. Curves. Silhouettes and Elegance. I caught myself about to discuss a passion for "art history" because I realized I was in it and couldn't do that! But I also shared with her my attraction to nature—the honesty of it.

"The trees, flowers, and even the dirt don't try to be anything than what they are. They just exist and are innately beautiful and necessary in their natural state. They don't need to prove anything to anyone to be admired and respected." I told her, taking a healthy sip from my drink. "I love the simplicity of fireflies dancing in twilight and the serenity of moonlit nights."

Imani's worldview was refreshing. She believed in freedom, the power and beauty of art to enact change, and the importance of living true to oneself. "You know. I don't know how the future will look back on this time, but I do know I want to be remembered for bringing art, splendor, and creativity into the world. Not for power or fame but for love...through my songs and through my campaigns." Imani told me. "I can't always be as free as I'd like to be, despite the admiration I get. I often feel trapped. Trapped...like a swan in a golden cage. But one day I hope to truly fly free, unbound from invisible societal chains. One day I hope people who love differently can exist openly, unshackled by the world's whispered judgments. I guess you can tell by now what I mean?" Her statement sounded more like a question.

"I do. And it's okay. You can soar with me," I told her, finishing the rest of my lemonade. I understood her more than she knew, even if it were for different reasons. I knew what it felt like to be jammed in a box you're too big to fit in. "You're so passionate. It's entrancing. Whoever you end up loving or even just liking would be so lucky."

"I can't help it. And you...you're so different. I can't put my finger on it, but there's something so uncommon about you. I don't know what it is, but I like it. You're stunningly beautiful, mysterious and magnetic, Trish," she said, her gaze intense yet soft. She brushed her fingertips against my knee.

Butterflies. They swooped up and down in my belly, making me blush. I felt an instinct to move closer to Imani and listened to it. Tension slowly built up. It had been a while since I'd gotten a direct compliment from someone new, and it made me feel amazing all over. Without thinking, I closed my eyes and let out a long exhale. I felt totally relaxed in that moment. "Thank you." It's all I could manage to say. I unconsciously ran my left thumb across the back of my other fingers to feel my wedding ring. Still there. Shit. I wanted to take it off. Imani glanced down at it and there was a pause in the conversation. "I—I don't think I noticed that earlier," she stuttered. "Oh my..."

My lips trembled as I searched for a response. "It's a deterrent! I wear it to keep men from bothering me," I lied. I didn't know where it came from, but it felt right. Imani had reawakened an eagerness in me, and I didn't want to ruin it with the truth.

She studied me, perhaps wondering if I was being honest or not; or if it mattered or not. I was unsure.

"I suppose so," Imani finally said. "I can't think of a man who would let a mesmerizing woman like you roam around these streets alone. How about a little music, or are you too tired? I can get you some blankets either way," she offered.

"Music sounds nice."

"Tell me if you know this one," she said, placing a record on a gorgeous gramophone.

I had no earthly idea whose voice I heard. Thankfully, it was a slow tune because I also realized I'd had no idea how to dance to fast music of the time.

"Nobody Knows You When You're Down and Out, Bessie Smith," Imani educated me.

This was a hell of a leap from Atlanta's trap music scene! It was incredible to experience the difference in musical tastes like this. I smiled inside. As Bessie Smith's soulful voice filled the room, Imani extended her hand towards me. "Dance with me, Trish?" she asked, a hopeful glint in her eyes.

I hesitated, feeling a rush of bashfulness. "I'm not much of a dancer," I admitted, my voice barely above a whisper.

Imani's smile widened, warm and encouraging. "Just follow my lead," she assured me.

Reluctantly, I took her hand, allowing her to guide me to a small open space in the living room. As we moved slowly to the rhythm of the blues, Imani's hands rested gently on my waist, guiding me in gentle, swaying movements. "Just like this," she encouraged. I followed tentatively; my movements awkward at first but gradually found the flow.

Her gaze was soft but intense, drawing me deeper into the moment. My heart pounded with excitement and a growing sense of closeness.

"You're doing great," she whispered, her breath tickling my ear.

I smiled, feeling more at ease. The music swirled around us, Bessie Smith's voice a haunting backdrop to our intimate dance. I could feel Imani's body heat through the thin fabric of our clothes. It sent a tingling sensation across my skin.

As the song progressed, our movements became less hesitant, and more fluid. Imani's hands slid from my waist to my back, pulling me closer. Our faces were inches apart, our breaths mingling. She smelled so good. So feminine. So enchanting. The tension between us was a silent conversation of desire and connection.

In a moment of boldness, I looked up into Imani's eyes. There was a vulnerability there, a longing that drew me in. Mid-sentence, as she was talking about the music, I leaned in and kissed her. I couldn't stop myself. I had to taste her. She moaned in surprise and gratitude.

The kiss was gentle at first, a tender exploration. But it quickly deepened, fueled by the pent-up yearning and the rapid emotional connection we'd built. Imani wrapped her arms around me, holding me close, her kiss passionate and affirming.

When we finally pulled apart, there was a silence, each of us catching our breath. Imani's eyes searched mine, a question lingering in their depths.

"I didn't mean to—" I started to apologize, but she cut me off with a soft finger on my lips.

"No, it was perfect," she said, her voice a sigh of pleasure.

We spent the rest of the night talking, cuddling on the couch, wrapped in each other's embrace. We shared stories, dreams, and laughter. Imani played more records, her head resting on my shoulder as we listened to the crackling tunes of the era. I could have gone for more but was content with the evening. We were just two souls, lost in the magic of Harlem's hidden heartbeat, exploring the depths of an unexpected, yet magical connection.

THE MORNING after found us half-clothed with curious hands exploring bodies. She was so soft, so sensual, so delicious. Imani told me how glad she was to run across me on the street yesterday, how she felt drawn to me from the moment she laid eyes on me.

"Even when you said you wouldn't be around long, I couldn't stop myself from wanting to know you," she confided. "I didn't know how the night would go but I'm beside myself waking up to you this morning. So gorgeous, mysterious, and magnetic. I sure hope you'll stay a while..."

A pang of guilt halted my passion.

"But if you don't," she added. "You'll be worth the trouble."

It was as if Imani knew she might get bruised. Like she knew she might get hurt. Like she *knew* she might get wounded but pressed forward anyway. She didn't care. Or...she accepted that I might be a fleeting bliss and wanted to have a good time without and emotional investment. I didn't promise her anything, not even a good time, but there we were on the edge of a waterfall of pleasure.

"Are you sure?" I asked her.

"I'm positive." She took my hand and led me to her bathroom. "Come. How awful of me to not show you where you might have freshened up last night. My apologies."

"We got lost in amazing conversation."

"We did. You said you liked design and architecture," she recalled "They make bathrooms like this down in Atlanta?"

I smiled. It was tiny but ornate, with accents of light yellow and dark azure. A small clawfoot tub with intricate designs at its feet was the showstopper followed by a classic white vanity basin. She had a little vase with wildflowers on a shelf with a few trinkets. A potted plant sat tall in a corner, grounding the space with earthy energy.

"I'd love to wash your skin," she said quietly.

"Oh wow..." she made me breathless, and started undressing me before I could say yes. My gasp and body melting were signal enough.

Imani filled the tub while slowly peeling off my clothing and even pinning my hair up so it wouldn't get wet. "Allergic to any essential oils?" she asked.

"No."

She smiled and put a few drops of lemon and eucalyptus emollients in the tub. Lighting three candles, she turned off the main illumination and retrieved a sponge from a package in a small cabinet. Imani helped me in the tubful of warm water and proceeded to tenderly bathe me. She kissed my forehead while squeezing fragrant water over my shoulders, watching it run over the slopes of my breasts and nipples. Her touches were so simple yet powerful. They were deep and intentional. Fully focused and almost like a meditation on my body, Imani tended to me. The bath felt sacred, and I lost myself in the glory of it. She stared deeply into my eyes, watching the quiet rise and fall of my chest as I breathed. She held my face, my hands, my feet. Imani adored me like she'd known me much longer than a day.

"Imani..." her name fell from my lips in a whisper. "Thank you." I suddenly felt an urge to release tears, but I held them. This bath was a healing I didn't know I needed. "Thank you so much..." It was a cleansing of pain from lack of attention at home.

"I sense a heartache in you. Not a big one. But it's there. I can feel it...better yet, I can see it. I recognize it as familiar..."

She hummed as she worked on my body, her beautiful voice filling the room with a soul-soothing melody. Her attention dropped us into a stunning stillness—into a presence that I wasn't used to. The more she hummed and nurtured me, the deeper we sank into a rapturous stillness of being. Into a pulsation of passion and life. No rush. Just patient attentiveness and sensitivity. She didn't move constantly, sometimes letting her hands simply rest on my body while our breathing synced. The fact that she *didn't* endlessly caress me was one of the most powerful things I'd felt in a long time. Stillness in intimacy was foreign to me. It was as if her hands were slightly dipping into my skin, joining our energies. And before the water became lukewarm, Imani carefully helped me out of the tub and towel-dried me while telling me how beautiful she thought I was.

"You are a walking work of art, Trish. I hope you know that." Imani complimented, and I nearly cracked and released the tears of wanting to be desired like this for so long. *Don't cry,* I told myself. Not here. Not now. But my body trembled, still trying to find a way to release the hurt.

"Thank you," I sniffled.

"Please, allow me to clean up in here a bit and tend to myself. I'll be out shortly. You can take anything out of the fridge you like. My room is right across from the bathroom if you'd like to lie down there instead," she offered.

"I appreciate it."

She was so incredibly gentle; it was mind-blowing. Not long after, she found me nude in her bed. Imani, were we on the same timeline, might have been a few years younger than me. Her body was petite and firm. Her energy was eager and youthful. Her smile was dangerously beautiful. She seemed so instinctual and wise for her years, especially considering the time. She was a mind-altering experience all in herself. Stunning.

"Are you alright?" I asked.

Though she'd tended to me so well, I sensed an aching and slight sadness in her, too.

"Yes. Just...amazed. At you. At this moment. It's like a dream," Imani confided. "I want it to last. Would you mind if I photographed you?"

Her request caught me off guard, but remembering her love of the arts, it made sense.

"Um..."

"It's just I got this camera secondhand the other day but haven't had a chance to shoot anything nearly as dreamlike as you."

"Uh...sure," I hesitated. What did this mean? Would the picture remain after I left? I had no idea, but I let her. Unlike the present, I couldn't see it right away, but she promised she cropped it at my shoulders—that it was just a portrait. Seeing her box Kodak camera was intriguing. I was looking at an antique in action to capture *me*. Wild.

After her mini-shoot, we got back to conversing. "Do you feel isolated sometimes?" I picked up where I'd left off.

"Very much."

"So do I...so do I, Imani. But you've been so amazing to me, that I want to love the loneliness out of you right now." The statement leapt out of my mouth with conviction. "I want to give you an experience you'll never forget. I want to make you feel seen, honored, wanted and deeply desired. Because you are worthy. I need you to know that." I paused to take her hand. "I want to fully experience you now."

Electrified by my words, she quickly joined me in bed. And in that instant, I knew our meeting was more than just a chance encounter. It was the beginning of something transformative, something that would challenge boundaries we'd known and accepted. Confines neither of us wanted. This was the beginning of our return to ourselves—sensual, passionate, loving creatures. I hadn't been with a woman in nearly sixteen years, but everything about this felt right.

The tides of our desire drove us to heights of pleasure unfathomed by the scales of time. Without music or any other distractions, we moved tantalizingly slow in kissing and tasting each other. Sighs, whimpers, and moans filled in the silence. I kissed her wrists, so sensitive and delicate. Her fingertips and forearms, the insides of her elbows, gently nibbling, whispering, and licking her earlobes, I massaged her scalp and ran my fingers through her hair while clinging to her.

In that moment, I didn't care that I was trespassing on the past. Imani and I furled, bent, curled, and blossomed into a gorgeous explosion of passion. Our orgasms rose like a giant sun, not needing a twenty-four-hour cycle to rise again. They repeated several times. We exhausted ourselves with tender strokes of affection and culminated with a feeling of being drenched and engulfed in a beautiful sea of ecstasy.

As we lay in each other's arms afterward, I felt a strange sense of lightness, as if I was floating. Imani's breathing was slow and rhythmic in front of me, a peaceful contrast to the cycle of emotions swirling within me. I held her, my little spoon, loving everything about our experience. But something was happening. I knew it. My eyelids grew heavy, and a soft drowsiness enveloped me. I fought against the sleep, wanting to savor every moment with Imani, but it was like being pulled by an invisible stream. I glanced at Imani, her face serene in sleep, her chest expanding and dipping softly. Our intertwined fingers felt like the last tangible connection in a world that was slowly slipping away.

It was a ghostly fade. The edges of reality softened, and I lost spatial awareness. My vision blurred. I was separating, like a spirit returning home through sparkly streaks of light. Eventually, those bright veins evaporated into cosmic dust. My tongue went numb and my extremities tingled as if awakening from a century-long sleep. Unlike the cannonball feeling of traveling here, my departure was unhurried and unwanted. My mind recoiled in abject displeasure, unwilling to accept that our affair was over just as quickly as it had started. Damn it. *Why so soon?*

I had wanted to wake Imani, to tell her everything, to say goodbye properly. But words were beyond me, and a part of me knew it was kinder to let her wake up without the jolt of my sudden disappearance before her eyes. Maybe, in her world, I would just be a beautiful dream, a fleeting shadow of what could have been. I didn't know, but I could only hope. The last thing I saw was Imani's peaceful face, bathed in afternoon light, and then there was a sensation of being unanchored from the world I had come to cherish.

Calls of jazz lingered in my mind, the melodies entwined with the distant sounds of Harlem's afternoon noises. But it waned like a song in its final seconds. My thoughts drifted to the night Imani and I shared – the morning too. The laughter, the dance, the tender kisses, the bath, and the indulgent entanglement, each memory was a brushstroke in a painting I knew I couldn't keep. I wondered, *what would happen to the photo she took of me?* Was it truly tangible or not? Would it be blank where I was or would she have a memory of me?

When my eyes finally opened again, I was sitting in the maroon recliner in Doc K's lab, the familiar surroundings were jarringly different from the vibrant world I had left. Disoriented, I sat up, the memories of Harlem and Imani both vivid and distant.

I touched my wedding ring, now feeling heavier than ever. Did I just cheat? Was it all real? The jewelry was a silent acknowledgment of the journey I had taken and the experiences that had changed me. Harlem in the 1920s, Imani, the music, the dance – they had felt like a dream, but a reverie that had irrevocably altered the fabric of my being. Those orgasms were authentic. I still shuddered at the memory. Even through the blurred vision, I could still see and feel Imani in my mind's eye. But I was home now. In my time, yet my life had changed.

"Welcome back, Trish." Gradually, Doc K's image straightened out into a more normal view. "How are you?"

"Confused," I admitted. I felt ecstatic, but guilty. Tired, but on edge. "How long was I gone?"

"About 23 minutes," Zephyra chimed in.

"That's it?!" I knew he said my perception of time would be off, but it still felt unbelievable that so much life could happen in twenty-three minutes.

Doc K, Jelani, and Zephyra watched me with concerned and curious eyes. I looked around, still processing my transition. I felt clammy, hungry to the point of light headedness, and overwhelmed with feelings of longing, gratitude, and fear. I missed Imani, Harlem, and the life I had briefly lived. But I knew time was still ticking for me. I had to get back to Atlanta before Jamie got home. Despite my haze and jumble of feelings, I glanced at my smartwatch, which magically reappeared on my wrist—funny how only my had ring traveled with me. There were four texts from Jamie. Fucking. Shit. God damn it! I had to snap out of this. I had to keep moving whether I wanted to or not.

"Here's some water," Zephyra offered me a glass.

"Thank you," I managed to say, taking the drink with slightly trembling hands. The cool water felt like a salvation, grounding me back in the present.

Doc K observed me intently. "Seems you had quite the intense experience," he noted, jotting down something in his notebook. "Physiologically, everything looks stable. No cause for worry on that front. Would you say you enjoyed yourself?"

I nodded, still trying to piece together the whirlwind of emotions and memories. "It was more powerful than I could have ever imagined," I admitted, my voice barely above a whisper. "Yes, yes, I did have a good time."

Zephyra leaned in; her eyes soft but curious. "Do you mind telling us about it? Anything that stood out, or how you felt through it all? You don't have to share everything. It's just so few people have had the experience, we're eager to learn about how Jump affects different people."

I hesitated, unsure where to start. My ethereal landing, the details of Harlem, the colors, the sounds, the emotions, Imani, and especially Charles – they were all so vivid in my mind. "At first it felt like being launched into outer space. Fast. Fiery. Furious. I had a feeling that everything was moving at a million miles per hour while my inner thoughts bent and warped inconsistently with the journey. It was everything all at once—my traveling environment—was incomprehensible and hard to completely explain. It was suffering before Stability. Before serenity and adventure."

"We understand it can be a lot to process," Doc K said gently. "Remember, this experience, though real in its own right, is a journey of your mind's creation, influenced by your subconscious. Was there anything that caught you completely off guard?"

"Yes. Charles. There was a man who knew about 'Jumpers' as he called us. Apparently, he saw me when I arrived, and it wasn't his first time. Did you know about this?"

Doc K looked shocked. He shared a stunned glance at Zephyra. "A man who knew about Jumpers?" he repeated, his voice stained with disbelief. "Well, that's...unexpected. We've never encountered this before."

Jelani didn't join the conversation.

Zephyra leaned forward. She was concerned and fascinated. "Sounds like your trip unearthed more than we anticipated, Trish."

I nodded, the memory of Charles and his subtle acknowledgement of my identity as a Jumper still fresh in my mind. "Yes, it was...more than I bargained for. But in a way, it made the experience feel even more real. There was a 'Jump house' with money to help me through my experience. I hadn't even thought about currency or acclimating in that way."

Doc K closed his notebook, his eyes meeting mine. "Trish, every person's Jump is unique, influenced by their deepest subconscious. It pulls brings to the surface what your soul may have been silently screaming for. And it seems your journey tapped into a deeper layer of this experience; one I'll have to make time to understand." Doc K's expression flipped to excitement and intrigue.

"And then there was Imani." A giant smile crossed my face. I let out a slow breath, remembering how she cleansed me. How time stood still while we loved each other so passionately. The image of her face—that bronze skin, short curly hair, and shimmery dress lingered in my mind. "We shared a night together, but it felt like more than that. Calling it a one-night stand cheapens the divinity of the experience. My time with her was gentle ascension. We needed each other." I didn't mean to tell them all of that, but I couldn't stop myself once the words started flowing.

All three of them shared a not-so-subtle glance and suppressed smirks as if they knew something intimate happened. Suddenly, I was flush with embarrassment. For the love of God, please tell me I didn't have an orgasm in front of these three strangers. I was mortified at the thought. *Oh my God, I couldn't have! Could I?* I wondered, aghast.

I cleared my throat, eager to move on. "I feel like I lived a whole other life in those twenty-three minutes."

Zephyra smiled gently. "That's the power of Jump. It's not just a trip to another time; it's a journey into yourself. It sounds like you've had deeply personal experiences and maybe lots to think about now."

"I did." I sat up straighter and glanced at my smartwatch again, the reality of my current life pressing in. "I need to get back to Atlanta. But...is it possible for me to buy another vial of Jump? I feel like there's more for me to explore, more to feel, and more to understand about myself. It's like I only scratched the surface."

Doc K's eyebrows rose slightly, but he nodded. "Of course. But remember, each Jump is different. You might not go back to the same place or time. It's actually highly unlikely that you do."

I understood, and it was disappointing to learn I may never see Imani again but the allure of self-discovery was too strong to resist. "I get it, I do," I said, a sense of urgency creeping into my voice. "And I'm ready for whatever comes next."

The life I had led in Harlem and my connection with Imani changed something fundamental within me. I was no longer the same Trish who had walked into Doc K's lab, uncertain and searching hours before. I was someone who had glimpsed another world, another life, and who was now eager to explore the possibilities of her own.

Doc K exchanged a glance with Zephyra once more. "Trish, I caution against hasty decisions. Each experience with the tincture can be vastly different and unpredictable. And you should have a trip sitter."

"But you said my vitals were fine, right? It's mostly my mental acclimation to the new world, and I think I can handle the surprises, especially now that I know there are Jump houses to help get me going. I understand the risks," I insisted, my resolve firming and urgency building in my voice as I knew I had to get going.

Zephyra sighed, her expression one of reluctant understanding. "We can prepare an extra vial for you, but please, use it carefully and in a safe environment, preferably with someone who can watch over you. Remember, the journey within is as important as the journey without."

"Thank you," I said, a wave of relief washing over me. The thought of having another Jump opportunity thrilled me to no end. I wanted to see Imani again, but knowing that was improbable, I looked forward to whoever I'd meet and whatever I'd learn on my next leap. Already, I was addicted.

As I gathered my things and prepared to leave, Doc K handed me the extra vial, its contents shimmering with the promise of another journey. "Take care, Trish. And remember, we're here if you need to talk about your experience further."

"Thank you." I beamed, clutching the tincture like a precious relic. As they escorted me out of the lab and back through the main house, the reality of my own time, my life with Jamie, and the responsibilities waiting for me clashed with everything I'd just experienced and craved to explore more. But I knew one thing for certain – my journey was far from over.

"Take care, Trish!" Doc K called as I stepped into the California sunshine. He, Jelani and Zephyra waved goodbye as I slid into my rental car, and headed back to San Francisco. I'd gotten a vehicle after checking out of the Frisco hotel rather than taking a chauffeur service all the way to Bolinas. It allowed me to be on my own time and was more comfortable. I had a few hours before my red-eye flight back to Atlanta, and took a deep breath after turning the vehicle in and making my way to the airport lounge. I wanted to be alone, but that was impossible.

So many thoughts raced through my mind, but my priority was formulating a story for Jamie. I had to be consistent and decided to text him rather than return a call from a noisy background. I also had to immediately get Bentley from doggy daycare when I got back to give myself time to "return to a normal" routine before Jamie got back later that night. I had a hell of a day ahead!

12

PRESENCE IN THE PRESENT

The harried buzzing of people around me was another stark reminder that I was back in my time, back to the world I had grown up in, and returned to a reality that now felt familiar but abnormally distant.

Pulling out my phone, I composed a text to Jamie, my fingers hesitating over the keys. After a few moments of thought, I sent him a message explaining a sudden work emergency that had kept me busy, apologizing for being out of touch. It wasn't entirely untrue; my time with Imani and in Harlem had been a sort of personal emergency, an urgent awakening of my deepest desires and dreams.

Staring out of the lounge window at the planes taking off and landing, I felt detached. The world around me moved on as usual, but I was different now. The experiences I had lived through, the emotions I had felt, the connections I had made – they were now a part of me, shaping my thoughts and feelings in ways I was still comprehending.

When I boarded, my mind flooded with thoughts from my Jump. The well-dressed children playing in the street, the carefree time at the jazz café, the community feel of everything around me vs. the cold, every-person-doing-their-own-thing culture I'd become used to.

My thoughts drifted back to Imani, clearly a woman-loving woman in a time when her desires were a danger to her existence. How lucky was she to have Charles around! Her voice, her smile, the way she moved – she was like a dream, a striking, hypnotic dream that I had woken up from all too soon. The memory of our night together was a vivid and poignant reminder of what life could be if you dared to step outside the boundaries of your reality. And that all the rules of reality and society are fake. Breaking them may land you in a personal paradise.

As I gathered my things to head to the gate, I felt pangs of anxiety. Going back to Atlanta meant facing my life with Jamie; reverting to the life I had momentarily escaped made me a nervous wreck. It also meant stepping back into a role I knew all too well, the role of Trish Gregory, the interior decorator, the wife, dog mom, and the woman who, on the surface, seemed to have a luxurious, predictable and stable life yet internally struggled with discontent and yearning for more.

But now, things were different. My Jump changed me. It opened my eyes to a world of boundless possibilities, feelings, and experiences that could help me feel more whole and freer. I felt more alive, aware of what I wanted, and more determined than ever to find it.

Once boarded and acclimated in my seat, I practiced deep breathing to relax. Memories of the workshop I'd attended with Lena found their way back to the front of my mind. When I thought of her, I thought of my body—paying attention to it from how I breathed to the shape of my back. No one had ever made me consider how much more aware I should be of my body than her. I needed to quell my anxiety about going home and appearing as if I'd never left. *Inhale. Hold. Exhale. Again...inhale. Hold. Exhale.* With each deep breath, I sank further into my seat and quietly expelled unwanted emotion from behind closed eyes. I let the airplane's hum lull me into a light sleep. By morning, I'd be back in Atlanta to my life with Jamie and Bentley.

~

I AWOKE to the dim cabin lights and a mild headache, the kind that lingers after a restless sleep. I wished I had a cup of good coffee. Something smooth, rich and invigorating would be ideal to jolt me back to reality. Damn. The in-flight option tasted the way cigarette ash smelled. I hated it! Before I knew it, we were descending into Atlanta's Hartsfield airport.

Landing was uneventful, but the drive home felt longer than usual. Though I only lived fifteen minutes away, each mile added weight to my uneasiness about facing Jamie. I rehearsed my story, embellishing details to make it more believable.

I didn't even bother going straight home, I drove a short distance further to get Bentley.

"Hey, Big Boy!" I hadn't realized I missed him until he did his goofy stroll to the lobby area to meet me. "There goes my handsome boy," I cooed.

He greeted me with his usual excitement, but something was off with his gate again. The daycare owner confirmed he'd been more reserved than usual—a bit lethargic and less responsive.

"Even with the meds I left for him?" I asked.

"Meds? You didn't leave any. I mean, he ate normally and went to the bathroom without issues. Maybe he just missed you is all," they told me.

Fuck! I forgot to pack his prescription, I realized. "Hm. Alright. Thanks so much." I paid for his stay and headed out with Bent.

Jamie wasn't due home until later that evening, giving me all day to settle in. Once home, I immediately unpacked instead of waiting several days like I normally would. I wanted everything in order, and I didn't want my Jump vial to break or spill in my luggage accidentally. As I shuffled through the bedroom, tidying up, my eyes caught a glimpse of something unusual. It was a small prescription bottle, partially concealed behind one of Jamie's books on his nightstand. Curiosity piqued, I reached for it, noting the label was slightly worn. I wasn't prying, but it struck me as odd.

Jamie had always been one to downplay his discomfort, rarely even reaching for aspirin. So, stumbling upon a bottle of painkillers tucked behind a book on his nightstand was unexpected. It was a prescription for a potent kind, likely from his motorcycle nearly a year ago. *I thought he had finished those. Hm.* The bottle wasn't empty, suggesting he might still need them. This quiet revelation stirred a mix of concern and curiosity in me – but I had my own behavior and story to worry about. I made a mental note to ask him if an appropriate moment came up—I didn't want him to think I was snooping. I wasn't. *What else was Jamie silently enduring?* I wondered. I hated that he hid his pain from me. He was getting better since starting therapy, but he still felt the need to be Superman most of the time.

I was still processing everything when my phone buzzed. It was a video call from Auntie Nia in India. "Trish, hey child! I just rode a camel through a desert, baby girl!" She was as excited as a teenager, her spirit seeming much younger than her years. "I sent you a pic!"

I couldn't help but burst out laughing at her excitement. "That's amazing, Auntie. How much longer will you be there?"

"Another week or two. Not sure. I bought a one-way flight, but I'm not staying too long. India is hard on the senses after a while. And you? I'm dying for an update. Spill it, child!"

"I did it, Auntie," I whispered into the receiver, my voice a mixture of triumph and turmoil.

"I'm sort of speechless at your speed. Proud of you for going after what you want, but nervous about you diving in headfirst. So. . . how was it?" Her voice was eager but cautious.

"It was...incredible. And complicated. Apparently, I discovered a layer Doc K knew nothing about—apparently, there are people in the past who know about those of us jumping back in time. They call us Jumpers."

"What?" She seemed just as shocked as Doc K and Zephyra.

"Yeah. And there are Jump houses with resources for us. Did you know that? I'm not sure how to feel now." Confessing to her felt like unburdening my soul.

"I did not. My jumps were quite different. The first time, I found myself in a small French village where life moved at a slower pace. It was during the late 1940s after World War II. My arrival must have been quite a spectacle, appearing seemingly out of nowhere. I remember a soft landing, like a magical feather twinkling and glistening in the sun until my body took its full physical form. There was a group of gawking villagers, dropping everything to eye me warily. Rightfully, so. Some even thought I was a spirit or an omen – a sign of change or a harbinger from another world. It was a time of rebuilding and redefining themselves, and here I was, an unexpected brown-skinned mystery in their midst. Most stayed away from me at first, but that didn't take long to change as their fascination overpowered their fear."

"Wow."

"I was there for maybe a week in their time, and I learned how to adapt, not knowing the language or having any resources. I learned patience, self-reliance, and humility because it was the kindness of strangers—who didn't have much themselves—that got me by. People were rebuilding and redefining themselves, and for those who thought I was magic, a belief that good luck would come back to them for helping me assisted us all. Those people taught me the value of community in the face of adversity. As time passed, my presence became a part of their post-war narrative, blending folklore with reality. Hell, I might still be a legend there today! Ha ha!"

"That's just so...oh my." I was speechless.

The second time was on a Greek island. I stumbled upon an abandoned hut and made it my temporary home."

"Seriously?" I was stunned. She hadn't shared the details of her locations before.

"Yup. I foraged for food, learned to fish, and even bartered with locals using skills I picked up. Oh, I had a time in Greece!" she said elatedly. "Fell in lust with a fine Greek man who taught me tantric eye gazing and sensual yoga practices, too. Whew! He was a beautiful specimen. But I digress," Auntie Nia caught herself going on a tangent. "The island really had a spiritual vibe to it though, and outside of that tryst, I spent much time in meditation and self-reflection."

"What year was it?"

"For France? It was 1967, so not that long ago. Still in my natural lifetime, but a completely different experience for me. Around that era, there was a global counterculture movement with hippies everywhere. I fit right in," she giggled. "It was beautifully quiet, and I met a few travelers drawn to the island for its tranquility. We shared stories, food, and some fleeting yet profound connections. It was a reflective experience with unexpected encounters, unlike the organized resources you discussed. It sounds like your journey was far more intricate and interconnected. I wonder if Doc K tinkered with the formula? Wow."

"I guess so..." I had even more to process now. She lived in an abandoned shack? I didn't know if I could do it. I guess I would if I had to!

"Listen, Trish, these journeys... they change you. Give it time. And be careful with Jamie. Secrets have a way of surfacing," she advised, her voice laced with a wisdom I wished I had. "Be careful not to get yourself in a web that ends up strangling you in the end. Take your time and approach everything with savoir-vivre."

"With what?" I'd never heard that phrase before.

"Savoir-vivre, Trish. It's a French expression on the art of living well, understanding the finer nuances of life, and conducting oneself with grace and empathy. It's what I hope for you on your journey – to not just experience, but to truly understand and appreciate the beauty and complexity of people—and the world – in whatever time period."

"Hm." I mumbled. "This was a lot."

"That means honesty too. Or at least as much as you can because it is freeing even when you think it'll hurt—hell, even when it does hurt. Pain doesn't last always, and then you can fly."

"Well, alright." I gave in. We ended the call with promises to talk soon, and I sat there, lost in thought until I heard the garage door open. The roar of Jamie's car pulling in made my heart bounce in my chest.

His entrance was typical – tired and distracted, but when he saw me, his face lit up. "Hey, you're home! Did everything clear up with your client?" he asked, embracing me.

I hugged him back. "It was hectic, but I managed. I'm just happy to be home." The white lies were getting easier to tell. Fuck. I didn't know if that was a good thing or not.

As we settled into the evening, Jamie's occasional glances at me and his hesitant responses added a layer of unspoken tension to our interactions. Later, while I was busy preparing dinner, his voice casually broke the silence. "So, what was the fire you had to put out anyway?"

"The Martins, you know, the couple with the estate in Buckhead, they needed a last-minute redesign of their guesthouse for a party. Coordinating with suppliers and contractors on such short notice was chaos, but we made it happen." I lied through my teeth, trying to keep my voice steady and matter-of-fact. I hoped to convey that it was just another day at work.

Jamie nodded, seemingly accepting my explanation. "Sounds hectic. Good job handling it," he remarked, returning to the stove. His response was nonchalant, but I thought I noticed a slight crease on his forehead.

The air between us grew thick with unspoken words. *Maybe he didn't buy it?* I couldn't be sure. Damn it. I couldn't read him. The next thing I knew we were going back and forth over something trivial—unwashed dishes—and it was dawning more and more there might be additional frustration beneath his surface. I also found myself further defensive than usual, battling my own guilt. The evening ended with us retreating to our respective corners of the house – him to his study with Bentley, me to our spa room. I sat—not relaxed—in the massage chair, contemplating my next move.

In desperation, I texted Yasmin and Amara as a group, "Can we meet up soon? I need to talk. It's important."

Yasmin's reply was quick, "Sure, Trish. Anything for you." But her words lacked warmth, leaving me wondering about her sincerity. It may sound silly, but I could feel her energy through the message. Amara's response tumbled in minutes later, "Of course, Trish. We're here for you. Let us know when and where, and we'll be there. Hope everything is okay."

I decided on a long, hot shower to settle my nerves. I couldn't tell if I was being paranoid if or this were Jamie and I's usual not-quite-right night. The tiff over the dishes was definitely new, but the awkward energy was not. I needed to rest. Harlem and sweet Imani were still on my mind and I was exhausted with conflicting emotions. Jamie took Bentley out for his final walk, as usual, and I crawled into bed hoping to be sound asleep before they both came in and went down with loud snoring. I was used to Bentley's gentle wheezing and noises in his sleep, but lately, Jamie had been adding to the cacophony.

As I drifted into a restless slumber, memories of the wild ride to Harlem echoed in my mind. It was crazy how warped the sounds, lighting, colors and my environment got. The journey was the most intense feeling I'd ever had in my life. Thoughts of being scared shitless blended with memories of being stupefied and entranced with feelings of oneness and love. The whole thing was unreal, yet very real. No matter its intensity, I knew one thing was for sure – I was going to do it again. The taste of freedom, adventure, exploration, and sweet seduction was too delicious to only have once. It may take me a while. I may slow down as Auntie Nia suggested, but there's no way in hell I wasn't going to do it again. I'd hid the vial from Doc K in my lingerie chest. Jamie would never look there.

HOURS LATER, the shrill ringing of my phone jolted Jamie and me awake. My cell phone automatically went to Do Not Disturb at 11 pm, so I wondered why it rang. I couldn't remember how long it had been since I laid down. The glowing numbers on the clock showed it was just past midnight. Fumbling for the phone, I blinked rapidly, trying to wake up. Any call that came through at that hour had to be family, and it couldn't be good news.

"Hello?" My voice was groggy, thick with sleep.

"Trish? It's Clint," said the unexpected voice. It wasn't one I expected at this hour. Clint was my mom's partner, a soft-spoken, gentle man who had been in her life for the past few years.

"Clint? What's wrong? Is it Mom?" I sat up straight, springing awake realizing there was no other reason for him to call me. The urgency in my voice mirrored the sudden fear gripping my heart.

"Well, yes, it's about your mom," Clint's voice was tense, underscored with worry. "She's in the hospital. She—she had a minor stroke, they say. She's stable now, but it was close, Trish. Can you come?"

My mind reeled, and a wave of panic washed over me. "Wait. What? A stroke?" The news made any remnants of fatigue vanish from my body. "Where is she? What hospital? I'll be there as soon as I can," I replied throwing off the covers.

"Jackson Memorial," Clint said.

Jamie woke up, his voice and eyes racked with curiosity. "What's wrong?"

"It's my Mom. She's in the hospital," I said, quickly pulling on some clothes.

"Okay," I returned my attention back to Clint on the phone. "I'll be there as soon as I can. When did this happen?"

"This evening," he told me. "I'm sorry, I should have called you sooner. I was just so scared and distracted. Plus...she and I aren't... well, we aren't as close as we used to be." He spoke sheepishly. "But I was still listed in her wallet as the person to contact."

That was news to me. I definitely needed to call my mother more often. God, I haven't been a good daughter lately. I felt ashamed of myself.

"I'll stay with her as long as I need to though." Clint's words broke through my pity party.

"I understand. Thank you for calling me."

"Of course, Trish. I'll see you soon."

Jamie sat up, his expression quickly morphing from confusion to concern. "I'll come with you," he offered, but I shook my head.

"She's in Florida, Jamie. You can't take off to fly there with such short notice, can you? What about your patients?"

"I don't have any surgeries scheduled for the next two days," he told me. "Besides, I don't want you to go through this alone. Who knows what kind of state she'll be in by the time you get there?"

"Clint said she's stable. Plus, Bentley. We can't just leave him..."

"So, we'll take him to daycare. It's been a while since he's been anyway. It'll be good for him."

Fuck! I can't go back there already. It has *not* been a while since he's been there.

"I'll look for the next flights out." Jamie sprang into action.

This man is too good for me sometimes. Remorse snaked throughout my body like a relentless vine, wrapping around my conscience. I was starting to feel the emotional squeeze of my trail of lies getting longer. Shit.

Jamie found a 7:45 am flight, giving us enough time to drop Bentley off at daycare. Our drive there was filled in with nervous chatter about my mother and Bentley's health. We brought his pain medication, which I'd forgotten in my haste to California. Jamie usually does everything like this with him, and I felt bad when I got home and realized it was my fault Bentley didn't feel well when I left him. *I have to get my shit together,* I thought to myself. *Get it together!*

Once we arrived, I grabbed Bentley's overnight bag while Jamie helped him out of the car. Stepping into the daycare, the owner greeted us with a puzzled expression. "Back so soon?"

Jamie looked at me in bewilderment.

I feigned surprise, "Oh, a family emergency came up. We have to fly out immediately, and unfortunately, Bentley can't come with us."

The owner nodded, a hint of slipup in her eyes, but he rolled with it. Thank God. "I hope everything's okay. We'll take good care of Bentley."

Jamie watched the exchange, his face unreadable. I could sense him wondering about Dexter's question—that was the owner's name. *Be cool. Be cool. Be cool. Breathe.* I told myself. *Make up a simple explanation. Be cool.*

"What did he mean by that, Trish? 'Back so soon'?"

I gulped. "I brought Bentley while you were away so I could focus on work without worrying about him being home alone. Remember I told you about the Martins? I knew I'd be running around Buckhead all day and didn't want to leave him without potty breaks, especially since he hasn't been feeling well," I explained.

I usually spent most of my mornings at home, so Bentley was good when I left at lunchtime because Jamie would be home just a few hours later.

"Hm." Jamie grunted. "Okay." He didn't speak again.

On the short ride to the airport, his silence grew heavier. It made me nervous. He was usually talkative, but the dead air hung between us like a tangible barrier. I stole glances at him, wondering if he believed my hastily concocted story.

"I hope things aren't too bad with my mom," I changed the subject. Plus, I really was worried about her.

Jamie finally broke the silence. "Try not to stress too much, Trish. From what you said, it sounds like she's stable. The doctors will do their best. We'll know more when we get there, and we can figure out what to do next," he said, his voice a mix of his professional calm and personal concern. Seemingly with hesitation, he put his right hand on my left thigh as he drove. But I noticed a slight deflation in his posture.

Jamie's comforting words and touch eased some of my anxiety. It was a reminder of his caring nature, despite whatever doubts and distance had crept into our relationship. His medical background always made him the rock in health-related crises, and I was grateful for it, even during my own inner mess. "Thank you, baby." I rest my hand on his.

The airport buzzed with early morning travelers. Jamie handled checking us in and ushering us through security, his efficiency a stark contrast to my inner chaos. We traveled lightly, with only overnight bags and no checked luggage. As we waited to board, the reality of seeing my mother, dealing with her situation, and the rift with Jamie weighed heavily on me. I tried not to feel trapped in my web of lies.

The flight itself got off to a smooth start. We were seated quickly, offered drinks and takeoff was on time despite overcast skies. About an hour in, however, turbulence hit, jostling the plane violently.

Immediately, the pilot came on. "Ladies and gentlemen, we're hitting a bit of rough weather, which is normal when passing over this part of Florida. We ask that you please return to your seats as we're now turning on the fasten seatbelts sign. I know it's uncomfortable, but please bear with us as we get through it. Please remain calm."

Just minutes after he made the announcement, the plane seemed to plummet a few hundred feet, and the air got worse. Jamie and I looked at each other.

"Stay calm, Trish. Everything is gonna be alright," he comforted me, looking directly into my eyes. He made me feel safe.

Boom! The plane shook again, and several people screamed. I clutched Jamie's hand. I could feel the hard air knocking the aircraft around in the sky as the turbulence got worse, not better. The pilot made another announcement, reminding everyone to stay calm and the flight attendants made their way to their jump seats. I swallowed hard. Nervous, even though the crew didn't seem too panicked. This wasn't your everyday turbulence, and we all soon knew it but at least they were calm. That was a good sign, right? Crash! The plane jolted violently, sending another wave of panic through the cabin.

"I want to get off!" a hysterical woman screeched, as if it were a fucking carnival ride the pilot could easily stop.

Swooplash! We forcefully swayed and bounced in the air, and the overhead compartments rattled loudly, and suddenly burst open flinging random bags and belongings on top of us. Coffee and other beverages rained over other passengers. Jesus Christ, does this happen to happen right now?! Oxygen masks fell next, and the cabin lights flickered. *Oh my God.* I gripped Jamie's hand, my heart bucking in my chest. Babies and grown-ass adults wailed in the background.

"Put your head down and brace, Trish," he instructed me calmly, but sternly. "It's gonna be fine, I'm sure the crew has gone through this a million times. Just put your head down to protect yourself. Everything is gonna be okay, you hear me?"

I sniffled but didn't respond. Terrified.

"Trish, do you hear me?" He asked again.

"Yes," I whimpered.

"Okay, I love you. Now, please do as I ask!" Jamie was firm.

"I love you, too." I responded, then obeyed his instructions.

While other passengers screamed and gasped and carried on, Jamie grounded me. I held his hand until my knuckles turned white. I was a mix of petrified and reassured because of his guiding presence. God, I loved this man. My stomach churned with every rock and shake of the aircraft, and I fought the urge to cry in fear. I just did what Jamie told me to do, and soon, the captain's voice crackled over the intercom once more. The air was smoothing out, he told us.

"Please just hang in there for a few more minutes, and everything will get much better," he told us.

The ordeal lasted what felt like an eternity but was probably only fifteen minutes. When it finally subsided, the cabin was filled with a collective sigh of relief, but fear still circulated through the air. And a mess of personal items, food, and spilled drinks littered the floor. At least two children howled in the main cabin around us.

"Are you okay?" Jamie asked, his eyes scanning my face for signs of distress.

"Yeah, just a bit shaken," I responded, trying to steady my voice. The last thing I needed or expected today was the threat of our plane falling out of the sky. I leaned back in my seat, close my eyes, and quietly thanked God for Jamie, and for stabilizing the aircraft.

Just when I thought he and I could relax for the rest of the flight, the crew pleaded for any medical professionals aboard to help. Another passenger was experiencing cardiac arrest. The call for help cut through the cabin's jittery atmosphere. Jamie didn't hesitate to identify himself and volunteer.

"I'll see what I can do," he told a flight attendant after explaining his credentials. Then, he unbuckled his seatbelt and followed them towards the passenger in distress.

As Jamie navigated up the aisle, I watched his retreating figure with a mix of pride and apprehension. Even from a growing distance – his posture was firm, his movements purposeful – he was in his element. Looking at him, I remembered the Jamie I fell in love with, the man who always took charge and stepped up in a crisis, whose compassion was as strong as his intellect. It had been a while since I saw this side of him, the decisive, caring side that could calmly handle emergencies. First, he displayed it for me during the turbulence, and now, for a stranger. *Mmph.* I missed him.

I couldn't see any of the action in real-time because the troubled passenger was in business class and we were in coach due to the last-minute booking. When the ordeal was over, however, Jamie told me all about it. He returned to his seat with sweat beads dotting his cocoa forehead. He looked relieved but exhausted. This wasn't the kind of trip either of us expected.

"Is everything okay? What happened?" I quizzed him for answers. It felt like he'd been gone much longer than a few minutes though I knew that's all it had been.

Jamie sighed, running a hand through his curly, salt-and-pepper hair. "It was a middle-aged guy. Overweight. A million stress lines on his forehead. Pale from lack of oxygen and faith he'd survive the flight. He was clutching his chest with stubborn tears falling from his eyes. Of course, I'm not a cardiologist, but I did what I could with the basics of emergency care," Jamie explained. "First, it wasn't a heart attack, thank God."

"No?"

"No. It just looked like one to everyone around him. And let's be glad it wasn't—for him or us—because that would have meant turning the plane around or landing at the closest airport after any attempts to restart his heart.

"So, when I got there, I asked his name, put my hand on his shoulder and spoke calmly to him. He wasn't immediately responsive. Then, I checked his pulse, requested the onboard emergency medical kit and monitored his breathing. People were screaming and whispering everything from 'is he gonna die? Can you do CPR!

Thank you, Doc!'" Jamie went on. "Look, death is not something I want to deal with today—not that I could control that—so I quickly assessed everything and saw that it wasn't that serious. His pulse was more erratic than absent, a much better scenario. I requested water and kept trying to talk to him, which soon worked. He spoke back, and I felt like his symptoms aligned more with a severe panic attack. His name was Paul, and I helped him focus on slow, steady breathing and asked if he had any medication."

"Wow," I whispered, fully tuned in.

"Turns out, he had anti-anxiety medication with him but couldn't get to it due to all the turbulence and items flying all over the cabin. We eventually found it, and with the water, his breathing eased. It was tense for a minute, though, I'm not gonna lie. Thankfully, he began calming down once the medication took effect," Jamie finished.

The juxtaposition of this Jamie with the one who seemed so distant and emotionally unavailable at home was jarring. But this wasn't emotion for him, it was instinct, and I had to remember that. As Jamie recounted his actions, the image of him working to help a stranger in a critical situation filled me with respect instead of envy. Despite our distance lately, this moment reminded me of his deep-seated sense of duty and his passion for helping others. It was a part of the magnetism that had initially drawn me to him. I sighed. The weight of his words also pressed down on me. They echoed in the hollow, deviant, and impatient parts of my mind and heart.

"It's incredible what you did, Jamie," I said, my voice coated with genuine admiration and a refreshed appreciation for my husband's complexities.

He offered a tired but honest smile, "Just doing what I should, Trish. Let's just hope he gets the care he needs when we land."

Jamie's life-saving actions calmed the entire plane down. The atmosphere went from fear to gratitude. The rest of the flight passed in a contemplative silence. Jamie kept his hand on mine for the remaining time. I needed that. Still, my mind couldn't rest. The commotion had rattled me more than I wanted to admit. It felt symbolic, like a physical manifestation of the hot mess of my life. Memories of my wild Jump, my spellbinding entanglement with Imani, my mother's health, and Bentley's condition all ambushed me. I needed time alone. I needed space to decompress and breathe. I needed a pause.

As the plane descended towards Miami International Airport, the tight knot in my stomach only grew. I steadied myself for what lay ahead, knowing that today's challenges might just be starting. Upon landing, Miami's humid air hit me like a stifling wave, a stark reminder of the seriousness of why we were here. Jamie hailed a cab, and we headed straight to the hospital, our thoughts and emotions a mishmash blend of worry, fear, and unspoken grievances.

After registering as guests and being directed to my mother's room, I braced myself for the sight of her lying there, frail and vulnerable. I wasn't ready for this, but I had to deal with it regardless.

"Trish, Jamie, hey guys!" Clint met us before we reached the room. I'd texted him that we were en route the moment we sat in the cab. His face etched with worry and fatigue. The sight of him, so nervous, tightened my throat.

"Hey, Clint," I greeted him with a hug.

"We got here as soon as we could." Jamie gave him a firm handshake and half-hug.

"How is she?" I asked, my voice shaky as we walked the final steps to her room.

"She's better, but it was a close call," he replied, leading me to where my mom was resting.

My heart sank when I saw her tucked under the thin hospital sheets. Her face looked sad and droopy, and it broke me. Jesus Christ, she looked so tiny. Seeing her lying there, not even close to her usual vibrant self, dumped a mound of guilt, fear, helplessness, and a deep-seated realization of the fragility of life over me. I should have been in better contact with her! The hospital's fluorescent lights and antiseptic smell made me feel even worse. These spaces were no place to heal.

"Thank you for being there for her," I spoke to Clint through tears. I couldn't stop them. "Do you know what happened?"

"Not exactly. I do know that she called for help herself. Through one of those life-alert things. She must have felt something off and it rang the front desk of her community. They then called 911 and got her here. Otherwise, I'm not sure what brought this on."

She shouldn't live alone anymore. The thought jumped into my head with haste. My mom and I weren't the closest, and it was true I gravitated to Auntie Nia more than I did to her, but it wasn't because she was a bad person. Our personalities just never gelled. She was the parent she needed to be to raise a successful daughter, but nurturing, fun and adventurous, she was not. She was stern, predictable and though I hate to say it, quite boring and rigid to me. There was a time when Clint fawned over her and it seemed to bring color to her black-and-white life, but clearly, that time came to an end. I wanted to know why but didn't think now was the moment to ask about their relationship. I was just grateful he still loved her enough to drop everything and see her when she didn't have anyone else around.

Of all the long-term neighbors and friends my mom had, she was the last one standing. Most of her friends had divorced their husbands, and one by one, they began transitioning to the other side or experiencing enough health problems that their children relocated them. But my mom always seemed physically stronger and more resilient than her compadres. Until now. Even she wasn't invincible. She and my dad were no longer close.

A nurse soon walked in and greeted us, getting to know our relationship with her. I caught her do a double take when Jamie smiled, and inched closer to him. I don't know why I felt territorial at the moment, but I did. My emotions were all over the place.

"Any idea on what caused the stroke?" Jamie asked her, his voice tinged with clinical curiosity.

"Doctors said it might be related to her hypertension, but we don't yet know for sure.

"Ah," Clint sighed and rubbed his chin thoughtfully. "That makes sense," he told Jamie and me. "She's been managing it for years, but lately, she's been under a lot of stress."

As the men talked, I quietly sat by her bed, holding her hand. The warmth of her skin was a small comfort in the cold reality of the moment. She was in a deep sleep, and I didn't want to wake her just yet. Meanwhile, thoughts of what needed to be done, the care she would require, and how this would change our lives bubbled in my mind. Soon, another nurse came in to check her vitals. She greeted Jamie and I warmly, assuring us my mother had stabilized and was doing well. It was at this time my mom fully woke up.

"Oh…" she smiled broadly when she saw Jamie and me. "Trish!" Her weak hand squeezed mine.

Something about the light in her eyes when she recognized us sent a rush of feelings through me. Her joy seemed to highlight my faults and failures. I felt awful. My life should have never gotten too busy to not know she and Clint weren't together, to not know that her health was deteriorating, to not know she'd be so thrilled to see me. Maybe I had an outdated version of her in my head. Sure, she never called me first, but maybe she wasn't as stubborn and non-expressive as I'd always known her to be. Maybe she'd softened in recent years. I would have known that if I kept in steady contact. I had to do better.

"Hey, Mama," I whispered, holding back tears.

Jamie, still standing, towered over us, one hand on the side of her bed and the other on me. He gave my shoulder a comforting squeeze.

"When did you get here?" She was confused.

"Just a few moments ago," I told her. "We came as soon as Clint called us."

"I'm so glad you're here." Fear glistened in her eyes.

"I am, Mama. I'm right here. And you're gonna be fine. Do you remember what happened? What were you doing?"

"Nothing worth ending up here, that's for sure. All I remember is putting on a little make-up—I was going to treat myself to see a performance at my community center. So, I was only fixing myself up a bit and all of a sudden, my vision blurred. I couldn't steady myself and I noticed the feeling go out of half my body. It was pins and needles everywhere. I knew what was happening from all the commercials that tell you the signs of a stroke, and I have a few help buttons in my apartment, so I pressed for an emergency. Truthfully, that's all I can remember," she explained.

Though I may not have been present enough, I did situate my mom in a nice retirement community. She had her own apartment, and access to fitness equipment, games and even a pool. It cost me nearly sixty thousand dollars a year, but I thought it was the best thing to do when it was clear she couldn't keep up the maintenance on her house, and she no longer had friends. She had no interest in moving to Atlanta to be with Jamie and me, and secretly, I worried how the three of us would manage. Plus, she'd met Clint and he was still pretty robust. I thought the setup would work for a while. And I guess it did, but this isn't how I imagined seeing her—or him—again. I sighed.

Hours went by with nurses coming in and out to check on her. The more they interrupted to help, the more it cemented for me that hospitals are the last place to get rest. The lights are awful, the noise is constant, the disruptions by well-meaning caretakers are constant, and the food is horrid. It would be terribly lonely for her without us there. I was grateful to the care team for stabilizing her, but I'd need to talk to both her and Jamie about if her current set up was still ideal. This wasn't a time for selfishness. Mortality stared me in the face with unflinching eyes, and I wanted to do right by my mom.

Eventually, Jamie and Clint went to find coffee while I stayed with my mom until she fell asleep again. It would be at least a week, possibly longer, before she was discharged. It was hard to watch her lying there weakly. Here was my mother, a woman who had spent her life being fiercely independent, now vulnerable and reliant on others. The irony wasn't lost on me; the roles had reversed, and it was time for me to step up.

Jamie, exhausted from the day's travel, excused himself to check us into a hotel while I remained at the hospital. Clint eventually left too, assured now that we were there. He was not a young man—likely close to eighty—and I could only imagine how tired he must be from the scare of it all.

"Clint, I can't thank you enough," I told him while walking him to the door.

"It's no problem. I'm grateful I was able to help. Helen and I may not be as close as we used to be, but I still love her. Always will," he huffed with resignation as though he wished they were more. "Please keep me updated."

"I will. I appreciate you."

By the time Jamie and I settled into our hotel room, I was spent. I wanted to stay the night with my mom, but her room didn't have a sofa and she wasn't awake much. So, I took the opportunity to rest in a proper bed rather than sleep in a hard hospital chair. Jamie didn't speak much, and I wasn't sure if I wanted him to. So much was happening; I found comfort in his silence. For now. In the back of my mind, I wondered how he felt about everything. While we didn't have a big conversation about what to do with my mom, I did mention my angst about continuing to leave her in a home.

"Let's see how she recovers and what she wants," was the extent of his response. He was fielding calls from his assistant and hospital, too. If it wasn't one thing, it was another.

When dawn broke, the reality of a new day made itself apparent. There was no peaceful birdsong and Bentley wasn't lazily lying next to the bed. I had to focus on my family and the challenges we faced. It was like I couldn't get time to relish the taste of heaven I'd experienced before the gates of hell opened in front of me.

As I put on my makeup for the day, I flashed back to my mom's story and the reality of doing something so simple being the last thing before she lost consciousness terrified me. Jamie was still unusually quiet, and it made me nervous. Before I could start a conversation with him, however, my cell phone rang with unwanted news from my assistant.

"Sorry to bother you, Trish. I know you're dealing with a family emergency bu—"

"But what, Marcel?" I didn't need this shit.

"It's the Martins. They're not happy with the job we did on their vacation cottage and refuse paying the final invoice."

"How much was the bill? $73,000."

"Oh, fuck no! I think the fuck not!" My attitude shifted quickly. You can forget about all my college education and ability to blend into any environment—I was still Trish from Dade County, Florida, and what I would *not* deal with is a client stiffing me for damn near a hundred grand. "Marcel, I really can't deal with this shit right now. Email me the details and I'll check it when I can. Thanks for letting me know."

"Of course. We need that or paying some of the vendors might be a problem."

"Okay, I got it," I grumbled. "I'll call you back." I hung up.

FUUUCCCCCK!

The contrast between the life I yearned for and the responsibilities I couldn't escape was heavier than a boulder on my chest. Overwhelming was an understatement. I felt like I couldn't escape. I needed to be strong for my mother, and for my family, but part of me wanted to run away.

As the avalanche of problems smothered me, I found a tiny breath of fresh air in the reverberations of my night in Harlem. Imani's soft touch and delicate whispers consoled me, although I wondered if she, too, felt confused by my sudden disappearance after our beautiful evening. Remorse was everywhere, but at least it was bittersweet with her. We were each other's safe space, if only for one night, and that meant a lot to me.

I was tired. The emotional rollercoaster of the night left me exhausted, yet sleep was the last thing on my mind. The obligations of the present demanded my full attention, but part of me still yearned for the freedoms and passions I had just begun to explore. I wanted another Jump, but I knew that wasn't an option, not now. Reality had a firm grip on me, and it wasn't letting go.

13

RIPPLES ACROSS REALMS

Jamie had to fly back to Atlanta that night because he had an important surgery the next morning and refused to pass his patient off to another surgeon.

"It doesn't work like that, Trish." He explained. "When a patient prepares for surgery, especially one as complex as this, they develop trust and a rapport with their surgeon. It's not just about the procedure; it's about the emotional and psychological preparation involved. Handing my patient off to another surgeon last minute would not only disrupt their mental readiness but could also potentially impact the outcome of the surgery. This is one of the Braves' players, too, not that it makes him more important than anyone else, but still. This isn't a decision I make lightly, but I have a responsibility to be there for my patients when they need me most."

He said he'd grab Bentley from daycare and for me to stay as long as I needed to. I didn't want to leave her alone, but I also had fires to put out for work. In the end, I decided to wait until she was discharged. It was past time for me to restructure my priorities. Yes, squabbling over a client with money that my business needed was important, but it wasn't as critical as being there for my mother. Money comes and goes, time does not. I was her only child, and it was my duty. She still wasn't quite herself after a few days—not regularly—in some moments she'd seem fine, and in others, she clearly had a foggy brain. I was exhausted from the chain of the events and didn't feel as sharp as I would normally be either, but I pressed on.

Regarding business, I scheduled a video call and steeled myself to be firm yet diplomatic. In times like this I wished Jamie could step in and help, but it would be highly unprofessional to get my husband involved with my client-facing business affairs. The conversation was tense, but I managed to navigate through their complaints and concerns, emphasizing the quality and effort put into the redesign. I proposed a walkthrough via video to address each of their issues, promising to rectify any legitimate concerns. It was a balancing act, but somehow, I assured them while standing my ground. I was proud of myself, doing better than the old me would have. I felt a gust of confidence that was unfamiliar but welcomed as I spoke to them. They agreed to release partial payment immediately and the rest upon resolving their listed issues. It was a compromise, but one that kept the business afloat and my clients relatively appeased.

For more than a week, the days blurred into a mix of clinical visits and remote work from my hotel. I became a fixture at the hospital, the staff recognizing me, offering sympathetic smiles and small talk. Each day, I saw slight improvements in my mom's condition, but her recovery was slow and inconsistent. Her moments of clarity were interspersed with confusion and fatigue, a constant reminder of the stroke's impact. Despite the circumstances, this time with her was a chance to reconnect, to repair bridges I hadn't even realized were in great disrepair. Her room was quiet except for the occasional monitor beep and pop ins from nurses. She stared at me fondly, almost longingly.

"So, how have you been, Trish?" Mama asked, her voice soft but clear.

"I've been... busy, as always. Work is crazy, but I manage," I replied, squeezing her hand. "And you? How have you been, besides this scare?"

She exhaled heavily, a hint of sadness crossing her face. "I've been okay. Keeping up with my little routines. But, you know, since Clint and I... since we drifted apart, it's been lonelier."

I felt a pang of shame for not knowing. "I'm sorry, Mama. I didn't realize things with Clint had changed. What happened? When?" I queried her.

My mom hesitated, looking away. "It was a couple of things, really. First, his grandkids wanted him to move closer to them out West. He didn't want to do that but started visiting them more, as they did with him. But we also had different visions for our golden years. He wanted to travel and see the world, while I preferred the comfort of our community here. I didn't want to leave Florida, you know? Maybe I should have. I wouldn't have been alone. I should have explored with him!"

Pain. Guttural pain squeezed my throat like the devil's hands. I was at a loss for words.

"You know, sometimes, making the tough choice leaves you wondering 'what if' for a long time," she murmured with a reflective tone. "Clint just happened to be in town when this happened to me, so he rushed over. He's a good man. I shouldn't have been so stubborn. I should have left with him," she rambled, seeming grateful to have someone to share her heartache with. "There's nothing for me in Florida. I should have taken the chance and gone on the adventures he craved. I miss him."

"It's not too late."

"Look at me, Trish!"

"But he came! Clearly, he still loves you. You can have a second chance once you get back on your feet." I found myself rooting for her, perhaps unconsciously rooting for myself. I would hate for her final years to be spent alone and with regret.

"Anyway, back to you," she pivoted. "There's got to be more going on in your life than work. What else is happening these days? How are you and Jamie?"

"We're okay. Still going, you know? And Bentley is still hanging on. Hey, I saw Auntie Nia the other day." I didn't want to talk about my marriage. "Have you spoken to her lately?"

My mother's eyes flickered with a complex mix of emotions at the mention of Auntie Nia. There was a hint of distance, maybe even a tinge of envy. "Not really. Nia has always followed her own path, very different from mine. But you two were always close."

"Yeah, she's been quite influential in my life," I admitted, treading lightly. "She's opened my eyes to new perspectives."

Mama's gaze softened. "I'm glad you have someone like her, Trish. I sometimes wish I could've been more... open, like her, for you. I'm sorry."

"Don't be. I turned out alright," I comforted her. I didn't want her to feel remorse. At least not now. Not ever, honestly. She did her best and she did it authentically. I shouldn't complain. If there's one thing I learned about parents, it's to give them grace. We can't expect them to be our everything as if they didn't have untold stressors while raising us.

"You were always a little wild child. Needing more than I could provide in that way."

"You gave me stability and balance...and work ethic. And I'm grateful for that." A swell of mixed feelings washed over me – sadness, understanding, and a newfound appreciation. This was the most heartfelt exchange we'd had in a long time. "It's okay, Mama. What matters is we're here now, connecting."

She stroked my hand, as soft as a feather, her eyes conveying a silent appreciation for this tender moment of honesty. It struck me then, the depth of what we'd missed in each other's lives for a lack of trying. Maybe this was the start of something new, an opportunity to mend and grow our relationship, one heartfelt conversation at a time. I'd have to figure out if she was going to remain in her retirement community, come live with me and Jamie, or...possibly reconnect with Clint. Who knew if he was even open, available, or even capable of taking care of her now? When she was ready for discharge, I saw her back to her retirement community for the time being. The relief was immense, but it was accompanied by a host of new responsibilities and decisions about her ongoing care. We shared more conscious moments, and I left it at "see you soon" instead of "goodbye." I had much to think about on my journey back home.

Jamie, meanwhile, was back in Atlanta, engulfed in his own world of surgeries and therapies. Our conversations had been brief, mostly updates on my mom and his work. The distance between us was noticeable for me, not just in miles but in the unspoken words and unaddressed issues. His absence, however, gave me time to reflect on our relationship. It was clear that something was shifting between us, and I wasn't sure how to fix it without a confession. I wasn't ready to do that.

By the time I got home, I was beat. I felt haggard and was running on fumes from not getting a full night's sleep for more than a week. From my return to the present, the scare in the sky, the unexpected reunion with my mom, and the mounting marital tension, I needed a break.

"Howooooo!" Bentley was so excited to see me, he greeted me at the door with a howl and wagging tail. His bright eyes were the best thing to happen to me in that moment. I loved that dog! His excitement was heartwarming, and a nice turn from the sluggish, in-pain pooch that we were getting used to.

But the happy moment was short-lived. As I made it past the garage entryway into the main house, Jamie stood there, leaning against the back of the couch with his arms folded. *Oh fuck.* I didn't know what was on his mind, but it couldn't have been good with that stance.

"What's going on, Trish?"

"What—what are you talking about, babe?" I dropped my overnight bag.

Jamie maintained his calm demeanor, his voice steady yet saturated with a quiet intensity. "You've been acting differently lately. It's not just this past week with your mom. Even before that, you've been...different." His gaze was fixed, analytical.

I shifted uncomfortably, feeling the pierce of his stare. "I've just been busy, Jamie. With work, newfound interests and everything..." My voice trailed off, not fully convinced by my own explanation.

He uncrossed his arms and took a step closer, his presence dominating the room. "Busy, I understand. But it's more than that, Trish." He tilted his head slightly, his expression unreadable. "Like your unusual hours, longer stretches in the spa room instead of hanging out with me."

"Is that what this is about?" I walked closer to him, sitting down on one of our kitchen chairs that faced the living room.

"What?" My question seemed to catch him off guard.

"Spending time together."

"No. Well, maybe a little, but not really," he backpeddled. "It was just an observation. I just want to know what's going on with you. You seem preoccupied and distant."

I clenched my jaw, trying to maintain my composure under his scrutinizing stare. "I've just had a lot on my mind. Plus, I didn't think you'd miss me much at night." I muttered.

"Hey!" He got defensive. Shit. That wasn't what I wanted.

"Of course, I'd miss you. Why would you say that, Trish?"

"And I've been meaning to ask if you've been feeling okay. I um...I found a bottle of prescription painkillers the other day."

His face cracked. I hadn't planned on bringing that up, but it flew out of my mouth before I could stop it. Jamie's expression faltered even more as tense seconds went by at the mention of those pills. "That..." he began, then paused, searching for the right words. "They're from the accident."

"But it's been a long time. More than seven months. You're not in pain anymore." I felt awful the moment I added that. He seemed to instantly feel pain at my questioning. But at the same time, I wondered, *why* was *he taking them?*

Jamie's features tightened, a mix of surprise and discomfort in his eyes. "It's complicated, Trish. Yes, the physical pain from the accident has mostly subsided, but there are times when it flares up. It's not just physical pain, it's... more than that."

His admission shocked me. It was easy for him to tell the truth. Guilt. Again, I felt like I was being waterboarded by shameful blame for my inability to do the same. I softened my stance, realizing there was more to his silence than I had considered. "More than physical pain? Jamie, what do you mean? Why haven't you talked to me about this? Does Dr. Rowe know," I asked, mentioning his therapist.

He sighed heavily. "No. He doesn't. I didn't tell anyone. I was embarrassed." He began pacing in our living room. "It's been tough, okay? The accident didn't just leave physical scars. There are days when everything just feels overwhelming. Constantly seeing blood, bones, and fear in my patients. It's a lot. It's more personal to me now. The painkillers... they help me get through the worst of it."

My heart ached for him, for the pain he had been silently enduring. "Jamie, why didn't you trust me enough to share this? I could have helped. I could have been there for you."

He looked down, avoiding my gaze. "I didn't want to seem weak, especially not to you. I'm supposed to be strong, for both of us. I thought I could handle it on my own."

"Being strong doesn't mean enduring quiet suffering," I said gently. "I'm your partner, Jamie. We're in this together, remember? No matter what."

Jamie finally met my eyes again, a vulnerability there. "I know, and I'm sorry. I'm working on not being so caught up in appearing 'strong' all the time."

I reached out and took his hand, the familiarity of his touch grounding me. "Let's make a promise, Jamie. No more dealing with our struggles alone. We face them together, as a team, okay?"

He squeezed my hand in response, a sincere smile breaking through. "Yeah. I promise, Trish. And I'm here for you, too, whatever you're going through. That goes both ways. So...seriously, you doin' ok?"

I thought for a moment, not wanting to rehash a conversation we'd had a zillion times knowing there wasn't a resolution yet. Intimacy. Passion. Lack thereof. "Yeah, babe. I'm fine," I answered quietly.

We sat closer together now, with Bentley chewing a rawhide at our feet. The conversation had shifted from my secrets to a shared understanding of our vulnerabilities, and I was grateful, even if not completely honest. Jamie wasn't ready to hear the new pathways opened by my search for fulfillment. He wouldn't get it. He wouldn't like it. He wouldn't understand it, so I kept it to myself. This was a small win, and I took it, but deep down, I knew my own secrets still loomed. And I worried about him taking painkillers while not experiencing physical pain. But I didn't want to be a nag. I wasn't sure what to do!

In the following days, work became my refuge, a place where I could exert control and find semblance of normalcy. I dived into the Martins' project with renewed vigor, determined to turn their dissatisfaction around. The mix of anger at their initial refusal to pay and the satisfaction of solving complex design issues created a whirlwind of emotions that I channeled into my work. I needed to keep busy while not dealing with Jamie and my mom—he and I had a discussion about potentially moving her in, and it ended with an embarrassing, not enthusiastic, "if that's what we've got to do" attitude.

I knew it was the right thing to do, especially if she was willing, but it was a big step and made me feel like I was back in a pressure cooker. I'd need to fly down several more times to coordinate her move, tie up loose ends at her home, review and update her legal records to ensure I had the power of attorney and authority to act on her behalf, and make rounds with her doctors to ensure I had all her up-to-date information.

Jamie and I would also need to convert one of our rooms to a safe, in-law suite—likely the room on the main level to avoid her having to take the stairs unnecessarily. All of this meant there would be one more dependent in the house when all I wanted to do was break free and enjoy myself. I had to do it, but I didn't know how I would.

As life kept coming at me, I found myself reaching back out to Yasmin and Amara for a much-needed get-together. I wouldn't say they were friends, but they were understanding of the direction I wanted my life to go in. Over drinks, I spilled everything – my mom's stroke, the Martins' fiasco, the growing rift between Jamie and me.

Yasmin listened, her responses measured. She was supportive but distant, her eyes occasionally flickering with an emotion I couldn't quite place. Disinterest? Disdain? It was hard to tell. Amara, on the other hand, was her usual empathetic self, offering comfort and solidarity.

"I'm sorry to hear about everything you're going through, Trish. You're strong though. You'll get through this," Amara said.

"Do you feel like you're living a double life by not telling Jamie about all your new interests and experiments?" Yasmin questioned me.

Amara shot her a disapproving look. "Look, we're not here to judge you, Trish. You're the only one who can make choices for your life."

Yasmin nodded. "True. Sorry about that. Well, that's life you know? Up and down, up and down. It's all part of the journey. Just be careful. Some adventures come with a higher cost than we expect." She smiled blankly. "Hey, did you ever decide on microdosing shrooms or going on one of the more sacred journeys like ayahuasca or peyote?"

"I didn't. But I did..." I stopped myself from talking about Jump, unsure I wanted to reveal that to anyone besides Auntie Nia yet. "But I think I do want to microdose."

"I think that'll be good for you," Amara offered.

Yasmin shrugged. "Maybe."

What was her issue, I wondered. *Maybe she's just weird. Or maybe she's just one of those people who get off on playing mind games with people.* I didn't know. I ended up buying a bottle of shroom pills from them to begin microdosing, as they'd mentioned long ago. I was hopeful that it would brighten my days.

I didn't stay with them long, didn't want to raise any more flags with Jamie. Plus, I legitimately wanted to call my mother that night and check on her. I needed to contact Clint, too. I had of list of folks to connect with before it got too late. By the time the evening wound down, I was exhausted. I took my first shroom pill, unsure of how it would affect me, but hopeful it would do something. But I couldn't sleep. I tossed and turned for half the night. Hot flashes irritated me. Slices of nonsensical dreams bothered me. Jamie and Bentley's snoring added to the chaos, and in a fit of discomfort, I went into my closet to open my lingerie chest and glanced at my vial of Jump. It looked so beautiful, glowing, and sparkling in the tiny glass. There was a hint of blue at the top this time – a new energy that I hadn't seen before—or was it the shroom pill making me see that? I was unsure, but it was magical.

In a dog-tired haze, I made a decision that would change everything. Again. I needed another Jump. This life was too much, and I wanted out for a little while. The allure of escape, of stepping into another world, even briefly, was too tempting. I rationalized it as a short break, a momentary lapse from reality to regain some semblance of balance. Twenty minutes, no more. What could go wrong?

The only thing that gave me pause was if I should take it right next to Jamie or go into my spa room where I had privacy. I remembered it hitting me hard and fast the first time, so on second thought, I decided to creep out and quietly slink into our relaxation chamber. It was more befitting anyway, and...I'd be seated in a reclining chair, similar to the first time. I didn't know if that made any difference, but I felt better with the consistency. Of course, I'd forgotten the multiple warnings to have a trip sitter that both Doc K and Zephyra gave me. I drank it without another thought. And this time, I landed in 1968 Mexico, and it was anything but ordinary.

14

MEXICO'S EMBRACE

Of all the places I could land, for some reason, I didn't expect it to be in an airport. Inside, surrounded by the hustle and bustle of travelers and announcements, the irony of it all struck me. But I guess it was better than arriving on a random street corner like I did in Harlem. Even though I knew what to expect when the Jump liquid hit my system, I still wasn't prepared for the world to turn sideways. It didn't go black this time; it flipped on its axis and exploded.

This time, I was inside a rotation of stained glass and flying Roman numerals. As it spun, I floated into a new world rich with scents, textures, and vibrations. The temperature dropped, and I shivered uncontrollably on my short trip. It felt cold enough for it to snow, but it didn't, and it was fast. Quickly, the winter feeling was eclipsed by heat upon landing inside a humid terminal. I was hot, dizzy, and confused. Even with partial but rapidly forming skin, I was a sweating, babbling fool dumped into vibrant Latin energy. Quiet gibberish quivered out of my mouth as I acclimated.

I don't know how I could make out where I was before my senses fully adapted—I just did. It was like an internal consciousness forming simultaneously with me gathering into shape. The airport was alive with the energy of arrivals and departures, a mix of English and Spanish, and a hum of activity. I staggered, waiting for my vision and hearing to adjust so I could better make out my surroundings.

"Bienvenidos a Ciudad de Mexico!" I heard that greeting on a loop as everything began coming together. Confirmation. "Welcome to Mexico City!"

As I glanced around, my gaze was drawn to an intricate art installation just outside of security and baggage claim. It was a stunning display of local culture, animated and booming with color. Among the myriad of designs, a hummingbird motif caught my eye. Intrigued, I approached it, feeling a familiar connection to the delicate bird depicted in mid-flight. There, subtly placed near the installation, was a small plaque. To a casual observer, it would seem nothing other than an artistic description, but to me, it was clearly more. Coded within the translated text a message in English hinted at the "Jump" location I needed to find. "A beautiful hummingbird jumps into flight...." it read, and that's all I needed to see.

Feeling confident, I walked in the direction of the bird's beak. I moved slowly and carefully, scanning everything until I caught a fleeting glimpse of another brightly colored hummingbird decal, almost hidden among the flurry of airport signs. It was positioned subtly, guiding me toward a wall of shops and booths. I followed the direction it pointed, feeling an inexplicable pull. I loved this adventure!

As I moved, another small decal appeared, this time leading me toward a quieter section of the terminal. There, nestled between a currency exchange booth and a quaint cafe, was a little-known traveler's assistance desk, less crowded and more discreet than the main information counters. A friendly attendant manned the desk, and a small envelope with the familiar hummingbird symbol lay on the counter, seemingly meant for me. Inside, I found a few hundred pesos and a simple map with a circled location near the Olympic Village. *Perfecto!* I thought, overjoyed with the ease of things this time.

"Buenas tardes, señorita!" several people greeted me.

I forgot what that meant, but I repeated it back with a smile—

minus the señorita part—I knew not to say that to men! Once outside, I was greeted with the chaos of a buzzing city. It pulsed like a living, breathing entity. Horns honked, people shouted, announcements echoed, and the air was thick with fumes. Whew! This was before people cared about car emissions, but I took it all in.

The city looked gray even though it didn't seem like it was going to rain that day. I looked around, seeing old taxis, busses, and a diverse collection of people gathering in front of signs that said "Puerta 1," "Puerta 2," and "Puerta 3." I searched my memory bank to go back to my eighth-grade Spanish lessons to remember "puerta" meant door. Got it. Everything should have felt utterly foreign, but for some reason, it didn't. I saw Black people, Asian people, European people, and of course, all kinds of Latin folks. It took me a few moments and several signs to realize why there was such high energy —it was late summer 1968 and Mexico City was the home of the seasonal Olympics.

The air buzzed with the electric fervor of the Games. Sounds of laughter, chatter, and distant music filled my ears as I glanced at the map and back up at available taxis, summoning the courage to get in one. I hadn't seen a paper map in decades, nor did I speak Spanish!

"You can do this," I whispered like an internal pep talk. I steadied myself, taking in deep breaths of the heavy air. My clothes were lightweight, bright and period-appropriate, but they clung to my skin due to the warmth. Despite the city's pleasant climate, the intensity of the sun made me sweat!

My 2024 urge to grab my cell phone and call an Uber had a hard time navigating this scene. I couldn't even rely on Google Translate. Shit. I knew about twenty Spanish words on a good day and cursed myself for not keeping up with my DuoLingo lessons at home. Fortunately for me, I overheard a group of Americans heading the same way I needed to go and pleaded with them for help.

I followed the Americans at a safe distance, my heart pounding with a mix of nerves and excitement. The packed pick-up/drop-off area of Mexico City's airport was just as busy and smoky as the interior halls I'd just left.

I managed to catch a taxi at the same stand as the Americans, grateful for their happy guidance. My driver, a middle-aged man with a warm smile, didn't seem to mind my limited Spanish. "Cuanto por Olympic Village, por favor," I asked, my accent butchered but hopefully understandable—basically, how much to go to the Village. I needed to know I had enough money before we drove off. Thankfully, I did, and hopefully, he didn't give me a gringo price because I only had so many pesos.

The taxi wound through streets filled with Volkswagens, Fords and Chevys, passing colorful murals and lively street corners. I was a silent observer, my eyes soaking in every detail. The car itself, an old Datsun, rattled and hummed, adding to the loudness of city sounds. I definitely felt the vibe of having traveled back in time. It was a bit grungier than Harlem in the 1920s. We passed slums and abject poverty just kilometers away from on-going beautification projects. Every now and then, someone was also riding a horse in the street. I saw vendors hawking their wares, street performers dancing and playing music, and the smells of sizzling street food tantalized my senses through the cab's open windows. I wondered if I could get a tamale somewhere! I hadn't been in Mexico for one hour and I was already looking for something to chow down on.

"De donde eres?" My driver asked. I only understood one word and couldn't answer right away. "Ah...Bueno," He paused, before trying again in English. "Yoo-nai-ted Stayts, si...yes? Aqui. Es." He spoke slowly. "Mexico City!" Then he pointed at me. "Ok... Don - de?"

"Oh, Atlanta!" I felt silly and triumphant that his extra effort helped me understand his question: where was I from *within* the United States! "Atlanta, Georgia!" I repeated, a little too proud of myself.

We both got a good laugh out of our kindergarten banter and soon, we arrived near the Olympic Village. The driver pointed to a small, cozy-looking restaurant just a few blocks away. "Comida buena," he said with a positive nod and scooping hand-to-mouth-gesture.

"Gracias," I thanked him, paying with the colorful currency from the envelope, and stepped out into the sun-drenched street.

The restaurant, a charming place with a rustic facade, seemed like the perfect spot to gather my thoughts and plan my next move. The menu was in Spanish, but I managed to order something that sounded delicious, even if I wasn't entirely sure what it was. The pictures helped.

As I ate, the flavors bursting on my tongue, I overheard multiple conversations about the Olympics. The excitement was incredible. From the window, I could see street artists hand-painting images of the Olympic rings surrounded by Mexican flags.

I learned from snippets of overheard conversations that there were free tours of the Olympic Village available to the public. Immediately, I knew I was taking one of those! It would be the perfect way to get closer to the action. I'd always wanted to go to the Olympics in my real timeline, but never made it. This trip was exhilarating. *Jamie would love this.* The guilty thought shot through my mind like a cannonball. I sighed, missing him in this unique moment. He would be beside himself being this close to so many elite athletes. It was too bad we couldn't jump together. Too bad I knew he was too skeptical to try something like this. It could be an amazing adventure for us both.

By the time I finished my meal and paid my bill, I was ready to find the tour. I glanced at the map I had and took a short walk to the entrance of the Village. There was a line, but I didn't mind waiting. The place was electrified with activity—athletes jogging, officials moving about, and tourists like me looking around in awe at the banners and flags fluttering in the breeze. I joined a group tour, my eyes scanning the crowd, wondering who I might meet.

The tour guide, a sprightly woman with a commanding voice, led us through various parts of the Village, explaining the facilities, who was living where—the Pakistanis, the Irish, the Vietnamese, the South Africans, etc.—and the work that went into construction. My gaze drifted over the young athletes in their training regimens, marveling at their dedication and focus. I don't think I'd realized how youthful many of them were—some barely 17-looking.

Athletes from all around the world, each deeply engrossed in their routines and preparations, created a fusion of focused energy and proud colors. I was so immersed in observing their world, a universe so different from my own, that the idea of meeting someone special didn't cross my mind. It was mesmerizing, watching these individuals who were at the peak of their physical prowess. My eyes were drawn to a boxing ring, where a sparring session was in full swing. One boxer, in particular, stood out with his fluid, almost poetic movement. He was older than most, perhaps in his mid-twenties, and radiated a mix of youthful energy, cocky confidence and seasoned skill.

The tour group moved on, but my gaze lingered on the vintage sportsman in his element. *He's kind of fine!* I chuckled to myself. The image of his perfectly chiseled, sweaty physique happily etched itself in my mind. As the session ended, the striking boxer noticed my interest. He cleaned up and chatted with his coaches before stealing a moment to approach me with an easy stride and a smile that was both swaggering and charming. *Oh shit.* I hadn't expected him to notice me let alone breakaway to come in my direction. *Be cool*, I told myself. *Breathe.*

"Enjoying the view?" he asked, a playful twinkle in his eye.

I suppressed the urge to bite my bottom lip. This young man was radiating big dick energy and I was already being pulled in. *Help me, Jesus. It has been a while!* I gulped, and laughed nervously. "Yes, it's quite something. You're very good."

"Thanks. I should hope so!" he replied, wiping sweat from his brow with a towel. "I'm David, by the way. David Dixon. But they call me Stargazer in the ring." His hair was styled in a way that spoke of both care and nonchalance.

"Stargazer?" I echoed, intrigued by the unusual nickname that happened to connect with my favorite flower. The parallel wasn't lost on me – a reminder of what I once cherished and now yearned for in life.

He grinned, his eyes crinkling at the corners. "Yeah, it's a bit of a story. I'm always aiming high, you know? Shooting for the stars."

"Or punching for them," I attempted to joke. I didn't land nearly as well as his hooks. "I see," I said, smiling at his enthusiasm. "I'm Trish. Just here taking in the sights."

"Well, Trish, if you're interested in seeing some real action, I've got a bout tomorrow. Fighting for the gold. Light-heavyweight."

"That sounds exciting," I said, genuinely impressed. "I might just have to see that."

"Please do," he encouraged. "It would be great to have you there. I'll make sure there's a ticket for you at the gate. What's your last name?"

I was surprised by his offer, but pleasantly so. "Gregory. Thank you, David. I'll be cheering for you." This felt so easy. I was elated.

"Well, I hate to run off, but I do have to get back to work. Coach'll be on my tail if he saw me out here flirting with you."

I smiled. Speechless and captivated. Butterflies rippled in my belly. Despite the age difference, there was an undeniable spark between us.

As we parted ways, he handed me a small piece of paper. "That's my room number," he said. "In case you want to get in touch after the fight. No pressure." He winked and jogged off, his firm ass looking beautiful in those little boxer shorts.

Damn! I hardly recognized myself. Our encounter was brief, leaving me with a heightened sense of exhilaration. As I continued with the tour, his invitation echoed in my mind. Considering how things went down with Imani in Harlem, I could hardly imagine the results of this, but I was ready. I was eager. I was starving for male attention. David was ruggedly alluring, yet boyishly handsome. Clean-shaven. Sinewy. He looked like a sculpture dipped in caramel, decadent muscles rippling beneath his skin. His eyes glimmered with a mischievous glimmer, suggesting a playful spirit beneath his disciplined facade. Watching him was a marvel and a turn-on. He moved with the grace of a panther, every stride a fluid exchange of power and allure. I was definitely going to see his fight.

I tried to remind myself that this was a fleeting moment in a world I didn't belong to. To only enjoy the moment, and not expect anything—even seeing Stargazer again—to actually happen until it does. Although, I hoped I didn't go through all of this to get here and not see any competitions! I clenched David's number in my hand, feeling every bit of twenty years old again. The prospect of watching him fight, the thrill of a possible connection, it was all so unexpected. An Olympic athlete?! I would have never dreamed, but I loved it. And I couldn't deny the magnetism of our encounter.

THIS TRIP, I was actually quite tired from my landing, interactions and so much walking around. After the Village tour, I explored the Cultural Olympiad, which was an incredible international exhibit of artist collaborations, science, culture and so much more. I heard famous non-athletes like Duke Ellington, Dave Brubeck and many others were there. This was the trip of a lifetime!

I used the remaining money I had to book a room at a local motel. Unfortunately, that was all that was available and I'd have to make do and lower my accommodation standards for the sake of rest. Besides, it was called "El Motel Colibrí," The Hummingbird Motel, so I felt a tiny sense of reassurance. I needed to give my body a break for the evening before going to the opening ceremonies the next day.

The tiredness from my adventurous day weighed heavily on me as I checked into the motel. While heading to my room, I saw a woman in the grubby lobby, her gaze intensely fixed on a colorful mural depicting a hummingbird. Her presence radiated an aura of mystery and adventure. Intrigued, I paused to observe her. She conversed with the motel manager in fluent Spanish, her gestures bouncy and expressive. As she finished her conversation and turned, our eyes met. There was a spark of recognition in her gaze as if she sensed something familiar about me.

"Excuse me," she approached with a confident stride, her voice tinged with a blend of accents. "I couldn't help but notice you seem a bit out of place here."

I nodded, slightly taken aback by her directness. "Yes, I am. Just arrived in town."

She laughed, a sound full of life and warmth. "I'm Soraya, from Cusco, Peru. This city is full of hidden wonders. I'm drawn to fellow travelers with an air of... let's say, curiosity. Did you Jump in today or..."

My eyes widened with shock.

"It's okay," she placed her hands up to put me at ease. I'm a Jumper too. You learn to recognize the signs, is all. I didn't mean to alarm you. This motel seems to attract our kind, is all."

My voice shook as I spoke. "Trish," I replied, extending my hand. *Our kind?*

Intrigued and relieved to meet someone who understood, I stepped closer to her. "I didn't know I would run into another."

Soraya's smile broadened. "Yeah, me too. We're quite the scattered bunch. This place is like a beacon for Jumpers, though it's rare to meet another in the same era and place."

Though I checked into the motel to rest, now all I wanted to do was talk to Soraya! As we chatted, her tales of her Jumping adventures captivated me. Her stories were woven with threads of dare, humor, and a zest for life that was infectious.

"So, are there more of us here now?" I asked.

"It's possible but unlikely. Our paths usually don't cross. Every Jump is unique, driven by our innermost desires and needs," Soraya explained.

I was fascinated. "And the motel?"

"More of a happy coincidence, a cosmic crossroad. We don't all land in the same timeline at the same place."

Her insights reminded me of what Jump was really about. Though fun, it wasn't only a fantastical escape; it was a journey of self-discovery and revelation.

"I'm here for the Olympics, but I don't have tickets," I mentioned.

"That's no problem. I have a way of finding things," Soraya said with a wink. "Let's meet for dinner later, and I'll take care of it."

Over dinner at the motel's quaint diner, Soraya's presence was like a breath of fresh air. She embodied everything I yearned to be: bold, fearless, and unapologetically alive.

"So, what really brought you to '68?" she asked, her eyes sparkling with curiosity. "What made you take a sip of that magical liquid?"

I exhaled, unaccustomed to sharing my personal life with strangers but grateful for the opportunity. "I'm searching for something to reignite my passion, to feel alive again," I confessed. "Intimacy. Feeling wanted..." my voice trailed off. "Not sure what that has to do with the Olympics, though."

"You're on the right path. Trust it," Soraya assured me with a knowing smile. "The unexpected is often where we find what we're looking for."

"Hm. And you?" I quizzed.

Soraya leaned back, her eyes drifting off momentarily as if recalling a thrilling memory. "For me? It's the thrill of the unknown, the joy of discovery. Each Jump is a new chapter, a story untold. I'm chasing experiences, learning, growing."

Her words resonated with me, echoing my own yearnings. "It sounds liberating," I mused.

"It is," she affirmed with a nod. "But it's not without its challenges. Every Jump teaches you something about yourself, something you might not have known otherwise. Make sure you're taking time to reflect when you're back home and in your own time."

I thought about her statement, noting that I'd learned about resilience and adaptability in Harlem. I'd learned about the power of leaning into the moment with Imani. She also taught me about empowerment—her subtle, but brave way of feeling me out and coming on to me despite the potential danger to her if I wasn't interested. I'd also gotten greater cultural awareness from being dropped into the time, which I planned to bring to my work if my life ever stabilized long enough for me to fully draw out the inspirations I'd gotten from that Jump. It was a fantastic experience.

My conversation with Soraya continued flowing effortlessly, delving into our lives, dreams, and the bizarre yet wondrous nature of Jumping. As we talked, Soraya's vibrant personality shone through – she was a traveler not just through time, but through the depths of her own spirit.

"I'm glad we met, Trish," she said sincerely. "It's rare to find a kindred spirit in these jumps."

"Me too, Soraya," I replied, feeling a bond forming between us. "Thank you for helping me with the tickets."

"Don't mention it!" she chuckled. "It's the least I can do for a fellow Jumper. We've got to stick together!"

I felt an amazing sense of camaraderie as we finished our meal. With plans to meet the next day for the opening ceremony, I retreated to my room, eager for tomorrow's adventures.

THE FOLLOWING morning would find Soraya and me in the crowded stands among a mix of well-dressed, fully-suited individuals and those in t-shirts and shorts. Sunglasses and sombreros, ecstatic applauses, cigarette smoke and happily energized children screaming at the top of their lungs engulfed us as we watched the amazing run of the female torch bearer from Greece make the long sprint to the cauldron. Dressed in all white, with a sleeveless shirt, shorts, socks, shoes, and a thin headband, she ran gracefully—her shock of dark hair bouncing in the wind. She never broke her stride around the track and up the steps all the way past the nosebleeds where she finally stopped, turned and proudly raised her right hand. Thunderous applause! I was a stranger there, yet the energy of the city embraced me like an old friend, inviting me to partake in its celebration.

The crowd was at capacity, as this was the first time the games were held in Latin America. And at the start, hundreds of doves were released as a symbol of peace and unity. In all my years of watching this event on TV, nothing compared to seeing it live. Seeing the trumpets with flags hanging from their valves. Watching the crowd cheer and take photos as if it were the event of the century—and to many of them, it was.

This was the year the iconic photo of Tommie Smith and John Carlos raising their black-gloved fists in protest of the national anthem was taken. Seeing that specific moment with my own eyes was surreal. I almost cried, watching them approach the white podium along with Peter Norman, the Australian silver medalist, and several officials and women in traditional dress. Immediately after the announcer said, "Los Estados Unidos de Norte America!" their black power symbolism shot towards the sky, and it galvanized me.

In that moment, I was reminded of the horrors at home of the time. The fact that Martin Luther King had been killed in April '68. That Robert Kennedy was also assassinated that year. That protests against racism, communism and the Vietnam War were in full effect that year. History overwhelmed me in the moment as I found myself living it in real-time. I'd learned there was a massacre of students right there in Mexico City—the Tlatelolco Massacre—just weeks before this Olympic ceremony. The world was on fire yet in this stadium and specific locations throughout the region, sports managed to bring people of all beliefs and nationalities together. Being a part of that would change me, I already knew it—the freedom of expression.

Soraya and I enjoyed the relay races, disc tosses and the ridiculously funny 20-kilometer walk. By early afternoon, we slipped out of the stands for lunch and eventually found ourselves where the boxers would brawl. I'd told her about Stargazer and without hesitation, she hyped me up to watch his bout. So, that's where we went next.

15

SEDUCTIVE STARLIGHT

As Soraya and I entered the boxing arena, the air crackled with anticipation and excitement. David "Stargazer" Dixon's bout was the day's highlight, and my heart raced with the thrill of what was to come. Having shared my brief encounter with him, Soraya teased me playfully, her words filled with encouragement and a hint of reckless mischief.

As we settled into our seats, the crowd's energy surged around us, a loudness of cheers and chants. The fighters entered the ring, and there he was – Stargazer, moving with a confident swagger that held the crowd in awe. His body was already glistening under the harsh lights of the arena. The stadium's noise blurred into a vibration when the refs called for order in the ring. All attention became riveted on the fighters. Stargazer faced his opponent with a steely stare, fearless looking. Ding! Ding! Ding!

From the first clang of the bell, Stargazer's movements were a masterful blend of precision and grace. He danced around his opponent, his feet gliding over the canvas with the lightness of a seasoned boxer. Each step was deliberate, a strategic maneuver positioning him just out of reach yet ever-threatening. His footwork was not just movement but language, speaking volumes of his experience and skill. The first exchange of punches was like a high-stakes dance. Stargazer's jabs were swift, a quicksilver flash that landed with precision, leaving his opponent reeling.

The crowd roared. But it was not a one-sided affair. His opponent met each advance with a ferocity that matched Stargazer's. Pop pop! Boom! He landed a few heavy blows, each a reminder of the bout's stakes. I found myself caught up in the moment, yelling and cheering with everyone else in the arena. I wanted Stargazer to win!

But for the second half of the first round. It didn't look too good. His opponent's cross punches landed with a thud and wallop that sent Stargazer towering back against the ropes. My heart raced watching the match, eager to pull for a man I'd just met. By round two, Stargazer was back in the fight, absorbing punches with a hardiness that spoke of his warrior spirit.

He bobbed and weaved, a fluid shadow slipping away from danger, only to reemerge and strike back with increased vigor. Bam! A hell of an uppercut to his opponent's chin put Stargazer back on top. Indeed, his rival's back was on the canvas while his eyes looked up at the stars.

"Get him!" Soraya screamed.

"That's it, that's it!" Yells fueled the arena. The crowd's chants followed the rhythm of the fight, crescendos of excitement peaking with each near-knockout moment. Sitting ringside, the energy was wild. I damn near lost my voice!

As the rounds progressed, Stargazer's strategy unfolded. His initial light jabs evolved into well-calculated hooks and uppercuts, each aimed with surgical precision. His eyes, sharp and focused, never wavered from his opponent, reading every move, anticipating each counterattack. In the end, it was a spectacle of sheer athleticism and strategic genius. The final blow sent his adversary staggering back, the impact echoing like a gunshot in the arena. Ding, ding, ding!

The final bell rang, and the showground erupted into a deafening thunder. Stargazer stood triumphant, his arms raised in victory, his chest heaving with the effort of battle. The sweat, exhaustion, and exhilaration were all etched on his face, and it was beautiful. *All that testosterone and aggression – umph,* his effect on me was also unmistakable. I was entranced, and the rush of sitting up close was overwhelming. I wasn't just a spectator; I had lived every moment of that fight, every punch, every dodge. Stargazer's victory was a thrilling climax to an already unforgettable day. As he exited the ring, his eyes met mine, and in that brief exchange, a connection was reignited, a spark that promised more than just a fleeting encounter. He smiled, perhaps surprised to see me so close so soon.

The ecstatic atmosphere of the arena gradually subsided as the crowd dispersed. Buzzing conversations and excited recounts of the match filled the air. Soraya, ever the instigator, nudged me playfully. "Go on, Trish. Now's your chance!"

But I knew better. The area around the ring was a flurry of activity. Reporters clamored for interviews, medics tended to fighters, and coaches discussed the next steps. There was no way to reach Stargazer during the post-match chaos. I needed a plan because I'd already decided I wanted to see him that night.

"Let's grab a bite. Maybe there will be a chance to meet him later," I suggested, trying to sound casual while my heart still pumped with adrenaline. This is when I really missed text messaging from my timeline. There was no way to message him instantly. I'd have to wait until I thought he was in his room and then find a landline to call him. The horror!

"Okay. Let's have an early dinner nearby." Once everything calms down for him, I'm sure he'll be out to celebrate. And likely not too far away from here.

As we ate, I couldn't help but steal glances at the entrance, half-expecting, half-hoping to see Stargazer walk in. Hell, this whole trip was about fulfilling my desires, right? Well, I desired him! And no sooner did the thought enter my mind, as if conjured by me, he appeared.

"The Champ is here!" someone screamed when Stargazer casually strolled in.

"Hey, hey, people!" David yelled. His presence was mesmeric, and as I watched, he interacted with those around him with an effortless charm.

Stargazer's gestures were grand and there was an arrogance in his stance that I both admired and found slightly off-putting. He had a few bumps and bruises, but his smile when he saw me was all that mattered. As he made his way over, the frenzy seemed to slow down. He became less the untouchable athlete now and more the accessible, roughly handsome man, a stark contrast to his earlier, almost mythic, ring persona and grandiose entrance. He sauntered over with an unmistakable swagger, a grin playing on his lips.

"Hey, Trish," he greeted me with a warm, inviting smile. "Fancy seeing you here."

"Congratulations on your win," I said, my voice a mixture of awe and excitement. "You were incredible."

"Thanks," he replied, his eyes never leaving mine. "I saw you in the crowd. Gave me an extra boost to beat that scumbag, knowing you were there—my good luck charm!"

Player, player! I didn't believe a word he said, but it felt amazing to hear. "This is my friend, Soraya," I introduced them.

"But I was just leaving," she quipped, not giving me a chance to expand. She grabbed her things, left a few dollars on the table, and winked at me. "Have a great night!"

And just like that, Soraya disappeared into the Olympic Village. I was surprised at how easy my conversation went with Stargazer. It flowed effortlessly, as if we were old friends catching up.

"Wanna go for a walk?" He asked. It was perfect timing. The eatery was getting too loud to hear each other.

"Absolutely," I beamed. A part of me hoped I'd have enough time to spend with him before being called home. Stargazer was a breath of fresh air.

"Call me David, by the way," he said on our stroll. "I don't want to be Stargazer to you. Just David."

"Just David?"

"Just. David." He confirmed.

His initial conversation was a mix of witty banter and insightful observations.

"You ever wonder if the stars above are nothing but the universe's way of winking at us, telling us there's more magic out there than we can imagine?"

I giggled, surprised he'd ask that. "All the time, David. All the time..."

David wasn't as art or community-focused as Imani, but he was intriguing, his words laced with humor and a tinge of bravado. We quickly moved on to chatting about the fight, his training, and my unexpected journey to the Olympics—I actually told him the truth, and of course he thought I was being silly and didn't buy a second of it.

"So, you gonna teach me some stuff from the future then?" he played a long for only a brief moment.

"Depends on what you want to learn," I flirted, feeling momentarily free from all thoughts and concerns in his company.

That's when our dialogue took a turn, veering into deeper, more intimate territories. I ditched the future talk so as not to play it too long and come off as a weirdo, but it felt good to be honest for a change. Our discussion became a tango of words, each sentence mixed with innuendo and a tantalizing promise of more. We delved into topics of passion and the thrill of the unknown. David spoke of his love for the art of boxing, how it was a dance, a physical conversation between two warriors.

"But I'm also a hell of a lover, too, you know? There's more than one way to get people on their back, and it doesn't have to involve pain."

I was NOT expecting those words from him. "Oh, really?"

"Yes, but my apologies. That was a bit forward. I just mean that I'm a passionate guy. I love romance just as much as I love rumbling. Haven't quite met the right female match for me though."

"What does she look like?" I was curious.

"Looks don't matter so much as her energy. Someone open-minded, willing to explore, confident in herself. Someone who just wants to have fun without making things all messy with territorial feelings. I want a woman who is free. Free to stay, or free to go. Just free, and ready to enjoy the moment."

"Hm." I was speechless. Not wanting to rush into a response, I let the air around us fill in the gap. It was thick with the unspoken tension of attraction and possibility.

As we talked, I noticed a small vial with white powder peeking out of his pocket. The way he occasionally tapped it with his finger didn't escape my observation, either. It actually triggered me to pay more attention to him sniffing. *Is that...nah?* I talked myself out of thinking it was cocaine, a habit I found repulsive despite my explorations with psychedelics. It was a contradiction I wasn't ready to unpack, and I hoped I was wrong. Besides, I knew athletes were drug tested before matches.

Eventually, David and I picked our banter and walk back up. It was daring, each phrase a step closer to something more profound, more intimate. As the evening wore on, the night air cooled the atmosphere.

"I have a room at a motel not far from here," I found myself saying, the words bold and uncharacteristic of me, yet thrillingly empowering. "El Motel Colibrí. Would you... would you like to come back with me?"

David's response was a smile that held a universe of possibilities. "I'd like that," he said, his voice a low, enticing promise.

The walk to the motel was a blur. Our connection was dynamically charged with anticipation. As we entered my modest room, the outside world vanished, leaving us to go on a journey of rapid, sensual discovery. And it was fast. David and I immediately dissolved into a passionate kiss against the door. It was deep, intoxicating, and woke my entire body up.

"I love how you taste," he whispered.

David's energy was desirous and intense but without haste. He focused on me, his fingers slowly creeping into my hair to rub my scalp as we kissed. It was a soothing massage that loosened me up. I felt him growing in his pants as his lips made their way to my earlobes and neck. I moaned, instantly feeling at ease. The hand he'd been using to caress my head made its way to the back of my neck—a gentle squeeze to contrast the tender kisses and licks he unleashed on my cheeks, lips, and even collarbones. My legs got weak.

"David," I gasped. Euphoria gripped me. Before I could speak another word, he slowed down to usher me to the bed.

The interlocking of our fingers, as we walked the short distance, felt playful yet sincere. Was I really doing this? He was half my age! *Yes, yes, you are!* My mind was far ahead of me. *Cougar!* It teased. *Get it, girl!*

"There's something special about you, Trish," David whispered. He knelt at my feet and removed my shoes as I sat on the edge of the bed. "Something irresistible, like a calling just for me. Don't mean to be arrogant, and I hope you don't take it that way." He said, beginning a foot rub that made me sink further into the moment.

"I don't," I managed to whisper.

David flooded me with attention. From my feet to my calves to my inner thighs. He rubbed and kneaded away tension with expert skill. "You smell good," he complimented, as his face came closer to me. "Lay down for me, would ya?" He asked politely.

I did as he instructed and watched him pull off his shirt.

"Ouch!" He flinched while pulling it over his head. "Occupational hazard," he quickly joked. "I'm a little busted up, obviously, but I still want to make this a special time with you." At that moment, the small bottle with white dust fell out of his pocket.

"What's that?" I pointed at the floor.

He gulped. "Oh, that...uh...it's nothing. Just a little celebration, party favor kind of thing for later," he explained.

"Is it..." I wanted to clarify, but at the same time, I didn't. Even if it was what I thought it was, clearly, he didn't plan on using it while with me. Shit. Well, that was a bit of a buzzkill. I sighed, disappointed.

"It's nothing, Trish. I'm sorry it upset you." He picked it up and chucked it in a chair before tossing his shirt over it. "Forgive me, please? I apologize. See, it's gone!" He flashed his open palms playfully.

I debated. The product threw me off, but it was also a mirror, and I was a hypocrite if I didn't accept his apology. "Yes," I closed my eyes and swallowed my pride and judgment. "I forgive you." I forced a smile.

David crawled into the bed and lay next to me, tenderly rubbing my arms, breasts, belly, and even my hip bones. He seemed so utterly absorbed in tending to me that I almost felt like it would be an intrusion to return the affection. But carefully, I let my hands wander over his perfectly muscular body. He did have a few visible bruises, but he was still beautiful. "I'm glad I met you," I confessed, turning to face and kiss him again.

"Mm hm," he mumbled while our tongues locked.

I was so aroused my panties were soaked. We hadn't even done that much but the little we did felt like a meditation in pleasure. It was so joyous and spontaneous that I couldn't stop myself from breathing heavier, rubbing his head, his chest and the solid bulge in his pants.

"Darling, you are so gorgeous," he complimented. "I feel like you've been wanting attention like this for some time now. And I'm here to give it. Matter of fact don't even worry about my pleasure. Seeing you respond to me is orgasmic all on its own. I want you to feel free tonight, okay, beautiful? Don't repress a thing!"

"Oh, David..." I couldn't stop the breathy moan if I tried.

I wanted to devour him, but realized he was quite delicate from his fight earlier in the day. It didn't matter that he wished to make it all about me. I wanted to experience pleasing him. In that moment, he was everything Jamie was not, and I had an insatiable hunger for it. Sensing my urge to move faster, David slowed me down by putting one of his hands on my heart while kissing my shoulders.

"Breathe with me," he murmured. "I want you totally relaxed. We don't have much time because I have to get back to the Village, but I want to make the moments we do have count. Breathe with me,

Trish," he instructed, and slowly, our breaths fell in sync. We became one—a balance of intensity and serenity.

I soon turned to face him completely, both of us on our sides, and stared directly into his eyes as I reached into his pants. Mirroring me, he slid his hands up my dress and tugged my wet panties down. Our gaze never left one another as we slowly began pleasuring each other. I felt his thumb delicately grazing over my clit as I carefully took his balls in my hand. I didn't want to go straight to his shaft. Unblinking and unflinching we explored each other to a point that quickly got close to the edge before he let out a heavy sigh and closed his eyes.

"Get the tip," he moaned once I began stroking him.

Both of our eyes were closed now, and I felt him slide a finger inside me after long moments of teasing my clit and lips. I was so wet, that I knew my juices covered his hands. We slowly went on like this for several minutes before he spoke again.

"There is something indestructible in you, Trish. It might be under rubble. It might be in the darkness. And it might be a little afraid to come out, but I'm telling you it's there..." he said. "I feel it." Right then I felt his finger gently putting pressure against my G-spot.

David spoke like no other person I'd been with.

"It's passion. Pent up and looking for a release," he continued while carefully putting another finger on my perineum, and the hole just below it. He massaged the opening, which was completely unexpected but incredibly erotic.

The surprise sensation of dual sensation made my body rock. I kissed him hard, and he inched closer to me—close enough that I could feel his dick on my thigh. "Take your pants off," I told him, but he waited a few moments. Instead, he slowed down his fingerwork to focus on my nipples with his tongue. It was heaven. I moaned uncontrollably from the attention.

Finally, David stood up to carefully take off his remaining clothes, as did I. I marveled at his god-like physique. The body of a champion. When he fully took off his boxers, his hard dick bounced up and down in a way that made my mouth water. He was girthy, but I wasn't afraid of him. This time, I sat him at the edge of the bed while I savored him in my warm mouth.

"Oh, hell yeah!" He exclaimed.

My ego stroked, I kept going. Not too fast, not too slow, not too rough, in rhythm with his thrusts. David put one hand on my head and the other on my shoulder blade and continued pushing into my mouth. Just as I felt precum drip on my tongue, he spoke. "Hold on, hold on...come off it. Not yet." He backed away, not wanting to climax. "Whew! Girl! You're definitely not from around here! The future, you say?" He laughed.

"I was just kidding!" I smiled, proud of myself.

David set my body on fire. His very vibration and existence were so potent that being with him gave me a contact high. The pulse between my legs grew harder and stronger each second with him. For the next half an hour, he made it a celebration of my whole being. Studying me, rubbing me, kissing me, and tasting me until I reached a body-quaking climax. We did everything except have actual intercourse, which was a pleasant shock.

"I want to. God knows I do, and I bet you've never heard this from a man before," he paused, "but I'm afraid of how much it might hurt!" David chuckled unashamedly. "My ribs. My back. My head...Everything is blazing, and I don't want to push my body too much with a lot more action, if you know what I mean. But we can keep this soul affair going," he finished, grabbing his own dick. "I like being watched...do you mind?"

"No, I don't." I was dumbfounded by his honesty and his exhibitionist admission. "That might be kind of hot." And it was! I was unprepared for how arousing it would be to watch him please himself in the bed next to me. He moaned, he grunted, and his eyes rolled back. I watched how he stroked himself and pulled up on his balls every now and then. David's self-pleasure ecstasy was so contagious, that I quickly neared orgasm number two just from watching him. But I didn't. Instead, I found myself doing the same with my body. Exploring.

"Oh my god..." I rubbed myself with two fingers, adding touches to my nipples with my other hand. The indulgence was a first-time for me and it sent me to heaven.

"Looks like I'm reintroducing you to your own body," he smiled pompously, but I liked it. I loved his cocky undertones. They made this affair even more powerful. "You see," he rubbed the head of his wood, "When you really, unapologetically become open to guilt-free pleasure... it will descend on you." David stroked and talked. He stroked and talked, only stopping to grab my thigh with his free hand. "You have to just go get it and not let anybody make you feel bad or like you're weird. That's why I just flat-out told you what I liked." David stroked and talked. "Now look at us!"

As he got closer to climaxing, his breathing got deep and heavy. He finally stopped talking. The muscles in his legs tightened. Watching him kept getting me off and I soon neared my peak too. David licked his lips, and closed his eyes, jerking himself off faster. "Come with me, Trish," he told me.

Caught up in the moment, I increased the friction of my touch. "I will..."

"Let's come together. Oh, fuck..." he was close.

"Yes!" So was I.

"Whisper my name."

"David..."

"Again..."

"David!"

Seconds later we both reached a feverish climax and David's seed shot onto my leg. It was warm, alive, and welcomed.

"Trish!" I heard my name, but it wasn't David's voice anymore.

My world was blurring. Space and time collapsed. Oh hell. Already? I felt like I was being sucked into a vacuum with a psychedelic sky. Pink and purple dogs with wings soared alongside me, and the air was thick with the sounds of a world untethered from reality. There were butterflies. Giant black butterflies everywhere. And bats! Warped eyes and contorted shapes. This was a tornado and I was naked among flying debris. Fuck! I wanted out!

"Trish!" I heard my name again, but this time I knew who it was.

Oh my God, no. No, no, no, no, no! Anxiety burned my body like acid, and I was shot back home.

"Trish!" The voice boomed one more time. "Who the fuck is David?" It was Jamie. He was standing in the doorway to our spa room incensed, staring at me with complete and utter disgust. And rage. "Who. The FUCK. Is David?" Jamie's tongue was a sword, and his eyes boiled over in fury.

I had no time to reacclimate. My orgasm must have been audible. Shit. Shit. Shit! "Umm..." I tried to speak, but couldn't. *Jesus Christ. Tell me I didn't actually say his name out loud! Damn it!* My thoughts berated me. Clearly, I did. How else would Jamie know it? "Jamie..."

My mouth went dry. My nerves were shot. The moment I'd never thought could happen was here. I knew I'd have to come clean one day, but never did I imagine I would be forced to do it like this.

I could see the up and down of Jamie's chest, the veins in his forehead and neck. Behind him, Bentley paced anxiously. This wasn't the soft and easy return I experienced before, and I wasn't ready to face reality. The harshness of present life hit me like a sledgehammer to the head.

"He's nobody." I gulped. My brief escapade in Mexico had suddenly turned my spa room into a courtroom, with Jamie as the judge and my guilt standing trial. By the time I realized my hand was still against my groin it was too late to try and hide anything. My shame and embarrassment were maddening. I wanted to drown.

Jamie walked closer to me. His frame, which usually felt like a comforting fortress, towered over me like a looming typhoon. Bentley whined in the background. It was too much. It was too much!

"I can explain! It's not what you think! There is no David!" I sat up straight, knowing I needed to talk fast. "But...you—you might want to sit down for this."

His brows furrowed in fury and confusion. I didn't even know where to begin. "Have you been cheating on me?" Jamie pressed me. He did not sit down.

"No," I answered swiftly, but didn't know if that was completely true. Did I cheat on him?

"Then who is he?"

"He's not real. I mean, he is, but not in this time."

"What the fuck are you talking about, Trish?"

I realized how disjointed and ridiculous I sounded. "Jamie... please, sit."

"No!"

I sighed. "Okay, it's not what you think. I took a potion. A...psychedelic."

"Oh, hell no. You did what?" Jamie was incredulous.

"And it allows me to experience things," I continued. "Different times, different places. To travel back in time."

"A potion?" Jamie's voice was a blend of disbelief and scorn. "Trish, do you hear yourself? This is insanity. Can you please just tell me the truth?"

"I am! I swear to God, I am. I can show you." I reached in the crease of the massage chair. Bentley sat by my side, protective. I quickly pulled the near-empty vial, its contents now a symbol of my tangled snare of lies. "Look! This is it. Someone I met through Auntie Nia gave it to me. It's real." Only a microscopic drop of the potion remained in the tiny glass. But it shimmered.

"Oh, for fucks' sake! This is bullshit!" His voice dripped with bitter sarcasm. "I should have known something was off with you as soon as you started talking about all this spirituality and energies and plants." Jamie eyed the vial, his anger simmering. "I don't buy it, Trish. This...this is absurd! You expect me to believe you're a time traveler or something? You're lying to my face!"

"I'm not!"

"This is the funkiest pile of dogshit I've ever smelled. I can't believe you don't have the dignity to tell the truth!" Jamie forcefully ran his hands over his head.

"I am not lying!"

"So what? You're having affairs with our ancestors? The fuck, Trish! Do I look stupid to you?"

"No, Jamie, you don't! I know it sounds crazy, but it's real. This was a plant-based potion and mixed with something synthetic."

He looked at me like I was out of my mind.

"It's real, Jamie. It's real! I was just in 1968 Mexico for the Olympics."

"Mexico? A psychedelic trip to the Olympics? Do you expect me to accept this... this horse shit fantasy?" Jamie looked at me without blinking. "And you were worried about *me* having a drug problem," he scoffed. His hands, once gentle, now flailed in frustration.

"I was only nervous about you getting addicted to painkillers."

"What do you care about me trying to ease my pain? Clearly, not one damn bit because you're fucking some other dude name David! Damn it, Trish!" Jamie's voice shattered. His eyes watered.

Oh my God. He was convinced I was having a real-time affair. "No, Jamie. It's not what you think—"

"And I immediately came clean about the pills, Trish. When you asked, I told you everything. No secrets, no lies. Unlike you—"

"Trust me, Jamie—"

"How can I?" He screamed.

Bentley, not liking the tension between us, barked impatiently.

"It's okay, big boy," I tried to calm him down.

"So, you've been drugging yourself? Escaping into fantasies while lying to me?"

"Yes. Well, no. Yes!" My tongue was tied. I'd lied myself into a fucking knot. A fucking noose! *Breathe.* I tried to calm myself, but struggled. My heart throttled in my chest. I fought to pull air from my lungs. My world closed in on me. "Jamie..." I sobbed.

"This is fuck shit, Trish! I know I haven't been the man you wanted me to be lately, I know that! But why did you have to do this? Why did you have to cheat on me?" Jamie rubbed his eyes, fighting tears. "I've been in therapy. I've been working on myself! Why couldn't you wait for me!? I would have waited for you, Trish! Why did you do this..." he could barely speak. "Why..." he cried.

Jamie was in shambles. And it was my fault. I felt like I died. I wanted to. "Baby..." My lips trembled in regret, sorrow, disgust, pain and every negative emotion I could possibly feel. Tears rushed from my eyes.

Unsure of who to console, Bentley let out a low, worried whine and nudged against Jamie's leg. The dog chose him. I was fucked.

"No, Jamie, it's not like that. I just... I needed an escape."

"Escape?" Jamie's voice splintered with emotion. "While you were 'escaping,' I've been here, dealing with reality. Dealing with pain."

"But you haven't! Don't think because your drug has a prescription label on it, you're better than me." I felt attacked.

Jamie flinched. I had struck a nerve. His face contorted into a mix of hurt and wrath. "Better than you? I've been fighting every day to stay afloat, Trish. To be here for you, for us!"

"For us?" I retorted, my voice rising. "Or for your own inabilities? You've been hiding behind those pills, Jamie, just like I hid behind this potion."

His jaw clenched. "Hiding? You think I wanted this? You think I enjoy being an emotional wreck? Being less than I was? Not being enough for you and being constantly reminded of it? You think I wanted that?" He got in my face – a first in our entire relationship.

Bentley barked louder, his unease growing with our anger. We were too heated with each other to quiet him.

"This isn't about your pain, Jamie. It's about us! You've been absent for almost a year, even when you're right here!" I shouted, my frustration boiling over.

"I've been trying, dammit! Trying to get better, to be there for you. But you? You've been off in your fantasy world, lying for God knows how long and cheating on me in your mind!"

"I wasn't cheating!" I insisted, my heart pounding. "It wasn't real, Jamie. It was an escape from emptiness! I just...I just wanted to feel something. To feel wanted."

"Well, if you felt it so deeply you moaned another man's name, I think that qualifies as cheating! How many times have you done this? How the fuck am I supposed to compete with some fairy-ass dude in another dimension." Jamie threw his hands up. "Pain. Emptiness..." He laughed bitterly. "You call this pain? You don't know what pain is, Trish!"

I resented him dismissing my feelings. "Fuck you, Jamie! That's why I didn't want to tell you. This is exactly why I didn't feel safe sharing any of this with you! I knew you wouldn't get it! I knew you would judge me and make light of something important to me! Fuck you!" I stormed out of our spa room, leaving him with Bentley. My body was an earthquake of emotion. Every cell rattled. I could barely stand.

Jamie followed me down the hall. "Trish! Trish!"

I refused to turn around. "Excuse me for hurting. Excuse the fuck out of me for trying to find peace while not trampling on your precious manhood and need to control everything."

Exhausted, I gripped the banister to steady myself as all the pain, fear, and uncertainty I'd felt for a year erupted. I faced an illuminated, artistic sculpture of our hands displayed in a wall cutout in front of me—I'd had it made for us years ago. I couldn't turn around to look at him but was still faced with an old symbol of our love. Gradually, I got control of my breath and spoke again. Slowly, and with an unsteady soul. "You know...until the last week, I couldn't remember the last time I woke up to a husband who wasn't lost in his own world of suffering, Jamie. I..." I couldn't talk anymore. I was tired and let out a heavy gust of air before going in my office and pushing the door shut. I didn't want to deal with this. But Jamie followed me.

"You're not gonna escape this, Trish. We're not done." His voice was venomous. "You think you're better than me while you're lost in your delusions. I took painkillers to cope and navigate, not abandon the real world. I went to therapy. I apologized!"

"Right, because you're so fucking perfect and I'm not!" I was devastated. "I'm sorry. I failed. I'm not perfect. I tried, and I failed. There! You want me to scream it! I'M NOT PERFECT AND I'M A FUCKING FAILURE AS A WIFE! I'M SORRY!" I collapsed, knowing it was honest. Finally, I got it out. The truth. Like a butcher knife slicing through a balloon. It was out, and my heart might as well have popped along with it.

"Trish..." His voice sounded muted under my agony and honesty. His eyes reflected confusion as to what he should feel.

"The real world is bigger than what we can see, Jamie." Tears welled up in my eyes. "There's so much more than this stupid routine life we have. There are amazing experiences out there. Different ways of thinking. Different ways of living and being. I'm sick of living in this box no matter how pretty it is." The moment I said the words I remembered Imani's sweet voice saying she felt *trapped...like a swan in a golden cage*. I understood her even more now. "I just wanted to feel alive again. I was desperate. I wanted to feel free."

Jamie huffed. He spoke quieter now. "Alive?" He shook his head, a mix of disbelief and sorrow. "I thought you were dying, Trish!" Bam. There it was. He sank down with me. "The only reason I came into the spa room was because I heard you making noises that sounded like you were in pain. You were sweating. Your breath was labored. You were tossing and turning. Your heart rate was elevated, and I couldn't wake you up. I shook you. I called your name. Nothing could wake you up. And then I ran to get my medical kit. By the time I came back, you were moaning another man's name while rubbing your genitals. Imagine my shock that you weren't dying...you were in the throes of passion with someone else. Someone, not me." His body caved in on itself. "And you were in so deeply my touch couldn't bring you back."

Anguish. Deep gut-wrenching anguish. It boomeranged from him to me, and it was heavy. "I'm sorry, Jamie. I was selfish—"

"No, Trish. You were more than that. You were reckless. What if something happened to you for real? Do you even know what 'synthetic stuff' is in this drug?" He cut me off, his expression hardening. "I can't do this. This... whatever this is." His words, sharp and accusing, cut through me. I saw the pain behind his eyes, the betrayal he felt. "I don't know who you are anymore. I can't even look at you right now. What if you would have died and I had to find you like that? I can't handle this! It's too much!" He was shaken, deciding to exit the room.

"Jamie, please, I'm sorry. I never meant to..." I cried, but he didn't break his stride or look back. In that moment, I felt the chasm between us widen, a gap that might be too vast to bridge. The truth was he didn't know about half my lies, and I didn't have it in me to tell him the whole truth he deserved. Not now. Not yet. My heart ached and tears sprang from my eyes knowing that I actively, willingly broke all trust in my marriage. My stability. My life. Jamie's steps were loud, leaving me in a silence broken only by Bentley's soft whimpers and the resonance of a love teetering on the brink of collapse. Fuck!

16

CONFESSIONS AND CROSSROADS

When you're married and childless, few things hurt more than knowing you are the reason for your partner's broken heart. The pain is hard to describe. It's bone-deep and it burns. The sting of knowing you failed them feels like acid relentlessly scorching through your veins. It's an awful emotional state to marinate in. For the first time in our entire marriage—with the exception of a deployment he had to Afghanistan, which he didn't like talking about—Jamie and I slept in separate rooms for days. I'd lost the game I'd been playing, both in a loud crash, and in the quiet closing of a door, leaving me alone with the weight of my lies and a loyal dog who couldn't comprehend the human heart's complexities.

Jamie didn't want to talk to me. He didn't want to see me. He didn't want to hear that sometimes good people do bad things when they're desperate for connection. I'd wounded him in a way that felt irreparable. I cried so much my temples felt like they'd become a gutter for an ocean of salty tears.

I had been so caught up in getting what I needed to feel whole—in quenching my thirst for affection—that I failed to grasp the unique significance of my actions. Saying yes to myself meant sacrificing

Jamie. It meant lying to him for months as if I had a superpower that would ensure he'd never find out. It meant the flesh and blood of our marriage would wither to ravaged skeletons and foul dust—a hopeless corpse of what it once was. I'd robbed him of the chance to understand and be empathetic, or even logical, by not being upfront with him. My assumptions eroded our decades-long foundation of trust, and I was ashamed of myself.

In the aftermath of that night's turbulent revelations, the world seemed unnaturally still. I'd never felt so unlovable and unworthy of the stability, provisions and care he offered. And I didn't know who I was anymore either. The version of me that existed before Jumping had been destroyed, yet, I wasn't disappointed with that. I wanted a change. I needed a new me. I was dying for more out of life. I just wasn't prepared to pay the full cost when the bill came due. In my dark moments, I decided to call the only safe lifeline I had. Auntie Nia.

"I'm not going to say I told you so. Don't worry." She comforted me.

I told her everything...all about the Olympics, the other Jumper I'd met, how my time with David evoked so much power that it ultimately became my demise—the very thing I craved ended up being my unpardonable sin. Jamie had had it with me. I'd messed his head up so badly he had to take more drugs to focus and make it through operating on patients at his job. Anti-anxiety meds this time. I'd driven him to haplessness, and that made anguish throb throughout my soul. I'd never seen Jamie like this because of me. He felt inadequate, jilted and diminished. And it was all my fault. White hot agony coursed through my body like venom. I was a greedy snake who had ruined my marriage. I failed.

"You know, you wouldn't be the first person with self-inflicted wounds because you were blinded by a starvation to get what *you* needed. Trust me, I've been married a few times. I know how hard it is to balance what you need versus what he requires, and what your union must have. Sometimes those things all align, and it's wonderful. Other times, they don't and that is the barbed-wire crux of marriage that's hard to navigate."

"I don't want to lose Jamie. I really don't," I whimpered. "I didn't think this through! It's just been one thing after another. The dog's been sick. Jamie's been absent. My mom had a stroke. I thought I was gonna die in a plane crash. My neighbors are fake. I don't have many real friends. My business is having issues. I was lonely, touch-starved, pitifully begging for attention from a man who didn't have it in him to offer. Jesus Christ, I just needed something to give!" I broke down. My heart was bleeding and I didn't know how to make it stop.

"Trish...life tosses us into deep waters, sometimes with sharks and other predators in them. Our demons. Our weaknesses. Our vain needs and even authentic soul's desires. But it's in these moments we discover our true strength—who we are, and what we're made of. Did you make mistakes? Yes, but who hasn't? It's human. What's important now is not to dwell on the 'could haves' and 'should haves.' You need to face what's in front of you, understand the consequences, and learn from them. You need to figure out what you must do to save your marriage if that's really what you want—but in a way that's evolutionary because you're not the same, Trish. You're just not." Auntie Nia spoke evenly, and without judgement. "Neither is he."

"But I don't know how."

"With all the schooling and life experience you have, girl, yes, you do!"

Her comment made me chuckle, a brief silver lining in a storm of doubt.

"You're in pain, I see that, and it's okay to acknowledge it. It's normal to feel lost and confused. But remember, healing begins with forgiveness – forgiveness of oneself. You have to forgive yourself, Trish. That's the only way you can start fixing what's broken. And you must be honest. Completely honest. No more lies," she said and stopped to let that sink in.

I inhaled and cupped my face with hands that covered my nose, and mouth and met at the corners of my eyes like an oxygen mask—my thumbs under my jaw. By the time I let out an exhale, I found myself massaging my forehead and eyebrows. "I understand," I whispered.

"Jamie is hurt, understandably so. You both need time to process this, to understand each other's hurts and needs. It might not be easy, and the path to reconciliation might be long and unsteady, but if there's unconditional love, there's a way. And Jamie, he needs to see your truth, your vulnerability, not just the mistakes. That's the key to unconditional love, and most people can't grasp that. But I hope for your sake he does," Auntie Nia went on. "And you're not a greedy snake, Trish. You're a human with needs and flaws, just like the rest of us. And I only call them flaws because of the societal structures we're forced live in. Desire is innate, and not truly a defect, but we don't live in a setup where you can have every desire you want, especially once you're in a monogamous marriage." She explained. "You did what you thought was right to feel fulfilled, and it worked, but not without casualties. Honesty is really the only way forward," she continued. "Now, it's about facing those so-called flaws, embracing them, and growing from them. Talk to Jamie, when he's ready. Don't push him! Be honest, be open, and be prepared to listen. Remember, it's not just about being heard, but also about hearing."

"I don't know how I'm going to manage it all. What if I have to move my mom in and there's no happy home for her to join?"

"Take each day as it comes. One step at a time, Trish. One honest, brave step at a time. You've got this. And if you do move her in, I'll come for a visit. She and I are long overdue for an honest talk and healing ourselves."

I wanted to know what she meant by that but didn't have the capacity to inquire or dig deeper.

"And Bentley," Auntie Nia added, "care for him, let him be the bridge where words fail. He's basically y'all's son. Maybe there's a way he can help in his own little doggy way. I don't know..." her voice trailed off. She'd run out of words, but truthfully, she'd said everything I needed to hear.

Slowly, the clarity of her thoughts began pulling me out of the tempest of emotions I'd been churning in for days. I knew what I needed to do, yet the weight of it pressed down on me with a heaviness I could scarcely bear. It was time to confront everything: the lies I had woven, the truths I had hidden, and the fractures in the life I had built with Jamie. The first step was the hardest, admitting to myself that my escape into other worlds wasn't just a flight of fancy, but a symptom of deeper desires in our marriage, wants I had been too afraid to tell Jamie had spun so out of control I was willing to take an elite drug to fulfill them. It was time to come clean...about everything, and hope for the best.

LATER THAT EVENING I would plead with Jamie to talk and promise to not hide a thing. I started with the day I saw Auntie Nia at the farmer's market and told him about the symposium I went to. I showed him my research and told him about my ventures with Yasmin and Amara. He still didn't want to believe in Jump, but as fate would have it, a news segment aired, featuring a scathing report on an exclusive 'playground' drug used by the wealthy to escape reality, sparking controversy and ethical debates.

"You spent how much on this?" He asked.

"Two thousand dollars a vial, but it really cost more. I got a discount!" I explained as if that would make it better.

Jamie had needed to step out of the room a few times when I told him about my trip to California to try Jump under supervision. He was disgusted and crumpled at the level of my deceit but partly comforted that I at least took that precaution. "You could have died, Trish!" He cried, clearly not wanting that for me despite being enraged by my actions.

"Doc K is a real scientist, not a quack," I assured him. "I was as cautious as I could be, I promise."

"But I wish you would have told me! I just wish you would have said something!"

"You wouldn't have believed me! You literally only just did because you saw it on the news!"

I was right and he knew it. I also knew how preposterous the whole thing sounded. "I am so sorry. And I can probably never apologize enough, but I need you to believe me when I say I didn't want to hurt you. I only wanted to heal myself."

"God damn it!" He threw his arms up in defeat. "I get it, Trish. I get it...I hear you." He paused. "And I'm sorry for not hearing you loud enough sooner. I didn't realize how alone you truly felt, and for that, I do apologize," he huffed. "But this isn't the way, Trish. I don't want you jumping into dimensions; having affairs with other people. Fuck that! Fuck ALL of that, okay? Because in my eyes that is still cheating!"

"But they weren't real!"

"The experiences felt real to you, and it affected our marriage. They're legit."

Before I could speak again, my cell phone rang, extracting me from our discussion on the definition of cheating. It was the care home where my mother resided, a reminder of another aspect of my life that demanded attention. I sent the call to voice mail. *Not now.* I knew that was equally as urgent, but it would have to wait a few hours.

"Cheating isn't just physical, you know that, Trish. And even though your cosmic flings only last twenty minutes at a time—or days or whatever—they were still an affront to our marriage. We're not in an open relationship! I don't know how to move on from this." He got up and paced. "I need space." Jamie's words cut through me. Just when I thought we could reconcile, he dealt a final blow to our fractured reality.

"I need space," he repeated.

Jamie was worried not just about infidelity, but about what biochemical changes the drug might have made on my body. He was nervous about me getting so much joy being with other people. He was afraid he could never measure up and be enough for the new me even if he became more intimate again. His world was stolen from him and he didn't know if he wanted to fight to get it back as it was clearly not the same.

While alone, I felt a sense of resolve solidifying within me. I wasn't going to lose him. I didn't care what it took, I was going to fight for him. When he was locked in his study or otherwise away from me, I got more details regarding my mother. I also called Clint. In the end, she'd need to stay a little while longer in her home while I got my life together. I would rather her be there than thrust into the clusterfuck that was my home environment, and that sucked. But it was the best decision for the moment.

I stopped buying drugs from Yasmin and Amara while my marriage was on life support, and I focused on my work while Jamie and I moved tensely throughout the house. But I couldn't help myself. During a few lonely nights, I began journaling about my trips to the past. I wrote down everything from the euphoric sensations to the disorienting transitions to deeply analyzing their effects on me, which is something I should have done all along. I needed to ensure I didn't create an addiction or dependence, because, despite all the damage they'd caused, I still wanted another taste. Jump was ecstasy and I wanted one last leap. I wondered if it could be the suture for my bleeding heart and if I could just get Jamie on board to try it with me. No more lies. No more secrets. I really thought he'd love it if he just gave it a chance!

The timing wasn't right for me to approach him with that, but I filed it in my mind for later if we ever got back on stable ground. My nights were lonelier than they'd ever been. I felt guilty when Jamie habitually put his hand on my back while asleep. But I also felt hopeful. He didn't hate me, he was defeated. And then there was Bentley, our loyal companion through the years. He was hanging on despite declining health and that meant something to me. As I watched him from the corner of my eye, I knew that if he could walk through pain every day and still find a reason to wag his tail when he saw us, I could pull it together too. *Don't push him!* Auntie Nia's advice regarding Jamie reverberated in my mind. I did tell him that she'd warned me to be honest with him from the very beginning. I didn't want him holding her in contempt. It wasn't her fault. My actions were mine, and I accepted the fallout without blaming anyone but myself.

Days later, a handwritten note from Jamie would change everything...

Dear Trish,

As I sit down to write this, a million thoughts race through my mind, each vying for attention, each demanding to be heard. But in the madness of emotions I've recently experienced, one truth stands clear and unshakable – I cannot live without you.

Our journey has been rocky. It has been sharp. And it's made me question my entire being and self-worth. Finally, something made me take a long, hard, sober look in the mirror—this. When I lost trust, faith and, really thought I lost it all, I forced myself to pause and lean on logic. I pushed myself to think this through before making any brash decisions.

Recently, you and I have weathered storms I never foresaw. We've faced challenges that tested the very foundations of who we are. Through all this, I've learned something crucial: trust doesn't mean people will always behave as I feel they should. It means trusting them to act according to who they are and accepting or rejecting their behavior. It's not about holding them to a measuring stick of my expectations. That's unfair to their needs. That's confinement. And I don't want that for you. I love you. I want you to be free.

I'm going to need to redefine what 'trusting you' means so it doesn't box you in. I'll have to trust you to be yourself, and accept whoever that is even as you evolve and want new experiences. I just wish you would have been upfront about everything, but I understand why you were afraid to. I am sorry for not being a safe space. I didn't know how deep the well of your loneliness went. I didn't grasp how much my absence and my own struggles drove you to seek solace elsewhere. And though this whole thing made me feel like a loser, I realized that defeat, though embarrassing and agonizing, doesn't have to be the end. I just have to control my ego. And work through my emotions to define a new normal.

In my pursuit of control and order, I forgot that life, at its core, is unpredictable and messy. I was so focused on maintaining a facade of strength that I failed to see the pain and isolation you, too, were experiencing. I failed to be there for you in the ways that truly mattered. And I made you feel like you had to keep secrets from me because you feared my reaction. For that, I am greatly sorry. Because if your home isn't the safest place to be your whole and evolving self, where is?

I've spent a lifetime building walls around my emotions, but you've always been the exception, Trish. You've shown me that vulnerability isn't a disadvantage, but an asset. That opening up doesn't diminish us, but rather enriches our existence. You've been my constant in a world of change, my anchor in the turbulent sea of life. Now, it's my turn to allow you to open up without hesitation.

I want to work on our marriage. I want to rebuild the trust that has been shattered, not with empty promises, but with actions and time. I want to learn about your journeys, your desires, and even about this "Jump." I won't pretend to understand it all, but I'm willing to listen, to really listen, and try to grasp what it means to you. I'll even do my own scientific and medical research into it.

Let's go to therapy together. Let's unravel these tangled threads and weave a stronger bond. I don't want a divorce, Trish. I want us. The real us, flaws and all. The journey ahead won't be easy, but I believe it's worth every step if it means having you by my side.

Bentley has been our silent witness, our furry companion through thick and thin. Let's be there for him, as he has been for us—he only has a few years left. And let's find our way back to each other, for him, for us.

With all my love,

Jamie

My hands trembled and my eyes overflowed with tears reading his words. A second chance. A chance to mend what I feared was irreparably broken. My body shook in release as I got up to find him. And as I walked toward his study, I found myself thinking the game—our life and marriage—wasn't lost. It was merely waiting for us to rewrite the rules.

Jamie was standing against his desk with his hands crossed in front of him, expecting me to come in. But I couldn't move. Jamie had shaved his head bald and it startled me. Noticing my alarm, he confirmed in just a few words.

"Yeah, I cut it. Irrational, maybe, but I felt like I needed to do something. I'm gonna grow my beard, don't worry. I won't look baby-faced for long."

"Um..." I had no words. Did my husband just have a *Waiting to Exhale* moment?

He huffed. "Come here, Trish," he spoke through tight lips. Slowly, he extended a hand, and sheepishly, I stepped into his embrace.

"Oh, Jamie." His arms never felt so good. They felt like home, a familiar space of strength and refuge. I cried profusely in his arms, grateful to be in them again and thankful that all wasn't lost. And I couldn't help myself, I touched his head. Things were definitely different!

In his embrace, a profound realization washed over me. The adventures, the sensuality, and the freedom I had sought in my jumps were not just about escaping my reality; they were about rediscovering the passion in the life I already had. Jamie's hold on me, once a symbol of the mundane, now felt like a salvation in a sea of uncertainty, steadying me in a world that was ours to redefine.

Bentley, our faithful companion, shuffled in with a gentle nudge seemed to say, "This is where you belong." As Jamie and I knelt to pet him, I saw in Jamie's eyes a glimmer of curiosity, a silent acknowledgment of the past and a tentative openness to the future.

"So...you really went to the 1968 Olympics and Harlem Renaissance?" He asked.

"Yes, I did."

"Hm." He grunted and fell back into silence.

I didn't offer anything else. Maybe one day, we would explore new worlds together, but for now, it was enough to rediscover each other and rebuild our world from the inside out. In that moment, in our quiet study with Bentley at our feet, we didn't need words to understand the journey ahead. It was a journey of forgiveness, acceptance, and above all, a journey of love renewed.

In our union, we found not just reconciliation but a transformed sense of adventure – one that didn't require jumping through time but diving deep into the complexities of our hearts. And in that realization, we found our true freedom.

THANK YOU FOR READING *TRIP*! I appreciate your time and support and hope you enjoyed this story. Would you like **free bonus content** (like character interviews, early access to book two in this series, etc.)? If so, click here or visit: https://BookHip.com/NLZLZVK.

If you enjoyed this book, please consider leaving a review on Amazon, Goodreads, or any other site that's easiest for you! Thanks again for your support. Book two is already in the works!

ABOUT THE AUTHOR

Born in Toronto, raised in Miami and now living in Puebla, Mexico, Cheril N. Clarke is the author of six novels, two stage plays, several short stories and poetry collections, and numerous children's books. She has been featured in *Curve* Magazine, *VoyageATL*, *The Princeton Packet*, *Philadelphia Gay News* (PGN), About.com, *Out IN Jersey*, *Burlington County Times*, as well as Phillyburbs.com, among others. Her creative writing website is CherilNClarke.com. Clarke is also an executive ghostwriter and the woman behind PhenomenalWriting.-com. She has written for Fortune 500 executives and entrepreneurs worldwide.

instagram.com/cheril_nicole_
tiktok.com/@cheril.n.clarke
threads.net/cheril_nicole_

OTHER BOOKS BY CHERIL N. CLARKE

Trick or Treat: A Halloween Quickie

Whiskey Dungeon

Corsets and Cognac

Sweet Dark Rum

The Edge of Bliss

The Beautiful People: New Orleans

The Beautiful People: Las Vegas

The Beautiful People: New York

Losing Control

Candle Wax

Bite the Pillow (Poetry)

Oxygen (Poetry)

Spoken Word albums by Cheril N. Clarke (as C. Nicole):

Honey

Drip

www.ingramcontent.com/pod-product-compliance
Lightning Source LLC
LaVergne TN
LVHW090606110826
845146LV00001B/277

* 9 7 9 8 9 8 9 5 2 2 5 0 7 *